THE OWNER
LIES DEAD

D1378090

THE OWNER LIES DEAD

Tyline Perry

COACHWHIP PUBLICATIONS
Greenville, Ohio

The Owner Lies Dead, by Tyrine Perry
© 2017 Coachwhip Publications
Introduction © 2017 Curtis Evans

Title published 1930
No claims made on public domain material.
Cover image: © GrandFailure

CoachwhipBooks.com

ISBN 1-61646-409-7
ISBN-13 978-1-61646-409-7

DON'T GO DOWN IN THE MINE

TYLINE PERRY (1897-1978) AND *THE OWNER LIES DEAD* (1930)

Curtis Evans

Don't go down in the mine, Dad,
Dreams very often come true;
Daddy, you know it would break my heart
If anything happened to you.
—"Don't Go Down in the Mine, Dad" (1910)

Tyline Perry had been residing in Colorado for a decade when she published her acclaimed debut novel, *The Owner Lies Dead* (1930), a murder mystery set in a Colorado coalmining town. During roughly those same years dozens of workplace fatalities had taken place at the state's many mines, grievously augmenting a grim roll call of ghastly tragedies: the 1917 Hastings mine explosion, the worst mining disaster in Colorado history, with 121 of 122 miners killed; the 1919 Oakdale and Empire mine explosions, which left 31 dead; and the explosions at the Sopris and Southwestern mines in 1922 and 1923, which laid waste to an additional 27 souls. Such calamities understandably did not promote harmonious relations between Colorado mine owners and laborers. A flare-up between the two frequently antagonistic groups led to armed state police shooting into a crowd of picketing colliers during the 1927 Columbine coalmine strike at the misleadingly named company town of Serene, located north of Denver; six men were slain in what has been dubbed the

5

"slaughter at Serene."[1] The miners' work stoppage, which had been made in compliance with the call by the Industrial Workers of the World (IWW, or Wobblies in popular parlance) for a general strike in protest of the state-sponsored execution of anarchists and international cause célèbre Nicola Sacco and Bartolomeo Vanzetti, spread rapidly across a state where deplorable working conditions in the mines had produced a work force which seethed with discontent.

Leftist crime writer Dashiell Hammett, a former operative for the Pinkerton National Detective Agency who during his time at Pinkerton had glimpsed darkness in the rapacious hearts of the rich and powerful, was familiar with contemporary clashes between capital and labor; and in an excoriating classic crime novel, *Red Harvest* (1929), he vividly drew on actual bloody violence that had erupted earlier in the decade at Butte, Montana, during the Wobbly-led strike against the Anaconda Copper Mining Company. A year after the publication of his acclaimed *Red Harvest*, Hammett reviewed Tyline Perry's detective novel *The Owner Lies Dead* in *The Saturday Review of Literature*, giving the novel what was for Hammett—who typically stinted praise for traditionalist, puzzle-oriented detective fiction—quite a strong notice:

> When the fire that had burned for weeks after the explosion in Haunted Mine was put out at last, and rescuers went down to take out the bodies of the dead, they found Tony Sheridan, the owner's nephew who had rushed down in the last attempt at rescue, dead at the bottom of the shaft. And old residents recalled the prophecy that the spirits of the miners killed long ago in Haunted Mill's first disaster would forever be at rest till the owner himself lay dead in the depths.
>
> But Tony Sheridan, after all, was the owners' nephew. Moreover, he had not died in the fire, he had been shot. . . . Ah! Go on from there; it's good. Toward the end the involutions become very involved indeed, but it all stays plausible, as mystery stories go.

Hammett was hardly alone in praising *The Owner Lies Dead*, which became one of the most lauded detective novels of 1930, in both the United States and the United Kingdom, an especially impressive achievement in a year that included Agatha Christie's *The Murder at the Vicarage*, Dorothy L. Sayers' *Strong Poison*, Ianthe Jerrold's *Dead Man's Quarry*, Anthony Berkeley's *The Second Shot*, Philip Macdonald's *The Noose*, R. Austin Freeman's *Mr. Pottermack's Oversight*, Freeman Wills Crofts' *Sir John Magill's Last Journey*, John Rhode's *Pinehurst*, Henry Wade's *The Dying Alderman*, Mary Roberts Rinehart's *The Door*, Mignon Eberhart's *While the Patient Slept* and *The Mystery at Hunting's End*, Helen Reilly's *The Thirty-First Bullfinch*, Alice Campbell's *Murder in Paris*, Earl Derr Biggers' *Charlie Chan Carries On*, Ellery Queen's *The French Powder Mystery*, S. S. Van Dine's *The Scarab Murder Case*, John Dickson Carr's *It Walks by Night*, Anthony Abbot's *About the Murder of Geraldine Foster* and Rufus King's *Murder by Latitude*—not to mention Dashiell Hammett's own remarkable stab at crime that year, *The Maltese Falcon*.

Like Dashiell Hammett, the reviewers for the *New York Times Book Review* and the *Detroit Free Press* were impressed with the bravura plotting and technical finesse of *The Owner Lies Dead*, wherein the inventive author managed to construct something of a "locked room" or "impossible crime" situation out of a mine explosion, as the latter paper explained:

> An explosion in a coal mine takes 17 victims. The owner's nephew insisted upon going down the shaft after the first explosion. Five weeks later his body is recovered—but it is discovered that he died from a bullet which went through his back! And murders are not committed at the bottoms of coal mines on the verge of blowing up. This is the start of one of the most intriguing murder mysteries lately published. Suspicion shifts about and the reader does not even stop to wonder who did it or draw his own conclusions because his interest in the story will not permit of any such interruptions. The name of Tyline Perry

is a new one, but his [sic] technique is certainly satisfactory.

"It will require a more than ordinarily astute mind to find [the
solution]," opined the *New York Times*. Meanwhile, in the UK,
where *The Owner Lies Dead* was published by Victor Gollancz, the
prestigious publisher of some of the most highly-regarded names
in British detective fiction (including Dorothy L. Sayers, Gladys
Mitchell and J. J. Connington), the novel received rave reviews
from the *Spectator* and from Charles Williams, editor of Oxford
University Press and an uncommonly astute critic of mystery fiction. Williams praised *The Owner Lies Dead* not merely for its
plotting and its "sinister opening," but for its verisimilitude, which
in his view made the murder problem actually matter to the reader
emotionally as well as intellectually. The "group of bewildered and
distressed people" in the novel, was, an awed Williams observed,
"much like ourselves. And to be like ourselves is a miracle—in a
detective novel." The reviewer for the *Spectator* concurred, declaring not only that *The Owner Lies Dead* boasted a superlative puz-
zle ("Mr. Perry's story will tax the ingenuity of the most cunning
readers and his book deserves more than one reading in order that
his brilliant manner of hiding clues may be appreciated"), but also
that it in fact constituted "that very rare thing—a first-class thriller
which is also a novel full of human interest and sound psychology."
For his part Dashiell Hammett perceptively noted that the plot of
the novel, which centers on three brothers and the mine-owning aunt
and uncle who adopted them, owes something to English author
P. C. Wren's hugely popular adventure novel *Beau Geste* (1924),
first filmed in 1926, with matinee idol Ronald Colman playing the
lead role.

As great a mystery in 1930 as that which was found in the pages
of *The Owner Lies Dead* was the matter of the author's identity.
Indeed, as the notices quoted above make clear, it was not even
generally understood by crime fiction reviewers that the ambigu-
ously named Tyline Perry was in fact a woman, not a man. Happily,
the author of this introduction has been able to solve what we
might term the mystery of Tyline Perry.

Tyline Perry was born Tyline Nanny on July 29, 1897 in the small town of Brownwood, Texas (burial place of fantasy writer and Conan the Barbarian creator Robert E. Howard, a fellow Texan), to dentist Thomas Frank Nanny and his former schoolteacher wife, Alma Boyd Rhoads. The couple originally had come from Muhlenberg County in western Kentucky, where they had been considered "two of the leading society young people" in that part of the state. Alma possessed a lineage of note in Kentucky, being a descendant of Rachel Boone Rhoads, a niece of Daniel Boone, and Henry Rhoads, Jr., a prominent Kentucky pioneer and politician of German descent. (The family surname Rhoads was originally spelled "Roth.") Frank had resided in the coalmining town of Bevier, Kentucky, where he was the railroad station agent and postmaster, before he wed Alma, in circumstances that were decidedly unusual, suggesting a vein of free-spiritedness and independent-mindedness ran through the souls of Tyline's parents. The couple had actually wed in 1891, but they kept the marriage "a profound secret" for over five years, during which time Alma graduated from Peabody Normal School (today Peabody College, which has been merged with Vanderbilt University and ranks as one of the country's top graduate schools in education), taking employment as a schoolteacher, and Frank graduated from the Vanderbilt College of Dentistry. Only after removing in 1896 to Brownwood, Texas, where Frank set up practice, did Frank and Alma announce the fact of their marriage. Tyline, the couple's only child, was born the next year.

Descended from a long line of devout Baptists (her German immigrant ancestor, Henry Rhoads, Sr./Heinrich Roth, was a Dunker minister), Tyline first attended Howard Payne College (now Howard Payne University), a Baptist school located in Brownwood (where a decade later her fellow pulps writer Robert E. Howard would take a stenography course); but after two years at Howard Payne she transferred to the University of Texas, where she received her undergraduate degree, before completing her institutional education with graduate work at Columbia University. By 1920, Frank and Alma Nanny had moved to Hollywood, California, where Tyline too was residing when that year she wed Ralph Drake Perry, a young attorney originally from North Dakota. The couple

TYLINE PERRY

relocated to Denver, Colorado, where Ralph became the sales manager of a paint store and Tyline began writing genre fiction for pulp magazines. Tyline would remain in Denver until the death of her husband from a heart attack in 1954, when she moved to the town of Plainview, Texas, near the Texas panhandle, where she had inherited 7500 acres of farmland from her Rhoads grandparents. Putting this land, which she named the Nanny farms, under the care of a manager, Tyline during the remaining 24 years of her life devoted herself to her daughter, Susan, and various philanthropic causes. Among other things, Tyline provided the money for the construction of the Castro County Library in nearby Dimmitt, Texas; established research fellowships, named in honor of her late husband, in parapsychology at Duke University (interest in the paranormal on the author's part is suggested by certain elements on *The Owner Lies Dead*); and sponsored a Chinese girl's education at Hong Kong Baptist College (now Hong Kong Baptist University).

From a very young age, when as a six-year-old child she performed as "Kitty Little" in *The Three Kittens*, a juvenile operetta staged at Howard Payne College, Tyline evinced an outgoing spirit and imaginative bent. She published the first of her many short stories (one source claims that she wrote 200 of them) at the age of 18, in *The Texas Magazine*. At Howard Payne, the mirthful and exuberant young redhead flourished, becoming a member of the Tennis and Movie Clubs and the West Texas Trampers (a female hiking club), as well as a contributor and cartoonist on the school yearbook, *The Lasso*. (She was also runner-up in the vote for the "Brightest" student of her class.) For the 1914 *Lasso*, a 17-year-old Tyline composed a humorous sketch, "The Midnight Mystery of the Malignant Mandarin," a parody of Sax Rohmer's offhandedly racist "Yellow Peril" tales of evil Dr. Fu-Manchu (aka "The Devil Doctor"), as well as contemporary damsel-in-distress film serials like *The Perils of Pauline* and *The Exploits of Elaine* (the latter based on a novel by American crime writer Arthur B. Reeve), giving early indication of her interest in the mystery fiction genre, which would come to ample fruition in the 1920s:

Chapter XXIII

"How came you here?" cried the lovely Gwendolyn Genevieve in agonized alarm, starting up from her seat by the Chinese lantern.

"I came to kill you!" fiercely hissed the Malignant Mandarin, drawing forth the three-bladed dagger.

"Unhand her, villain," spoke a cool, deliberate voice.

The Mandarin turned wildly around and his gleaming, squinted eyes met the serene blue ones of Algernon Archibald.

"Drop that knife, you dog," calmly commanded our hero.

The dagger upraised fell from nerveless yellow claws and the Malignant Mandarin slunk away. With a thrill of ecstasy, Algernon Archibald caught in his arms the swooning Gwendolyn Genevieve.

"O. Henry won't have anything on Tyline in a few years," avowed the University of Texas school yearbook, *The Cactus*, in 1916, referencing the famous pen name of the late William Sydney Porter, the hugely popular and prolific American short story writer. Under the pseudonym "Peter Perry" and, a little later on, her own name, Tyline in the 1920s began publishing genre short fiction in the pulps; her two known detective novels, *The Owner Lies Dead* and *The Never Summer Mystery* (1932), also were published under

TYLINE NANNY, B.A.
Brownwood.
Φ M.
TYLINE—The girl with the Titian hair. O. Henry won't have anything on Tyline in a few years, judging by the University Mag. She has the true artistic temperament, being able to get an inspiration for a story out of a tack. Tyline "busted" into Texas from Daniel Baker two years ago.

TYLINE PERRY, COLLEGE YEARS

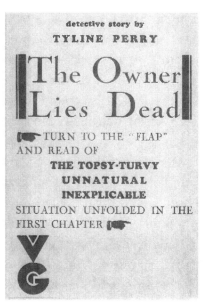

her own name. Evidently Tyline's best known serial character was a tough though colorless police detective named Douglas Greer, who cracked nearly forty cases in the pages of *Flynn's Weekly Detective Fiction* (also known as *Flynn's*, *Flynn's Weekly* and *Detective Fiction Weekly*) between October 24, 1925 ("Trapping 'Mousie'") and December 22, 1928 ("The Nicked Blade"). In *Yesterday's Faces*, volume 4 (*The Solvers*), Robert Sampson asserts that the Greer tales are packed with "lunatic ideas, inadequately worked out, substituting energy for the illusion of reality, and gore and violence and shock for rational plots"; yet he avows that they nevertheless "have their moments." The frantic action of one of the Greer stories, "The Forty Thieves," culminates in an abandoned coalmine, anticipating the milieu of the coalmining town of Genesee, Colorado in *The Owner Lies Dead*.

Two years after the appearance of *The Owner Lies Dead*, Tyline Perry published her last known detective novel, *The Never Summer Mystery*. Like its predecessor, *The Never Summer Mystery* is set in Colorado, this time in the mountains around Never Summer Camp, home of a wealthy octogenarian businessman whose fortune is coveted by the dependents with whom he has surrounded himself. Although this is obviously a familiar situation to mystery fans, *The Never Summer Mystery* is an excellent detective novel in the classic mold, complete with a map and floor plan. The *New York Times Book Review* deemed the plot "ingenious" and the story "skillfully constructed" and predicted that even were the reader to deduce the identity of the murderer, the reader would almost certainly find herself "completely at a loss to explain [the murderer's] method."

After the publication of *The Never Summer Mystery*, however, Tyline Perry seems to have largely abstained from writing fiction. An additional story, "The Holy Child of Agincourt," appeared in the popular general-interest magazine *Liberty* in 1940, but I know of no additional published fiction by Tyline Perry after that year. Her obituary states that she actually wrote four detective novels, however, so mysteries enshroud the author still. Were two novels published under another, unknown pseudonym, or perhaps were they never published at all? Given the quality of Tyline Perry's two known detective novels, one hopes additional books turn up again someday.

ENDNOTE

[1] See Lowell May and Richard Myers, eds., *Slaughter in Serene: The Columbia Coal Strike Reader* (Denver, CO: Bread and Roses Workers' Cultural Center and the Industrial Workers of the World, 2005). My mother, who grew up in a small town in Pennsylvania town where many of the men, including her carpenter father, supplemented their income by working in local coalmines, recalled to me that in the 1930s, when she was a young child, "when you heard an ambulance going down the street, that meant there had been another one [injured] in the mine."

THE OWNER LIES DEAD

To Ralph

I

"MEN HAD DIED BEFORE IN HAUNTED MINE, BUT NOT BY BULLETS"

The hills rose gaunt and gloomy against the stars, dwarfing the crude buildings of the mine, even the high tip tower, and making the town in the valley below, with its church spires and its lighted windows, look like a toy village. Against that mighty backdrop, the group of people, huddled about the mine shaft, seemed pitifully helpless, puny humans at grips with nature. Most of them had been there already twelve hours, waiting, panic-stricken, but with stoicism bred of habitual danger, for news of those below. Feeble electric bulbs, strung up hastily, furnished inadequate light for the rescuers. Voices were low and tense. Somewhere a woman sobbed convulsively. Another disaster had been added to the black history of Haunted Mine.

Acrid, sulphurous odors of coal smoke hung in the air. Wraith-like clouds rose from the shaft in little spindrifts and whirlwinds. An ambulance waited. Men, white-faced and tight-lipped, passed and repassed on hurried errands. Useless errands, perhaps. Men came and went with the ceaseless busy movement of ants around an ant hill disturbed by a heavy foot. Blades of light from restless cars along the road stabbed and probed through the shadows, and sometimes lit up for a moment the drawn, pinched face of a woman. It was like the sudden shameless baring of a soul, these quick glimpses of faces squeezed out, wrung like a rag by fear.

A ripple of excitement flowed over the crowd; the mass surged closer to the shaft. There had been a signal from below; the cage was coming up. Three blackened figures, like strange goblins, in gas masks, staggered into the arms of the waiting men. A stretcher was lifted from the floor of the cage.

A woman clawed through the crowd. Her voice was lifted hoarsely, fear and joy mingled in her tone. "Billy, Billy—it's my Billy!" Her hands reached out for the still form. Then her voice changed. "Oh—my baby," she moaned.

"It's Big Bill's boy." The word went around.

"Done for, too. Nobody could live long in that hell hole."

Silence settled, pall-like, as the stretcher was slid into the ambulance.

The rescuers who had brought out the body lay exhausted on the ground, masks removed, faces distorted as they sucked great gasps of air into tortured lungs.

One sat up, panting. "No use—tryin' again." He took a gulp of scalding coffee a woman brought him. "Fire's spreadin'," he said jerkily. "Can't get past the first crosscut. The kid—" he jerked his head towards the ambulance turning into the road—"we stumbled over him. He'd almost reached the shaft. Too late, though, I guess. Smoke is bad—after-damp, too. No chance for the rest—can't get to 'em, poor devils."

But three firemen in oxygen helmets had already plunged into the smoke-filled blackness. A fire hose was dropped down the shaft. The crowd waited tensely. Would it mean others rescued or more lives added to the toll of Haunted Mine?

Fire had broken out with a small explosion in the two-hundred-foot level shortly before noon. No one knew just how it had started. Spontaneous combustion or a short circuit in the wiring might be responsible, or a pipe lighted in defiance of rules. But fire is tragedy in the subterranean maze of a coal mine. Powdered coal dust and inflammable gases had spread the blaze with lightning rapidity. The forced draft, fan-driven, sucked the flames along timber-lined passages. Smoke clouds, rolling through the workings, had overtaken the men before they could reach the shaft. The hungry flames were not far behind, licking at the ancient dried timbers.

Most of the men in Haunted Mine had been in the work rooms along the east crosscut of the hundred-foot level. They had escaped. But a second and greater explosion—from fire-damp—had caused a cave-in below in the two-hundred-foot level, and had poisoned the air with the deadly after-damp. Eleven lifeless bodies had been taken out of that level. Five other limp forms had been revived only with untiring effort. But seventeen men who had been working there were still unaccounted for. Whether they had been overcome by smoke and gas like the others or killed by falling rock, or whether they had, by quick thought and work, managed to wall off the flames and the smoke from some part of the workings was still uncertain. The fire, breaking out in the loose waste of a goaf, was swept into the gangway by the draft from the ventilating fan. Those in its path had succumbed. But there was still a chance that the others, cut off from escape, had retreated into the workings where the air was still good. If they were uninjured, their first thought would be to throw up a bulkhead across the drift. They might be alive and safe yet, but slowly perishing from want of air. If they could be found, an effort would be made to sink a shaft to them. But there were miles of workings honeycombing the mountain and the valley, and no hint of where the men had taken refuge—if, indeed, they were alive at all.

The rescuers who had attempted to fight their way through had been driven back by the smoke and the choking after-damp. The last three to descend came up empty-handed, gasping for air, tearing off their helmets. They had been unable to penetrate the remoter drifts.

"We reached the air shaft all right," one reported. "The smoke is cleared away there where the draft works right. But we couldn't get close to the fire—it's hotter'n hell in the gangway. And the cave-in's changed the draft."

There was no hope left. The seventeen had been working at the far end of the gangway, beyond the waste-filled excavations, where the blaze had started. They might have built a barricade against the smoke, but the insidious gas would find an entrance somewhere.

The old miners shook their heads.

"Ain't no use riskin' more lives. Ain't a chance in a hundred there's a soul alive—with all that smoke."

"Not in Haunted Mine."

"Haunted Mine has killed a lot of men."

"It's got a bad name."

"That pit ain't ventilated right. A mine where there's fire-damp ought to have a bigger fan. I seen a fan once as was four times as big as this."

A hush fell on the group as a woman plodded past, eyes staring at nothing. The miners shuffled uneasily in heavy shoes.

"We was just sayin' the boys might've throwed up a bulkhead," one began.

The woman turned dull eyes upon him. "I told my ol' man Haunted Mine would get him sooner or later, and I guess it has. I'm goin' home." She moved on.

The men were silent. Shoulders hunched in blue denim coats against the cool night wind, caps pulled low over tired eyes, discouraged, passive, they waited with dog-like patience for news of their fellow workers—news that only by some miracle could be good.

Matthew North, owner of the mine, was there. He had done all that could be done. His long lean face was grave and stern; there were dark circles under his pouched eyes. He chewed moodily on an unlighted cigar.

"Well, boys, it looks like we're beaten—no more volunteers." He shook his head.

Then a young man strode up to Matthew North, his nephew, young Anthony Sheridan.

"Uncle Matthew, I'm going down again." There was determination in his voice.

Matthew North stared at him, then laid one hand on the boy's shoulder. "Tony, it's hopeless."

Anthony Sheridan flung off the restraining hand. "I must go! I know every inch of the workings. I'll try to get through—"

"Tony, it's foolish," the older man snapped. "What can you do? You couldn't drag a man out through that gas."

"If I can find out where they are—if they're still alive—perhaps we can sink a shaft through to them—"

"It's suicide!" cried North. "The fire's worse!"

"Don't try to stop me. I'll be back in ten minutes."

With long strides Anthony Sheridan moved towards the shaft. People made way for him.

"Tony, Tony!" A girl's voice rose, panic stricken. "Don't go! Tony!"

Anthony Sheridan seemed not to hear. His face was grim and set, so that he looked older than his twenty-six years. His firm chin was thrust out determinedly. His brown eyes seemed more dark and glowing than ever. Tony Sheridan had never looked so handsome as when he pulled that hideous gas mask over his face.

Men who had called him wastrel and snob forgave him now. Women prayed for him.

It was midnight when Tony Sheridan was let down into the black pit of Haunted Mine. A full moon was just rising. The bare top of Moon Mountain gleamed ghostly above the dark splotches of the pines, while the valley below was shadow filled.

The crowd waited restlessly. Five minutes passed. Moonlight flooded the grim scene. Girls, flushed from the open fire, ladled thick greasy soup into tin cups. Tired men gulped down the food silently.

Twenty minutes. Twenty-five. There was no signal from the pit bottom. The oxygen helmet carried only a half hour's supply. A man called down the shaft, but only the echo of his voice came back.

Matthew North paced up and down before the shaft, stopping occasionally to peer into the black chimney from which poured smoke and dangerous fumes. He held his watch in one hand. At the end of thirty-five minutes, he ordered:

"Bring the cage up anyway. Maybe he made it to the cage, but was too weak to signal."

The cage rose to the surface—empty. It was lowered again quickly, in the hope that Anthony might yet reach it.

"Who'll go down?" challenged Matthew North.

The volunteer workers were silent. Discouraged and dog-tired after a night of frantic labor, all felt the uselessness of the struggle. The only men saved had been brought up ten hours ago. To venture down now meant endangering other lives.

"Nobody could get through the gangway now," one said. "The after-damp is awful. Even a gas mask ain't much good," added another, still breathing with difficulty. "There's goin' to be more explosions," another muttered.

"There's five thousand for the man who brings up Tony!" Matthew North announced.

Still the men hung back.

Then, as if to settle the matter, there was a rumble like thunder, an explosion that rocked the ground and wiped the color from Matthew North's face. The cavernous mouth of the pit belched forth black smoke.

Though Matthew North was not liked by all his men, none saw him but was sorry for him now. A stern old man of forbidding aspect, dictatorial and self-righteous, he had ruled the mine and the town with autocratic benevolence. But now that the evil shadow of Haunted Mine had fallen on him, he was one with the others. None had guessed he cared so much for his nephew—his wife's nephew in reality. Matthew North looked suddenly aged. The muscles of his face twitched; the skin seemed to hang in loose folds and bags; his eyes had a dazed frightened look. He was a broken old man. His head jerked feebly from side to side as if he were trying to shake off nightmare memories.

The fire raged now with new fury. There was no more pretense of hope. The ventilating fan was shut off, and both downcast and upcast were covered over with boards, but even that did not stop the flames. The first rays of dawn slanted into the valley. The unpainted wooden shacks about the pit mouth and the tall skeleton of the tip house were ugly and commonplace in the early light. Only the curling black wisps of smoke rising from the crevices around the boards, and the tense lined faces of the little groups still gathered there hinted of the tragedy below.

For three days the fire raged unchecked through Haunted Mine. Then it was decided to seal the shafts. Forms were laid and concrete was poured. Even then the coal might smolder for years. But, as it happened, the fire in Haunted Mine was soon smothered. In five weeks the shafts were opened; air was forced though the drifts, and men went down to clear out the wreckage.

Then began the search for Anthony Sheridan's body—a search that ended in a shocking discovery. The smoke-blackened form was found at the foot of the main shaft. After it was brought to the surface, it was discovered that death had been caused by a bullet through the heart.

Incredible as it may seem, there was the bullet wound.

No one had gone into the mine that night after Anthony Sheridan. The seventeen men whom he had tried to rescue were dead before he went down. Their bodies were found behind a half-built barricade that showed they must have succumbed within an hour of the first explosion. They could have done Anthony Sheridan no harm.

No one could guess how Anthony Sheridan had met death. The gas mask had been torn from his face. It was found beside the body, the tank still two-thirds full of oxygen.

He could not have shot himself. The bullet had entered just beneath the left shoulder blade and passed though the heart. No man could fire a bullet straight into his own back. If such a thing were attempted, the bullet would inevitably take a slanting course. And no gun was found near the body nor anywhere in the mine. Nor was any other body found except those of the trapped miners.

Old women recalled all the long lists of deaths and disasters in Haunted Mine. Whispers went around that an evil influence was responsible and that Anthony Sheridan had died to right an ancient wrong. Old women's talk. And yet—what had happened to Anthony Sheridan in those black depths underground? Men had died before in Haunted Mine, but not by bullets.

II
"WE ATTACKED THE FORT"

Some of my earliest memories are connected with Haunted Mine. I can remember, when I was six or seven, venturing near the edge of the black pit and listening to the men's voices and the hollow sounds of shovels and trams that echoed up the well-like shaft, and growing numb with fear, wondering if Tony and Uncle Matthew would ever come up from that fearful darkness that seemed to me the bottom of the world.

Tony was always adventurous. He was about eleven then. And Rush was two years younger. Ever since we had come to live with our mother's sister, after our parents died, Tony had been consumed with curiosity about mining. And after his first visit, he never tired of talking about it.

"The miners wear little lights in their caps. And they don't wear any clothes except overalls and undershirt. It's hot down there and smelly. I had a cap with a light in it, too. But you can't see ten feet ahead. There's tracks like a railroad, and horses pull the coal in little cars. The horses stay down there all the time. There's miles and miles of low black tunnels—but they call them drifts when they're all underground and don't open to the daylight. Uncle Matthew had to bend his head in some places. You can hear groans and queer noises. And things pop overhead. Uncle Matthew said it was the 'working' of the mine. Sometimes the big timbers creak and crack right over your head till it sounds like the mountain is falling down. And once I saw a big rat. But I wasn't afraid."

Tony, I think, was never afraid of anything. He was the leader in all our little escapades. It was one of these which had won me the title of "Captain," later shortened to Cappy, which I still prefer to Henry. It began with Mr. Townsend's new bulldog and ended with a scar Tony was to carry the rest of his life.

Regina Townsend, who lived next door, climbed up on the high iron fence that separated our yards. Her greenish-gray eyes were bright with excitement. Her heart-shaped face with its little pointed chin and freckled up-tilted nose gave her a mischievous, elfish appearance. She had a tiny little red button of a mouth, almost round. Her ash blond hair fell in long limp bangs to her eyebrows. It was never straight, always blown awry in little ragged wisps like some woodland creature's. When she went to Sunday school or to a party all her hair except the bangs was elaborately curled like a bisque doll's, and she walked with her chin up and a little self-conscious twist of her shoulders and hips like the older girls. But that was not the Gina who was our playmate, who could whistle and climb trees and whittle a stick and turn cartwheels and stand on her head as well as Rush or I, though never half so well as Tony.

"We've got a great big bulldog," Regina had announced proudly. "And his name's Bum. My papa brought him home last night, but you can't play with him till he gets used to us."

"Why can't we play with him?" Tony demanded.

"He's f'r-rocious!" Regina puckered her lips and blew out a great breath with the word to emphasize it.

Caution was ever a challenge to Tony. "Huh, who's scared of a dog? Where is this wild animal?"

"In the old chicken pen behind the garage."

"Let's have a look," said Tony.

We raced after him.

"My papa says you mustn't let him out!" Regina screeched warningly, showing even then her understanding of Tony's character.

We rounded the garage. Rush and I stopped short as the great white bulldog lunged at the chicken wire that imprisoned him. It may have been a friendly demonstration, but I saw only the bared white fangs, the great red mouth, and the powerful strength of the jaws snapping at the fence. Tony stood close to the wire, feet wide apart, and regarded the brute speculatively.

"I don't believe he's f'r-rocious at all," Tony decided. "He's just mad because he's in a cage. He's no lion. Are you, Bum? Here, Bum— Bum—" Tony thrust one finger through the wire and touched the dog's black snub nose, while I grew stiff with fear. "See, he won't bite!" Tony stepped back proudly. "We'll play the chicken pen is a fort," he decided. "We'll storm it. And Bum's the enemy, shooting at us."

The dog uttered short impatient yaps. He hurled himself at the wire again and again and tore at it with his great protruding teeth. There was unholy glee in his misshapen ugly face. I have since seen English bulldogs display the same paroxysms in sheer excess of emotion. But this was my first experience, and nothing could have convinced me the beast was not raging to sink the great fangs in my throat.

"I'll be captain," said Tony, seizing a broom. "You're the soldiers. Get your guns! Present arms!"

"I don't like to play soldier," I mumbled with assumed indifference.

"Then you can be captain," said Tony magnanimously, "I'll be the general. Regina will be a major. And—" he saw Rush retreating slowly—"Professor will drive the ambulance." There was real generalship in the way Tony marshalled his unwilling troops. "You stay behind, Professor, and be ready to carry off the wounded. Get the ambulance!" pointing to our battered toy wagon.

We attacked the fort, poking our guns through the wire and shrilling our fear and excitement as the dog crunched the wooden sticks in his powerful jaws. With our yells, the beast grew more frantic. He tore at the wire and threw himself against it till one corner ripped away from the post, and, with a lunge, he was upon us.

The others ran, but I stood frozen with fear. Fifty chunky pounds of muscle catapulted at me, knocked me down. I lay on my back staring into the dripping red mouth. I felt his hot breath. The white teeth almost touched my face. The broad, powerful chest was just above me. Then, most terrifying, the long wet tongue was slapped across my face like a rough towel!

Then, Tony's voice in my ears, high-pitched to the breaking point, but courageous still: "Stop that, you damn dog!"

He kicked the animal squarely on the sensitive stubby nose.

Until now the dog must have been activated by playfulness, for I had not received a scratch. But whatever amiability he felt was forgotten in the indignity he had suffered. With amazing quickness for so short legged and heavy set an animal, he sprang upon Tony. The white fangs ripped down Tony's thigh.

Regina's screams rang in my ears, and I added my howls to the pandemonium. I don't think a sound escaped Tony's lips. I heard him bringing the broomstick down in desperate, frantic whacks. I heard the dog's teeth snapping at the wood and his sharp growls as he sprang again and again at the stick.

At last Tony cried out triumphantly. "Bite my brother, will you? You damn Bum!" His words ended with a sob.

I saw the dog scrambling under the low kitchen porch. From this retreat he looked out, still growling. I suspect now that Bum had suddenly realized the enormity of his crime or Tony could not have beat him off, but no doubt of Tony's prowess troubled me then.

Half a dozen grown people, aroused by our screams, came running.

"Tony whipped the bulldog!" I crowed.

Then the sight of blood streaming down Tony's leg filled me with fresh panic. Tony dropped down on the grass. His face was white and set. Then suddenly he went limp and toppled over sideways. My heart turned over in me.

Aunt Addie lifted him up and carried him across the lawn to our house.

"Phone for Dr. Ames," she said to Rush.

When I peeped through the door of Tony's room, Aunt Addie was tearing strips from an old tablecloth. Regina's mother was pouring hot water in a basin. I crept back to the stairs and sat there wretchedly on the top step. Rush had disappeared. He always crawled away in a corner by himself when there was trouble.

After long minutes Dr. Ames came. He passed me on the stairs without even seeing me, and went into Tony's room. I heard him bustling about. He was very energetic for a stout man. He took quick short steps across the room. After an interminable time, I heard his laugh—a hearty laugh, infinitely reassuring.

I pushed open the door and sidled into the room. The air was filled with terrifying, doctor-like smells. But Tony was propped up on the pillows reciting his adventure with appropriate gestures.

"The enemy burst from the rampart!" he cried. "The captain covered the retreat, but was attacked in the rear. He called for reinforcements. And I went to his aid."

"And you were attacked in the flank," Dr. Ames chuckled.

He shook all over when he laughed. He was a round, pink-cheeked, roly-poly little man. I used to wonder if he bounced when he fell down.

Tony spied me flattened back against the wall. "Come here, Captain, and look at this mess Doc put on my leg. There's three stitches under there, too," Tony announced proudly.

We did not see Bum again. He was sent away in disgrace. But Tony's scar and my title remained as honorable souvenirs of the battle.

III
"NOT TILL THE BODY OF AN OWNER LIES DEAD—"

Rush was different from Tony and me. We were normal healthy little animals. Rush was not gregarious. He went for long walks by himself. And sometimes we found him in dim, out-of-the-way corners, straining his eyes over a book. Professor, Tony called him, because of the big glasses which gave him a solemn, owl-like look. Rush had a little of the artist, a little of the poet and a little of the musician in him. But he lacked that wholesome boyishness which always made Tony the favorite.

Rush had brown eyes like Tony's, but darker and larger—too large for his thin pale face. Tony was sturdy and strong and tanned. When he flexed his biceps proudly, the muscle rippled under the smooth brown skin. I was neither temperamental like Rush, nor heroic like Tony, but it was Tony I tried to emulate.

It was Rush, of course, who ferreted out the legend of Haunted Mine and how it had got its name It was an old mine that had been worked for more than four generations. There were abandoned shafts and forgotten levels where the roof had long ago fallen in.

An old woman who lived at the edge of town had told Rush the story. She had been born here in Genesee when the town was only a huddle of rough shacks, and Haunted Mine was the only mine in the valley. It had not been called Haunted Mine then, but Genesee Mine. Her father had cut coal there before she was born, and he was one of the few who escaped the disaster that gave the mine its name.

It had happened more than eighty years ago. There were no shafts then nor electric hoists, no coal cutting machines, no ventilating fans nor air compressors. The tunnel led into the side of the hill from an

outcropping of coal on Moon Mountain, and followed the steep slant
of the seam into the earth. For ventilation a fire was kept going under
a huge chimney so that the heat sucked the air up from the long black
corridors.

The seam of coal was very thick then and the tunnels were high.
Pillars of coal were left to support the roof. But the roof was soft and
nearly half the coal had to be left in pillars. These could not be got
out until the roof had fallen, the waste settled and new roads driven
in, which would, of course, take a long time.

The owner of the mine was greedy and did not want to wait.
There were no laws in those days governing the working of mines
and no organizations to protect the miners. The owner of Genesee
Mine wanted to get out all the coal he could. The pillars were cut
smaller. There were "creeps" in the floor as the great weight crushed
the pillars down and forced up the strata between them. The roof
crumbled in a few places, but without injury to the men. There were
rumblings and hollow sounds and deep mutterings in the earth. The
miners grew uneasy and complained. But the owner laughed at their
fears. He ordered more pillars robbed.

Then one day, without further warning, the pillars crumpled under the mighty pressure of the mountain. The roof came down everywhere. There were no more tunnels. Seventy-nine men were buried
alive. If any escaped the fall of rock, they had died slowly and more
horribly of suffocation. None was ever seen again. Their bodies were
never recovered. The mine owner would not open that level again
because the coal there was almost worked out, and it was more prof-
itable to drive a new level into another seam.

After that disaster miners sometimes heard moans and muffled
cries like those of imprisoned men. And Genesee Mine began to be
called Haunted Mine. Old women shook their heads and said that
some day the owner of Haunted Mine would pay for those lost lives.
But that owner had died peacefully in his bed, and never yet had any
great calamity befallen the owners of Haunted Mine. Now the prophecy was forgotten by all but a few ancients.

Rush repeated it to us one summer evening as we sat on the porch
steps. Rush with his thin bare knees clasped under his chin, gazing
up at the top of Moon Mountain and the stars.

"And she says the ghosts of those miners are still in those abandoned tunnels. And some day yet Haunted Mine will be a grave for its owner," Rush intoned solemnly. "And not till then will the spirits of those lost miners be at rest."

"Shucks!" muttered Tony. "There's no such thing as ghosts. And if I did see one, I'd kick him in the shins." But his voice had a queer uneasy sound. He picked up a pebble from the walk and shied it into the live-oak where a screech owl hooted dismally.

Rush pushed back the lock of straight brown hair that fell over his forehead. "Turribul things have happened in Haunted Mine," he chanted with quiet intensity. "Turribul things are going to happen." His voice sank to a troubled whisper. "'Not till the body of an owner lies dead,' he said, 'will the spirits rest in Haunted Mine.'"

"Aw, dry up," said Tony. "You sound like an old woman, Professor."

But in spite of Tony's assurance, I was impressed and frightened as I often was by Rush's tales. For years I really believed he could see strange things invisible to ordinary eyes.

After that the cold dank air that came up from the shaft always seemed to me to carry the smell of a tomb. Not until I was nine or ten years old could I be persuaded to descend into the mine. And then I think only Regina's taunt bolstered up my courage.

"Baby—'fraid cat!" She softened the sting by holding out her hand to me.

She and Rush and Tony and Big Bill, the engineer who was taking us down, were already standing in the big grimy cage that would presently sink down into the earth. Rush was afraid, too— I knew by the way his lips were pressed together. But Regina was venturesome like Tony. She was only a year younger than he, and almost as tall now. She had grown amazingly in the last year and had assumed a patronizing air towards Rush and me which I did not like at all. I pulled away now when she put her arm around my shoulders.

"Hug Tony if you want to hug somebody," I said.

And to my surprise, Regina's face went red.

Tony gave my arm a vicious pinch. Then the cage sank slowly into the darkness. I heard Big Bill chuckling to himself.

It was the lunch hour below, and the talk and laughter of the men who sat about eating and swapping yarns, the sight of familiar grimy faces, the friendly greetings reassured me, but did not completely banish my fear of the underground. Big Bill showed us the horses munching corn in their stalls, and let us ride in one of the empty cars down the long sloping track to the face of the coal where cutting machines were eating into the black seam.

The low passage seemed to take form under our Davy lamps and to vanish again behind us. The black walls soaked up the feeble light like blotters. The mysterious darkness was all around us. The whistle of the draft, the strange dead smell of the underground, the creaking of the timbers overhead filled me with dread. I kept close to Big Bill.

He was a great homely fellow nearly seven feet tall with bushy sandy hair and a broad smiling mouth—a favorite with all of us. His hands were thick and stubby with immense freckles and tufts of sandy hair on the backs. He had a boy about my age and was always telling me about him. Billy could play three pieces on the harmonica. He could play *Auld Lang Syne* so it sounded almost like the organ at church, Big Bill said. Billy was not afraid of the dark or the mine, Big Bill told me, so I kept my own fears to myself. But I was glad when it was all over and we were out in the sunshine again.

That day was Rush's birthday, I remember, and therefore a holiday for us all. It was for that occasion we had been permitted to visit the mine, though it was Tony who wanted to go, not Rush.

It was in the afternoon of the same day we had our first encounter with Pat Brace. We had gone home to a birthday dinner with cake and ice cream, and, afterwards, the surprise of a glittering new bicycle for Rush. The frame was scarlet and nickel plate; there were big rubber grips on the shining handlebars, and a bell, and a coaster attachment. We took turns at riding it.

Tony was doing circles on the lawn with his arms folded and his feet on the handlebars when we first noticed the boy watching us through the fence. His hands grasped the iron bars, and his eyes followed Tony with a peculiar intensity. Dark brown eyes they were—the kind usually called black—shadowed by dark lashes under straight heavy brows and a tousle of black curls. His face was thin, but not delicate like Rush's, a stern strong face for a boy, square jawed, square chinned, with prominent cheek bones, a face all straight lines and angles, a face that seemed too old for his years—he was about Tony's size.

Regina, seated on the grass, greeted him with a casual, "Hullo. Some bike, isn't it?"

"I bet it's the finest one you ever saw!" I crowed boastfully.

"Yes." The strange boy bit out the word without looking at us. He glowered through the iron fence at Tony.

"It's mine," Rush confided shyly. "Like to try it?"

"No; thank you," curtly.

Regina glanced up, surprised at the tone. "Why not?" She was all curiosity.

Tony had swung his feet down to the pedals. He circled around now and brought up beside the fence. "Why not?" he repeated.

"I don't want to," was the surly answer.

We looked at him curiously. Never before had a child refused to play with us. We were the rich children of the town—Regina's father owned the Genesee Bank. We had the nicest playthings, the widest lawns, and the most fun, I think, of any children in Genesee. We were democratic, as children naturally are, but we expected as much from others. And the boy was poor, as we saw now. He was shabbily dressed, and his coat sleeves lacked inches of covering his bony wrists.

"Are you afraid?" asked Tony. It was not a challenge, only a puzzled question.

Then Rush, with his quick intuition, inquired gravely: "Why don't you like us?"

The boy's gaze was still fastened on the bicycle. "It ought to be mine!" he said fiercely. "And the house, too." He stared hostilely at the red brick, turreted old mansion, then turned his frowning glance on us. "Yes—and Haunted Mine, too!"

We stared back, wide-eyed.

"What do you mean?" Tony challenged belligerently.

The boy laughed harshly. "You don't know, do you?" He climbed up on the fence so that his square frowning face looked down at us from above. "Your uncle stole the mine from my father—that's what I mean!"

Tony had slid off the bicycle. He stood with his feet planted wide apart, his head tilted to one side. "Come on in the yard and say that!" he invited.

The boy's lip curled. He had fine white teeth. "What good would that do? It wouldn't get the mine back, would it? You got to go to law about things like that. My mother hasn't any money for lawyers now, but when I grow up, I'm going to be a lawyer, myself. And I'm going to own Haunted Mine." He turned deliberately and walked away.

Regina drew in a long astonished breath. "The little devil!" she exclaimed. She climbed on the fence and called after him: "Hey, kid, what's your name?"

The strange boy glanced back. His tense frown relaxed a little. "Patrick Brace," he said, and walked on.

Regina shook the hair out of her eyes and smiled her elfish smile. "Isn't he the killingest thing? I know who he is. He lives in that funny little stone house on the hill. And—" Regina broke off suddenly, and her voice sank to a whisper. "And his father killed himself!"

"How? Why? When?" we demanded.

"I don't know why. But he turned on the gas in the kitchen one day, and Mrs. Brace found him lying there dead. It was a long time ago, when Pat was a baby."

"Poor kid," Rush said slowly. "He looks so—honest—and brave—"

"And he has such pretty curls," said Regina. She smoothed down her silken bangs and twisted the locks that made two slender golden half-moons around her piquant face. "I love curly hair," she sighed.

"Curls!" snorted Tony. "Curls!" He sprang on the bicycle and pedaled furiously across the lawn.

At dinner that night, I asked suddenly out of my puzzled thoughts: "Who is Pat Brace? Why did his father kill himself?"

The question dropped into the middle of a brief silence. Uncle Matthew laid down his fork and looked at me from under his shaggy brows—black brows in strange contrast with hair already gray.

"Pat Brace?" he repeated thoughtfully. Then nodded. "O—Brace. Ummm, I suppose he brooded over fancied wrongs till he believed everybody was against him."

When we were older, Uncle Matthew told us how he had taken over Haunted Mine from Pat's father on a foreclosure.

"There is an old Chinese proverb that says: 'Lend your money; lose your friend'," Uncle Matthew quoted sadly. He stared into the fire, and his long slender fingers tapped the arms of his chair. The firelight threw into relief his long, aristocratic face with its high-bridged nose and fine dark eyes.

He wanted us to understand all about the deal, he said. He had made too large a loan on the mine, partly through friendship for Pat's father. The mine had been in a bad way then. Pat's father was a poor manager, but Uncle Matthew hoped the loan would enable him to pull through. The money had been sunk in idealistic improvements, but still the mine was not on a paying basis. It happened at the time of the panic in 1903. Dallas Brace could not get another loan anywhere. And when he could not meet his obligations, Uncle Matthew was forced to take over the mine to protect the money he had invested.

"When the mine began to pay, Dal Brace was bitter—that was only natural, I suppose," Uncle Matthew said. "He did everything he could to ruin me in Genesee. He even brought suit against me, but the case was thrown out of court for lack of evidence. Dallas Brace was never practical. He had wild dreams—Utopian plans. 'Mad Dal Brace' he was called." Uncle Matthew sighed and shook his head. "I'm afraid Pat has inherited some of his father's instability."

IV
"CAPPY, I'VE BEEN HANDED A STIFF JOLT"

We rarely saw Pat Brace during the years we were growing up. We had almost forgotten there was such a person when Rush brought him home from college for the Christmas holidays.

"Pat's mother died two months ago," Rush explained to Aunt Addie. "He didn't have anywhere else to go, so I brought him here."

Pat was twenty-four or five then. He was working his way through the state university, studying law, and was in the same class as Rush. This was their senior year.

Uncle Matthew had decided we needed a lawyer in the family, and, since Tony was all for mining and I, of course, had chosen the same, it fell upon Rush to study law—Rush who wanted only to dabble at art and music and poetry. Naturally, Rush was not doing particularly well with the law, and I suspect depended a great deal on Pat to tide him over the rough places. At any rate, a close friendship had sprung up between them.

They came home in an old racing car that was Pat's chief pride and trouble. Its battered body told the story of its last run on the track. Pat had it geared down now to something like a sane speed. "Tiger" he called it, and had painted ridiculous black stripes on its tawny body and added a long tin tail curved up at the end realistically and menacingly. Pat spent hours tinkering with it—he was a good mechanic—and sometimes on a straight stretch of road let it out to suicidal bursts of speed.

Pat was almost handsome now. He was as tall as Tony, as broad-shouldered and as muscular. The hollows under his cheek bones had filled out. His eyes had lost some of their fierce, hungry look. But the overhanging black brows still seemed to be frowning. They made a straight black line across his face. His mouth was straight and firm, too; thin lipped and rather wide, it made a parallel line. His square chin added a third.

When I first recognized those uncompromising lines as he came up the walk with Rush, I experienced a few minutes of misgiving, an uneasy fear that our vacation was going to be spoiled. But I was soon put at ease.

I liked the straightforward way Pat Brace greeted Uncle Matthew:

"I told Rush I couldn't accept your hospitality, Mr. North, without apologizing for some of the things I've said and thought about you," he began before us all.

Uncle Matthew cut him short with: "No use digging up the past, Pat."

"But I want you to know," said Pat earnestly, "that I looked up the records of the case, and I found all the papers in order and perfectly legal. I don't know what the evidence was my father thought he had against you—my mother said he was always hunting for a letter or something he thought he had lost—but whatever it was, I don't see how it could have helped any. I think he just brooded over his failure till he was morbid."

Uncle Matthew still held Pat's hand. "Thank you for saying that, my boy. Now we'll forget all about it."

That was my sophomore year at the School of Mines. Tony had received his degree three years before and was now superintendent of Haunted Mine. He was not so well liked in Genesee as I had expected. Some of the older miners seemed to resent having so young a man in charge. But Uncle Matthew was satisfied. He was depending more and more on Tony in managing the business.

Responsibility had had a sobering effect on Tony. He seemed older, and there was a worried look about his eyes. He did not join in our fun as Pat did. But Tony's seriousness seemed to me becoming in a man about to be married. He was engaged to Regina, and the wedding was set for June.

Regina was bubbling over with plans. I found her in the library one evening poring over her messy, much-erased sketches for their house, brows puckered studiously, lower lip caught in her teeth, and looking prettier than ever. The light gleamed on her ash gold hair, waved now with astonishing naturalness and drawn into a little knot at the nape of her neck. The freckles had vanished from her nose. Her expression was no longer saucy, but sweetly serious.

"Look, Cappy," she traced a line with a much-chewed pencil, "do you think Tony ought to have a little dressing room or just a big closet? Is he messy with his clothes, or is he orderly?" She was very much in earnest.

"Messy? Not Tony. Uncle Matthew is the only one in this family who is untidy," I told her.

"But do you think Tony would like a dressing room?" she persisted. They were very much in love.

Tony drove me out to the spot they had chosen for the house, two miles up the valley on the winding Hill Road, away from the slag piles and the smoke stacks of the mine and the ugly little town, yet only a hundred yards or so from the paved highway.

"I wish we could be married now," Tony said. "I don't like to wait so long. But Gina wants the house built first. We're going to call it Happy House."

Tony smiled a little crooked whimsical smile that curved only one corner of his mouth. Tony laughed with both sides of his mouth, but a smile always came out of the left corner first. It was a happy, shy smile that somehow warmed me. It was good to have Tony confide in me again.

I did not dream that anything was wrong. It was Rush who discovered that. He came into my room one night after I had been asleep. He sat on the edge of my bed.

"Cappy, what's wrong with Tony?"

I rolled over. Rush's brown eyes were troubled. "You're always imagining something," I grumbled. "Go away and let me sleep."

"I think it must be the business," said Rush. "It couldn't be on account of Regina."

"Of course not."

Three months later I remembered the conversation. In March the Genesee Bank failed. Regina's father was ruined. Aunt Addie wrote that he had given up the big stone house next to ours and had moved into a cottage at the edge of town. Regina's mother was ill. Regina was needed at home to care for her, and the wedding had been post-poned indefinitely. Tony had stopped work on the new house, though it was nearly completed.

These explanations were far from satisfactory.

Tony did not write till May. His letter ended with:

> Cappy, I've been handed a stiff jolt. Regina blames me for the whole thing—the crash. I saw it coming, but I couldn't help it. I never dreamed it would be so bad. It was that Baker and Rice business. They had the idea they were going to handle about half our output as usual, and sold the coal on contract, then borrowed money on the contracts at the bank.
>
> But Uncle Matthew never agreed to let them have any coal this year. Wages and costs have increased so he couldn't let them have it at the price they expected. After the strike Uncle Matthew signed other contracts at nearly double the old price. Baker and Rice couldn't get any coal to fill their contracts and, of course, the bank lost all the money advanced. But what could I do, Cappy? I begged Uncle Matthew to sell Baker and Rice enough to fill their contracts, even if we lost money. But I couldn't insist when coal has gone up so. Uncle Matthew said if Regina really cared, she wouldn't let this business come between us. And I don't think she would. That's what hurts most.
>
> I don't want to be bellyaching—but—to pass Gina on the street and have her look the other way—to live here in the same town and not be able to talk to her—to count the profits piling up from Uncle Matthew's contracts and know that Gina and I are paying for it all—it's enough to drive me mad. Maybe when you and Rush come home, I'll buck up and be more amiable.
>
> Tony.

But Tony did not buck up. He was changed. He did not confide in me any more. He had other friends, older men. He was going with the smart, fast young married crowd of the town, and drinking entirely too much. He looked older and not so fit. I would have given my own hope of happiness to see him and Regina together again as they had been at Christmas.

Happy House stood ironically lonely, deserted, unfinished, its empty windows like sightless eyes staring hopelessly through the high weeds sprung up around it. I thought if Regina could see that wreck of her dreams, she might forget her angry, wounded pride. Surely Tony had been punished enough.

I walked out to the place at the edge of town where Regina and her father were trying to start a chicken ranch, but as I drew near the low, rambling unpainted cottage, I saw Pat's ridiculous striped Tiger there in front. I did not go any farther. I felt suddenly powerless and wretched.

That summer I saw Regina often beside Pat racing through town in the long low car, her chin, held high, the wind whipping back her hair.

Once I met her on the street. She tried to hurry past me, but I turned and walked in the same direction.

"Why didn't you come to May's party last night?" I asked.

She said stiffly: "Mother isn't well."

"Your mother is up," I argued. "Yet you never go anywhere."

Regina stopped and turned on me savagely, little lights running through her greenish eyes. "If you must know, I haven't anything to wear. And I don't want to be pitied. And I don't want people asking me why I don't make up with Tony Sheridan."

She pursed her mouth into a little round button and tilted her chin defiantly. She looked like a naughty little girl who needed spanking. Her hair was short and straight again and framed her heart-shaped face like two parentheses. And I saw now that she was wearing a faded old green linen dress. If she was not so pretty as she had been at Christmas, she was more like our old playmate.

"Gina," I began impulsively, "if you could see Tony—"

But she cut me short. "It's no use, Cappy." Her voice was hard and level. "Tony and your uncle let my father be ruined because they saw a chance to make more for themselves. I couldn't marry a man like that." Her eyes looked straight ahead. She walked on rapidly and did not seem to notice when I said goodbye and turned back.

In August she married Pat Brace. They went to New York for their honeymoon.

V
"PAT'S SUSPICIOUS"

Pat's old hatred of us seemed to have flared up again. He had taken an office in Genesee—a dingy, high-windowed place over a grocery store. And we heard he was going to bring suit against Uncle Matthew in behalf of Baker and Rice and the bank.

Uncle Matthew was of the opinion the suit would never be filed.

"Pat hasn't a shred of evidence. I wouldn't have made such an agreement with Baker and Rice without a deposit to bind it. But if it does come to court, we have a lawyer in the family, eh?"

He laid an affectionate hand on Rush's shoulder. Rush stared wretchedly at the floor.

"It's that spirit of revenge in Pat," Uncle Matthew continued sadly. "He wants to stir up hard feeling against me. It's to be expected though, I suppose, since he married Regina. And I've lost another old friend in Regina's father. But a man can't make a success without making enemies. I'm sorry. But I couldn't sacrifice my own business to pull him out of the hole. I have Addie and you boys to think of, too."

In September I went back to school, and, as boys do, threw off the depression of the summer. I spent the Christmas holidays at a houseparty; Tony and Rush rarely wrote, and not until I returned to Genesee in June did I realize the state of affairs at home.

Uncle Matthew was no longer satisfied with either Rush or Tony. And no one could blame him. But I was equally sorry for my brothers. Tony, who had never been wild in his youth, was drinking and gambling to such an extent that he was unfit for work much of the time. I knew that secretly he blamed Uncle Matthew for the loss of Regina.

And Rush, never suited for the law, had been unfortunate with his cases. Though Pat Brace had never filed suit in behalf of Baker and Rice, he had raked up and championed several minor cases against Haunted Mine—claims of adjoining property owners. Pat had taken them on a contingent basis, it was said. The suits had cost Uncle Matthew some annoying, though not serious, losses. And Pat had profited handsomely by them. Uncle Matthew blamed Rush for not making a stronger defense and accused him even of disloyalty.

Pat had written editorials for the Genesee paper declaring Haunted Mine unsafe, and the ventilating system inadequate, with the result that the insurance rates had been raised, the miners were becoming dissatisfied, and Uncle Matthew's prestige in Genesee had decreased noticeably.

There was a threat of trouble in the air, as vaguely disturbing as distant thunder in a summer sky. Tony was taking the precaution of watching the shifts as they went down, as we always did when there seemed a possibility of disturbance, to make sure there was no stranger among the men, for wherever there appears the slightest breach between employers and workers, there are professional agitators ready to plant their charge of social dynamite. And Pat's attacks had supplied that breach.

The necessity of opposing Pat Brace made Rush unhappy. But in spite of his own distaste and Uncle Matthew's displeasure, he was struggling with dogged determination to earn his salary. And he had, in his quiet, thoroughgoing way, fallen hopelessly in love. The girl was Norma Elliott, Uncle Matthew's secretary.

Norma had gold-red hair that waved naturally, amber colored eyes, and a beautiful profile with a delicately curved upper lip. Her eyebrows were plucked into dainty arched lines. She was very smart looking for our small town and had a city bred assurance of manner which excited both admiration and distrust. She was tiny, pert, vivacious, and, I feared, inconstant. If she were, she had it in her power to hurt Rush even more than Regina had Tony.

I think now that Regina realized her marriage was a mistake. She did not look happy. There was a line between her brows. She was thin; her cheek bones had become too prominent, her fingers too slim and nervous. She and Pat were living in the "funny little stone house" where Pat had been born.

Regina came to our offices occasionally—we had a suite over the bank—and, though her manner was still frigid towards Uncle Matthew, she had forgiven the rest of us. I was acting as cashier during the summer months, and from my desk, I could see everyone who came and went. Regina came ostensibly to see Rush. She usually had some excuse, a borrowed book to return, a message from Pat, an invitation of some kind. But her eyes, I noticed, always sought Tony's door, and twice I saw her drop a note on his desk as she passed. But Norma, who did not realize how matters had stood between Regina and Tony, missed these nuances and was a little jealous of Regina.

"Why does she have to pick on Rush?" Norma pouted, amber eyes gleaming under lowered lashes. "Why can't she sob out her troubles on some other man's shoulder?" Norma banged out a few words viciously on her typewriter.

I tried to turn the matter aside with: "Regina's like a sister to us—"

But Norma gave me a sidelong, amused look. Her short little upper lip curled derisively. "When a man says that, I suspect the worst." She put a new sheet in the machine. "Regina isn't happy with Pat Brace. Nobody would be. He's quarrelsome—always afraid someone is going to insult him. Pat's suspicious, too." Norma leaned over her desk and lowered her voice. "What I can't understand is why he doesn't get on to Regina and Rush. Glory, I'd be scared if I were Regina."

I couldn't tell her it was Tony, not Rush, Regina came to see.

Later Norma stopped by my desk to whisper: "Regina ought to be more careful. She won't fool Pat Brace long. Those black eyes of his just look clear through you. He simply glares. He reminds me of a hypnotist I saw in vaudeville once."

I was to remember her words later when I saw that steely black gleam in Pat's eyes.

I did not realize then that Regina was meeting Tony. But a few evenings later as I was sitting on the steps enjoying a cigarette before turning in, I heard Tony's car coughing painfully in the garage. He got it halfway down the drive, and then it expired. The spark plugs needed cleaning, I knew. They had been missing for weeks. But Tony hated soiling his hands with so menial a task. I heard him trying in vain to coax the motor into a semblance of regularity.

I threw away my cigarette and strolled out to the drive.

Tony looked up, surprised. "Just when I'm in a hurry, the darn thing has to throw a fit," he grumbled, jerking impatiently at the choke. "Haven't had the old bus three months, and she's got the asthma."

It was a handsome little Pearson coupé, rich tan in color and up-holstered in brown. I lifted the hood, tested the plugs with a screw driver, cleaned four of them on my handkerchief and replaced them. The cylinders throbbed regularly.

"Good boy," said Tony appreciatively.

"Where are you going?" I asked, closing the hood.

"Got to give the graveyard shift the once over."

"Then why all the haste? You've over an hour yet."

Tony glanced up quickly. He had forgotten his muttered words, I suppose. The upward rays of the switchboard light accentuated his surprised look.

"Oh—thought I'd drop in at a movie—if it isn't too late—"

He was elaborately casual, I realized later.

"Then I'll go with you," I said, one hand on the door.

"Oh, I meant to tell you," Tony exclaimed suddenly. "Aunt Addie wants you to drive her over to Mrs. Barnes' a little later. Aunt Addie is going to sit up with her."

We still do such old-fashioned things in Genesee as sitting up with sick neighbors.

Before I could answer, there was a grinding of gears and the car slipped away from me. I stood watching the vanishing red tail light.

Aunt Addie was mildly surprised when I mentioned the matter of Mrs. Barnes. "But Tony knows I sat up with her last night," she said.

"He probably forgot," I mumbled.

Tony was not going to a movie. The sudden conviction that he was going to meet Regina flashed over me sickeningly. Tony had never lied to me before.

VI
"THE REVOLVER WAS GONE"

As I look back, it all seems to begin with our amateur rehearsal—a rehearsal for a play that was never to be put on. It was a spectacular, pageant-like affair laid in the days of chivalry, knighthood, intrigue and romance, one of those showy pieces where costumes can compensate largely for poor acting. Tony was the dashing, adventurous hero, and Norma Elliott was the golden-haired heroine for whom he dared all. An actor from the city had been engaged as director. It was great fun—until we began to rehearse the third act.

It was Friday evening. The barn-like stage of the Opera House was mercilessly exposed in the glare of footlights and an erratic spot someone was experimenting with. In the shadowy cavern of the auditorium were scattered half a dozen little groups of performers and friends. Whispers, sibilant and gossipy, busy chatter and little bursts of laughter rippled through the vast empty space.

I was sitting alone in the darkness of the last row trying to recall the few lines I had to speak, for I was to play an ancient astronomer in a long white beard and a monklike robe. As I mumbled over the queer stilted phrases, I saw Regina come in alone.

She was wearing a rose shawl with a long fringe over a sleeveless white dress. She drew the shawl around her shoulders as if she were cold, though it was a warm July evening. Her glance darted about the auditorium. Then as her eyes grew accustomed to the dark, she saw me in the corner and came over.

"Has Tony come yet, Cappy?" she asked. Her voice was a little breathless.

"Not yet."

My eyes met hers and I saw she had been crying. I pushed down the seat of the chair next to mine.

"What's the matter, Gina?"

She glanced about quickly as though she would like to escape, then changed her mind and dropped down in the seat. Her right hand rested on the back of the chair in front, and she leaned her head over on her arm, turning her face away from the aisle towards me. She tried to smile, then wiped her eyes with her handkerchief.

"There's no use trying to pretend with you, is there, Cappy?" She laid her left hand on mine, and I felt the little wad of linen in her palm wet against my fingers. "I must see Tony," she whispered. Her hand gripped mine tighter. "Pat told me not to come here to-night. He's forbidden me—*forbidden* me—to go on with this play. If I drop out now, everyone will know it was because of Pat's jealousy and because he forced me to. I couldn't bear it. I told him it would cause talk. He said he'd give people more than that to talk about. Oh, Cappy, I must tell someone. I can't stand it any longer. I'm afraid of him when he's like that—I'm afraid there's a streak of insanity." Her words came in a quick, choking rush.

"Listen, Cappy, two weeks ago I saw Pat loading a revolver. I didn't even know he had one. I told Tony—I begged him to leave town, or at least be careful. But he laughed at the idea. 'Run away from old Pat?' he said. Then I begged him to carry a gun—to protect himself—for my sake. But he said I was worrying over nothing. 'Pat's bark is worse than his bite,' he said. 'I'm going to put a muzzle on him some day.' You know how Tony makes light of danger."

"But maybe there isn't any danger," I argued, though my heart seemed suddenly squeezed dry by icy fingers. "Maybe Pat just—just—"

"But wait—you don't know—" Regina stopped me. "I haven't told you all. Pat put the revolver in his chest of drawers. I looked every day to see if it was there. To-night after he left, I looked, and the revolver was gone!" Regina pressed her handkerchief to her quivering lips. "Pat's out with that gun, Cappy. He's looking for Tony. Oh, I must see Tony! I must tell him. I can't stand it! Why doesn't he come?"

There was nothing I could say to reassure her. I was numb with dread. My throat was pressed dry. I sat there dumbly wishing I could do something to save her and Tony—and afraid I might never see Tony again.

But presently he came in. Thankfulness welled up inside me. He saw Regina instantly and stopped beside her. His hand covered hers on the back of the chair. Regina looked up. They did not notice me. I slid out down the long row of seats to the other aisle.

Aunt Addie, who had come with Tony, was surrounded by a group of women discussing costumes, programs, tickets and other details of the performance. Aunt Addie was mildly excited, very busy and gently dictatorial. She stood primly erect, a tall, angular, dignified woman. Her brown hair was barely streaked with gray—two silver wings flowed back from her temples—and it was still coiled in a big knot on top of her head in defiance of custom or style. Her skirts fell uncompromisingly to her ankles. Yet, somehow, as always, she gave the impression of being well dressed and almost handsome. Perhaps it was the simplicity and the richness of material she affected. She was wearing a platinum and diamond pin, which looked almost magnificent against the severe black satin of her dress, and a single ring Uncle Matthew had given her.

Aunt Addie, arguing politely, insisting firmly, intent on the unimportant problems of our amateur performance, had no idea of the real drama, and the more important one, being enacted behind her back. Neither did anyone else know that in the darkness of the last row Tony was sitting with both arms tight about Regina.

I wandered up to the stage. Norma was there flirting with the director while Rush looked on helplessly, too wretched to realize she was doing it for his benefit.

"I'd just love to see you on the stage," Norma cooed, opening her golden brown eyes very wide and gazing admiringly at the director, an elegant little man of about forty with sleek mouse-colored hair and a close-cropped mustache. She took a cigarette he offered her and lighted it from his. "I know you must be simply wonderful." She glanced around at Rush, blowing a little cloud of smoke at him, and asked: "Don't you?"

"Yes," said Rush tonelessly, his great dark eyes, patient and unsmiling, fixed on Norma.

The rehearsal began with a love scene between Norma and Tony, a secret meeting with Norma fearing discovery by her ducal uncle, the villain of the piece. Tony rattled off his lines absently at first, but Norma threw herself into the spirit of the play.

"'My love, my love, I fear for thee! But feel the beating of my heart!'" She clasped Tony's hand to her breast and raised pleading eyes to his. Under the fragile chiffon of her dress her slight bosom rose and fell with quick tremulous breathing.

My glance sought Rush standing in the wings. His sensitive mouth was drawn into a tight hard line.

The scene went on, with the director, oblivious to undercurrents of trouble, waxing enthusiastic.

"Cling to him," he ordered Norma. "Remember you may never see him again."

Norma clung to Tony, both slim arms around his neck. She was very fresh and dainty to-night in transparent, cobwebby chiffon flowered in yellow and brown, clinging revealingly to the budding young curves of her body. Tony was no saint. Neither was he an actor acting away for so much a week. A kissable girl in his arms brought the natural reaction. Tony kissed her. And it was no perfunctory stage kiss.

"Not yet—not yet!" cried the director. "Your lines—you say—"

There was a snicker from the audience. Then a round of applause drowned out the director's words.

"What's your hurry, Tony?" someone called.

Tony was never embarrassed. An excited recklessness seemed to take possession of him now.

"I like this scene," he confided to the audience with an engaging crooked smile, one arm around Norma.

He went on with the part. His low words seemed meant for Norma alone. He kissed her again—lingeringly.

"No, no," protested the director. "Not so much moonlight and roses. Not so dreamy. Remember your life is in danger. You're desperate! You kiss her fiercely—like this—see!" The director illustrated the action.

"Oh, yes," murmured Tony. He drew Norma towards him. "'Be brave, my sweet, for I must fly! From thy encircling arms I go unto the arms of fate!'" He pressed his lips to hers.

Then Rush strode out from the wings. "Is it necessary to rehearse this scene so many times?" he demanded of Tony, his voice deadly cold. "Don't you get enough practice off the stage?"

A hush fell over the little audience, who, until now, had been thoroughly enjoying the scene. A dull red crept up Tony's face, but he choked back his anger.

"Don't look so fierce, Professor. This isn't mellerdrammer."

Rush was pale. He held his clenched hands close to his sides. "I saw you—" he began, slurred, began again, "I won't have—-"

"You ain't done right by our Nell!" Tony mocked lightly. But I could tell he was furious with Rush for making a scene.

Norma laughed nervously. "Glory, why shouldn't I kiss Tony? What's the harm? He's going to be my brother anyway, isn't he? And he's awfully good looking," with a sidelong glance at Tony.

"Too damn good looking," Rush muttered. His head was flung back with that quick nervous motion. He stepped closer to Tony. "You've played around with a lot of girls lately, but there's one girl you're going to keep your hands off—"

Rush had forgotten himself completely. I gripped his arm.

"Get hold of yourself, old man."

He ignored me. "You've had your own way about most things with Cappy and me because you're older and stronger—but if you think you can take Norma away from me—if you think I'm a coward—I'll—I'll—"

"You have nothing to do with it," Tony retorted recklessly. "As long as Norma doesn't object, I'll kiss her all I please."

"Norma is going to be my wife," Rush began in a strained voice, "and I won't have—"

"Oh, you won't!" Norma laughed shrilly, her eyes like flames "Well, you don't *own* me, Rush Sheridan!" There was a catch in her voice. She tossed back her red gold mop of hair and snatched the ring from her finger. "You're not going to dictate to me!"

For a moment Rush stared at the little circlet of gold in his palm. Then turned and strode off the stage. No one spoke while he walked the length of the aisle. The outer door slammed. The hollow sound reverberated through the empty building.

Then Norma laughed a little hysterically. "The silly old thing! Will you take me home, Cappy?"

Tony shrugged. "Who'd think the old Professor would fly off the handle like that?"

We went on with the rehearsal, but it was a spiritless affair.

I saw Regina and Tony together again in a corner behind some dilapidated scenery back stage. Regina had not fully recovered her composure, but her face was no longer crumpled with crying. Her eyes, though troubled, were clear and brave. She opened a little round silver box, and gazing into its tiny mirror, powdered her face. Her hands trembled slightly. The rose shawl slipped down, and Tony replaced it, his hands lingering on her shoulders. She looked up at him. When their eyes met, something seemed to pass between them.

No one seemed to notice the tenseness in her manner as she went through her short part in the play. When it was over, she wrapped her fringed shawl about her and strolled down the aisle with the slow undulating twist of hips and shoulders which, as a little girl, had marked her self-conscious moments on dress parade. She was acting now, I realized, and marveled at her self-control. She paused to speak to several people before she passed leisurely out into the night.

It was half an hour before I discovered that Tony had disappeared mysteriously—he must have slipped out the stage entrance. I was worried; I had wanted to talk to him, to urge him to be careful. But he had probably gone to the mine, I reflected, to watch the graveyard shift go down. With unrest in the air, we could not be too careful. And especially during the graveyard shift, which went on duty at eleven, for somehow trouble always seemed more likely to occur during this shift. There was no definite reason to fear a demonstration, but trouble, like fire-damp, may seep into a mine, invisible, impalpable, undiscovered, lurking in obscure nooks, till, touched off by a naked flame of hate, it wreaks destruction.

I tried to console myself with the thought that Tony would be at home when I got there. But I could not forget that look that had passed between him and Regina. There had been that old, familiar, reckless light in Tony's eyes. I knew he had been meeting Regina. What if Pat should find them together? I thought the rehearsal would never end.

Aunt Addie and I walked home with Norma—it was only a few blocks. Norma lived in a little brown bungalow with her mother and two younger sisters. The family had moved to Genesee a year ago, Mrs. Elliott to take a position in the high school. I had admired Norma for her willingness in helping her mother support the family—the two younger girls were still in school—and for her cheerful light-hearted disposition. But to-night I was alarmed for Rush's happiness. I reflected that Norma must spend all her salary for clothes. To-night I disapproved of her as much as Aunt Addie—more perhaps, for Aunt Addie understood her better, as she proved when we reached the little bungalow and stopped to say good-night.

Aunt Addie lifted up Norma's chin until she could look into the girl's eyes. "You've hurt Rush to-night, my dear. But I think you did it because you love him. Maybe you can tease some boys like that, but you'll only kill Rush's love. He doesn't make friends easily or quickly, but when he does, the roots strike down deep. Please don't hurt him deliberately."

I saw the tears glisten in Norma's amber eyes. She winked them back.

"He can't talk to me like that," she insisted stubbornly, but with quivering lips. "I didn't know he was such a prig."

She turned and fled into the house. After all, she was only nineteen.

"She's a vain little minx," said Aunt Addie, which, I think, explained part of the trouble.

But Aunt Addie didn't know that Norma imagined she had some justification for hurting Rush. Neither would Rush have dreamed of Norma's being jealous of Regina. I meant to explain it to him when I reached home, but in the events that followed I almost forgot so inconsequential a thing as Norma's childish jealousy.

Aunt Addie and I walked on towards home. As we crossed the avenue, a wedge of light cut a swath in the darkness, a car swerved from the driveway of our house, a few blocks away, and, gaining speed, bore down upon us. I recognized the powerful throb of Pat's racer—the same old Tiger but the outlandish stripes had given place to a sedate gray, and a tiny roadster top had been added. We hurried to step up on the curb as the machine roared past. There was a screeching of brakes as Pat, recognizing us, came to a stop with tires skidding on the gravel. We waited while he backed up.

Pat leaned over towards us. "Have you seen Regina?" he demanded. His brows came together and made one black line across his face.

Even in the dim light, the steely needle points in his black eyes sent a current of fear through me, and I recalled what Norma had said. But Aunt Addie seemed unaware of anything amiss.

"Regina was at the rehearsal to-night," she said innocently. "But she left early. Maybe she went to her mother's; I heard Mrs. Townsend was in bed again. Is she having one of her bad spells?"

Pat ignored the question. "Where is Tony?" he snapped.

"I'm worried about Tony," Aunt Addie confided gently. "He and Rush quarreled to-night—"

She stopped in surprise as Pat's car shot away, and I jumped to the running board.

"Pat, what are you going to do?" I demanded.

"Get off," ordered Pat. He speeded up.

I tightened my grip on the door. "I won't till you tell me—"

"I'm going to kill that God-damned brother of yours!"

"Pat, you're crazy! You don't know what you're doing!" I seized his arm. "Give me that gun!"

I tried to reach his pocket. But he flung me back and skidded the car around a corner. I lost my hold and was thrown into the street. I picked myself up, shaken by the fall, but more by fear. The Tiger's tail light, like a vengeful red eye, vanished in the night.

I went back to Aunt Addie. But I couldn't tell her of Pat's threat. My heart was churning under my ribs. I wanted to call the sheriff. But it seemed like disloyalty to Tony to reveal his affair with Regina. Tony wouldn't want that—no matter what the cost. And in a few minutes it might be too late to do anything.

Aunt Addie had not seen me fall. But she was puzzled by Pat's actions.

"What a queer young man he is," she remarked.

VII
"DR. AMES WAS WOUNDED"

As we reached the corner of our yard, we saw Uncle Matthew's sedan roll out of the drive and turn down the street away from us.

"That's Matthew!" exclaimed Aunt Addie. She lifted her voice in an ineffectual call: "*Yoohoo!* Matthew! Here we are!" He went on without hearing. "Now, isn't that too bad?" Aunt Addie murmured. "He's gone to the Opera House to get us."

But another explanation occurred to me. Pat must have been at our house looking for Tony, and Uncle Matthew, alarmed, had started out to try to stop Pat or to warn Regina and Tony. I ought to go to Regina's house, I decided—they might be there. I left Aunt Addie at the steps.

"Want to get a package of cigarettes," I mumbled with the air of just having thought of it.

I almost ran up the steep sloping street that climbed the hill above town. As I did, Pat came racing recklessly down. He did not see me in the shadow of the great elms along the sidewalk. I called to him. But the purr of his motor drowned my voice. The car swerved at the foot of the hill and was gone.

I hurried on towards the stone cottage at the top of the street, fearful of what I might find. The high narrow windows were dark. I rang the bell and tried the door. No one answered. I went to the back and called. The door was locked there, too. There was no light or sound, no sign of life. I was afraid Tony and Regina might be lying dead behind those curtained windows, those locked doors.

I could not call for help without bringing disaster upon Tony and Regina. I could not break into the house without attracting attention.

57

After all, I tried to argue, Tony might be safe at the mine. I decided to phone there first. I struck a match and looked at my watch—eleven-thirty.

As I dropped the match, I saw Uncle Matthew drive by, and, for a moment, I thought he was going to stop, but he recognized me, I think, and drove on. I didn't say anything—I didn't want to tell him why I was there. I dreaded putting my fears into words. Uncle Matthew, realizing evidently that Pat was not here, continued his search elsewhere.

Down the hill I went to the nearest drug store. I phoned the shift boss at the mine. Tony had not been there to-night.

"But say," the shift boss exclaimed, "we got a guy in the hospital here with a smashed foot—got it caught in the cage as the graveyard shift was goin' down. See if you can get hold of Doc Ames, will you?—and hurry him up. He said he was comin' and bringin' a nurse, and he ain't here yet."

But before I could phone the physician's house, a car stopped in front of the store. In the street light outside, I recognized Dr. Ames' red coupé. A nurse got out. There was an exclamation of surprise from the group of boys on the sidewalk. They rushed to the coupé. I saw them helping out Dr. Ames. His plump face was strangely pale. His lips were pinched together. His coat, which was thrown loosely about his shoulders, slipped down. His left arm was pressed close to his side. His right hand held a soggy red wad of handkerchief pressed against his left shoulder. His shirt sleeve was soaked with blood.

They brought him into the drug store. He slumped down on one of the little iron chairs by the row of ice-cream tables.

"Can't understand," said Dr. Ames jerkily—he had a clipped way of speaking. "Can't understand why anybody would plug me. Better send another doctor to the mine. Better call the sheriff, too."

The nurse cut away his shirt. In the soft flesh of the upper arm just at the shoulder, a round red wound gaped like a painted mouth. Blood dripped in a little pool on the white tiled floor. The druggist brought a basin of water, antiseptic, bandages, cotton and adhesive. The nurse worked with quick, sure fingers cleansing the wound. And while she worked, she talked.

"It must've been a gang of bandits," the nurse declared emphatically. She was a small, energetic woman with a prominent nose and very little chin. She had mouse-colored hair, and her movements were quick and mouse-like, too. She turned her head with swift, sidewise glances as she talked. Her name was Madge Dunlap. "We were just slowing down to turn in at the mine gate. I heard a car behind us, but I didn't look around. It had been following us all the way, I think. Then that shot?" Her voice was shrill and piping. "It broke the glass in the back of the car. I ducked down in the seat. Dr. Ames just grunted. But I knew he was wounded. He nearly ran the car in the ditch. I expected to hear another bullet over my head. I thought we'd both be killed! But the other car didn't pass us. It turned off and went up towards the Hill Road."

"Didn't get a look at it," Dr. Ames put in. "It wasn't far behind us, but before I could stop, it was out of sight. Cross road comes in there near the mine. The car was running without lights, too."

Miss Dunlap had driven Dr. Ames back to town and to the first drug store. The wound was not serious. The bullet had cut a clean bore through the flesh.

"Look in the car, will you, Cappy," Dr. Ames asked me, "and see if the slug is there? Like to have it for a souvenir."

But I knew he wanted it for a clue through which he might possibly trace his assailant. Dr. Ames was coroner of Genesee County, had been for many years. His efficient inquests had led to a number of arrests and convictions. A man who investigates crime naturally makes enemies.

I did not find the bullet. Its diagonal course through the glass at the rear and through Dr. Ames' arm at the shoulder would have carried it out the open left window of the car. Without even that bit of evidence, there seemed little chance of discovering who had made the attempt on the doctor's life. If he had been followed from town, the attack, evidently, was planned. But I could not understand why the would-be murderer had not made certain of his crime with more shots, and concluded that the bullet might have been a warning. But for what? There was a possibility, too, I reflected, that the shot had been meant for Miss Dunlap. But the nurse was such a capable, business-like woman, it was difficult to imagine her as the center of any crime of passion.

This swift striking in the dark by an unseen enemy left me more anxious than ever about Tony. I hurried home, hoping to find him there. But the garage doors were open, and the empty blackness beyond showed me his car was still out. I did not stop. I retraced my steps up the hill to Regina's house. I did not know where else to look for Tony. I could not go home till I had found him.

The old-fashioned cottage stood gaunt and lifeless in the bluish midnight gloom. Its locked doors, its blank windows, its cold walls gave back no answer. The town below was a huddled jumble of roofs and trees and dark amorphous shapes. The bright patches that were windows had vanished. The shadows seemed full of hidden stories and passions. I wondered if Tony and Regina were down there somewhere and what had happened to them.

The clock in the town hall made a doleful business of striking twelve. It was the beginning of the worst twenty-four hours of my existence—the day of the disaster at Haunted Mine. At twelve-five the midnight express came down the valley from the north. The bright sword of its headlight slashed the night. Its shrill whistle echoed in the hills. It plunged into the town and came to a grinding stop. I heard the solemn ringing of its bell at the station. A minute later it went roaring south.

Before the rumble of its wheels died away, I heard a car on the hill—the Tiger—I could tell its purr. The headlights swept over me as it turned into the drive.

Regina was at the wheel. She stared at me.

"Cappy!" she cried startled. "What are you doing here?"

"Where's Tony?"

She brushed the hair back from her forehead. "I don't know—he's gone home. No; he's not home yet." Then her voice rose sharply, as if in fear. "Why do you ask?"

"What's happened?" I cried. "Where's Tony? Where have you been?"

I gripped her arm. She was trembling.

"Let me alone!" she sobbed hysterically. "Please go away."

"But—Tony? Tell me where Tony is," I pleaded. "Pat said he was going to kill him."

"Tony is all right. He's all right," she repeated anxiously, as if she were trying to convince herself.

I knew something had happened.

Regina crumpled down in the seat limply and leaned her head on the steering wheel. The rose shawl slipped from her shoulders. A tremor passed through her. She pulled the shawl tight about her again.

"Where's Pat?" I persisted.

She sat up, staring straight ahead at nothing. Her hands were clenched together. Her voice had a dazed, dull sound.

"I drove Pat to the train," she said slowly and deliberately. "He left on the twelve o'clock train."

"Why did he leave?"

"Because—because—he had business."

"Why didn't Tony bring you home?"

"He couldn't. He—" She hid her face in her hands. "But Tony's all right. I'll tell you about it—in a minute. Just put the Tiger in the cage first. I—I'm—I'm tired, Cappy." She climbed out of the car.

"But you're not going to stay here alone?" I protested.

"I don't mind," impatiently.

"Come home with me," I urged. "You know Aunt Addie would want you to."

"I'd rather stay here." She turned away abruptly and walked towards the house.

I took her place at the wheel and eased the car into the garage. When I came back to the front of the house, Regina was sitting in the porch swing. The big maltese cat she had adopted rubbed against her, and she snatched it up, hugging it tight in her arms and burying her face in its fur. She did not look at me.

"I saw Pat—" I began.

She looked up quickly. "Where?"

"I met him on the avenue. He was looking for you and Tony. I tried to stop him, but— Where did he find you?" I asked bluntly.

After a moment she answered: "At the office—your office. Tony had some letters he wanted to write, and I went with him. Pat saw the light and came up."

"What did he say?"

"What does it matter?" she cried impatiently. "Why do you ask so many questions?"

"But I've been nearly crazy, for fear—"

"Yes, yes; of course. I'm just nervous, Cappy that's all." She was apologetic. Her voice seemed heavy with the weight of unshed tears. But after a moment she gained control of herself. "Pat was looking for me because he wanted me to drive him to the train. Some business came up. He had to go to the city to get some evidence for a case," she explained carefully.

My fears flared up again. "Gina, you wouldn't lie to me about Tony?" I touched her hand.

She jumped up, letting the cat drop to the floor, and covered her face with both hands. "I told you Tony was all right!" Her voice was high-pitched.

I was a little ashamed of my fears now. "I've been imagining things, I suppose—after seeing Dr. Ames wounded—"

"Dr. Ames?"

"Someone shot him—"

"Don't tell me. I can't stand it," Regina interrupted. "Please go now. I'm all in. Good-night."

She unlocked the door and went in so quickly I could say nothing.

Tony had not come in when I reached home. I found Uncle Matthew and Aunt Addie in the library. Aunt Addie had on a kimono, and her hair hung down in two tight braids. Uncle Matthew was sitting in a chair staring morosely at the floor.

"I should think," said Aunt Addie, drawing herself up stiffly, "a man in your position would be ashamed to break the law. I'm surprised and shocked to find you drinking intoxicating liquor."

Not until then did I realize Uncle Matthew was drunk. Aunt Addie turned her aggrieved gaze on a quart bottle standing conspicuously on the mantel.

"Felt like I was taking cold," Uncle Matthew enunciated carefully.

I had never seen him even slightly intoxicated before, though he always kept whisky in the house for medicine. Like Aunt Addie, I was surprised, though not shocked.

I couldn't ask if he had found Tony. I didn't want to worry Aunt Addie.

"I saw Regina," I ventured. "Pat's gone to the city to get some evidence on a case."

Uncle Matthew looked at me with a surprised, bleary eye. "Gone to the city?" he repeated.

He looked infinitely weary and old. His long face with the little pouches under the eyes was creased by a thousand wrinkles. The fold of flesh under his chin was like empty skin, loose and flabby. The veins stood out on the backs of his thin yellow hands. I felt rather sorry for him as Aunt Addie continued her patient censure:

"We saw you leave the house. I thought you were going to the Opera House for me."

Uncle Matthew nodded.

"Then where have you been all this time?"

"Drivin' 'round." He made feeble circles with his hand.

I knew, of course, he had been worried about Tony and Regina, as I had, and it was rather fine of him, I thought, to keep the trouble from Aunt Addie, in spite of her accusation.

I told them the news about Dr. Ames.

Uncle Matthew started up from his chair. "What's that?"

I assured him it was nothing serious. He pulled himself up from the arm chair, murmuring: "Bless my soul, bless my soul!" and groped his way towards the door.

We heard his dragging footsteps on the stairs.

"I just couldn't believe my eyes when I saw him," said Aunt Addie, primly indignant. "I came down to put my pin and my ring in the safe—and found him—like that."

Aunt Addie drew off the ring Uncle Matthew had given her recently, and with it and the pin in her hand, crossed the hall to the dining room. I heard her opening the small wall safe built there for the jewels Uncle Matthew insisted on her wearing occasionally.

"It seems a shame," Aunt Addie complained, as I followed her upstairs, "to keep such valuable things where a burglar could get them so easily. It's like putting temptation in people's way."

But I hardly heard. I was still worrying about Tony.

There was a light under Rush's door, but as I moved down the hall towards it, it disappeared. I rapped, then called. There was no answer. I pushed open the door.

The moonlight slanting through the windows fell across the bed. Rush was lying there face down. He did not look up.

"You needn't pretend to be asleep," I told him. "I saw your light." I sat down on the edge of the bed.

"Let me alone." His voice was muffled in the pillow.

"Have you seen Tony?" I persisted.

"No."

"What time did you get home?"

"About eleven."

"Was Pat here?"

"Yes."

"What did he say?"

"Don't know. Didn't see him. Saw his car. I came in the side door and up the back stairs." He rolled over. "Where've you been?"

I told him about Dr. Ames. "He was going to the mine," I added. "One of the graveyard shift was hurt—smashed foot."

"Why does everything have to happen during the graveyard shift?" Rush murmured.

I did not suspect then it would be many weeks before all that had happened that night would be known.

I was going to tell Rush about Norma when I heard Tony's step on the stairs. The sound brought a rushing flood of relief and thankfulness. I flung open Rush's door as Tony passed. But he strode on without even glancing at me and went into his own room. I followed. I had my hand on the doorknob when I heard the key turned in the lock. That cool little click seemed to make a wall between us. Tony had never locked me out before. I stood there a moment, bewildered. Then I realized that whatever had happened between Tony and Pat was none of my affair. Tony was safe—that was enough. I turned away.

Rush was sitting up in bed. His hands gripped the covers. "Tony's been with Norma! I know he has," he declared with conviction.

"You're crazy." I scoffed.

"Then why did he go straight to his room without stopping here?" Rush faced me tragically. "He heard you open the door."

"It's late," I argued weakly. "It's after one."

"Tony never did that before, did he—without even stopping to say good-night?"

"Aunt Addie and I took Norma home," I told Rush shortly. "Tony was with Regina—they went to the office together. I saw Regina—she told me Pat found them there. I went to Regina's house."

"What time did Regina come home?" Rush asked.

"A little after twelve."

"Then where has Tony been since then? Not by himself," said Rush bitterly.

"But you can't believe Tony would do that—try to come between Norma and you?" I protested. "That isn't like Tony."

"Wouldn't he come between Regina and Pat?"

I felt helpless. "But Tony's always loved Regina."

"You always take Tony's side," said Rush accusingly. In the dim light his great dark eyes were black and reproachful. The slim oval of his chin was set firmly. "Tony avoided us. He's afraid we'll ask where he's been. But I know." Rush ran a hand through his hair, and his head jerked back defiantly. "He's been driving around with Norma!"

In the face of such conviction, what could I say? I had no idea where Tony had been. Besides, Rush was so often right in his intuition.

VIII
"THE PAY ROLL HAS BEEN STOLEN"

There was no opportunity to talk to either Rush or Tony at breakfast, with Aunt Addie, neat and prim, at one end of the table, and Uncle Matthew hiding behind a newspaper at the other, and Hilda, our big red-faced cook, plodding heavily in and out with muffins and bacon.

When I reached the office, Tony was dictating to Norma.

Saturday was pay day. I had to make out the pay roll and take it to the mine before one. It was my habit to bring the money from the bank at about ten o'clock in a soft leather bag used for the purpose, and put it in the safe until I could make out the envelopes and check over the amounts. I always went as soon as the bank opened because Saturday was a busy day, and later I might have to stand in line and be late with the pay roll.

And to-day I wanted time to look over the money for possible counterfeit notes. I had the serial numbers of an issue of ten-dollar banknotes, the signatures of which had been forged. They were issued by a Chicago bank, but had been stolen from the engravers before the signatures were affixed. They had been circulated in our part of the country recently, and I was rather curious to see one. I ran through the sheaf of ten-dollar notes first and discovered three issued by that bank. The signatures were the same as those of the forged notes, but when I compared the numbers, I found none was of the stolen issue, though one missed it by only a single figure—its number ending in 200 while the stolen issue began with 201. I ran through the other notes hastily and returned all to the leather bag.

There was $8,319.85 in the bag when I placed it in the safe and turned the combination dial.

The safe stood in the outer office, which was used for a reception room. Norma had a desk here. There were two small offices on each side. Uncle Matthew and Tony occupied the two larger ones in front; Rush had the cubbyhole back of Tony's, and the bookkeeper and I shared the fourth.

I made out the checks for us at the office, and for the engineers and the foreman, and took them in for Uncle Matthew to sign. Only the miners and the laborers were paid in cash. I took Tony's in to him, hoping I'd have a chance to say something about Rush. I didn't want that quarrel between Tony and Rush to go any deeper.

Tony was standing with his hands in his pockets, looking out of the window. He was wearing knickers and a sweater, as he usually did on Saturdays, and I supposed he had planned a round of golf or some excursion for the afternoon. He turned around as I entered.

"Do you like mining, Cappy?" he asked reflectively, taking the check.

"Of course," puzzled.

Tony laid a hand on my shoulder affectionately. "There's nothing about this job you couldn't handle now." He flapped the check across his fingers. "One good thing about this game," he said as if to himself, "you can go anywhere." A one-sided smile twisted his lips, a strangely unhappy smile, I thought.

"You aren't dissatisfied here, Tony?"

"Well—no," he answered meditatively. "But—I suppose there are more interesting places to work."

The door opened then, and Regina stood there. She closed the door and leaned back against it. I don't think she saw me standing a little to one side. She looked only at Tony. There were dark circles under her eyes as if she had not slept.

"Oh, Tony!" The words were a cry, a moan, not a greeting.

Tony was at her side. "Cappy's here," he whispered.

He led her to a chair. She sank down limply.

"Here, here, this won't do!" Tony patted her hands briskly. "You've been running around in the hot sun too much. If you don't do better than this, I can't let you make my costume for the play!"

"That's what I came for," said Regina dully. "I want to get your measurements." She drew a tape line from her shopping bag.

"Get Gina some water, Cappy," Tony ordered.

I brought a paper cupful from the cooler in the outer office, but Tony took it from me at the door, then closed the door. There was no one in the reception room now. Norma's chair was empty. I heard Uncle Matthew's voice through the closed door of his office, dictating a letter.

I returned to my own desk and continued making out the pay envelopes. A few minutes later I went to the safe for the money. The leather bag was gone.

I looked through all the compartments carefully. I didn't want to raise an alarm unnecessarily, and I couldn't believe the bag had really disappeared. I had put it there less than an hour ago. I remembered whirling the dial and turning the handle to make certain the safe was locked. Certainly, it had been locked just now, for I had spent half a minute opening it. The doors to the four offices were closed; the reception room was unwatched, but people had been coming and going. I had crossed the room several times, myself. Norma had been at her desk part of the time. It was absurd to imagine a burglar's manipulating the dial and discovering the combination under these circumstances. Yet no other explanation suggested itself. I went to the hall door and looked out bewilderedly, half expecting to see the fleeing burglar. But no one was in sight—except the patients in a dentist's office across the corridor.

Then I went to Uncle Matthew's door and opened it.

"The safe's been robbed," I announced. My voice sounded husky and rather scared.

Uncle Matthew whirled his chair around sharply. "What's that?" His shaggy black brows went up and down.

I repeated my message. "The pay roll has been stolen."

"Bless my soul!" He pulled himself up stiffly from the chair.

I followed him to the safe. He had to search the compartments as I had, to make sure it was gone.

Then he called worriedly: "Tony—Rush—come here!"

Norma and the bookkeeper were already in the room. Only the six of us knew the combination, which had been changed about a month ago. We looked at each other inquiringly. Uncle Matthew's suspicions seemed to fasten on Tony.

"Is this meant for a joke, Tony? If it is—"

"It isn't," Tony answered shortly.

Uncle Matthew walked up and down the room, clasping and un-clasping his hands behind his back. He stopped before the bookkeeper.

"Fenton, it wasn't you?"

Otis Fenton shook his head and answered: "No, sir," without rancor.

He was a stooped, worried looking little man with a shining pink bald head too large for the lower part of his face, a domed crani-um that should have belonged to a great scientist or a mathematical wizard. His forehead was creased with many wrinkles caused by his habit of ducking his head and looking over the top of his spectacles. He had an insignificant nose and a weak chin and was almost servile in his desire to please. He always spoke hesitantly with many "ah's". But to my mind, there was no doubting his honesty. He had been with Uncle Matthew fifteen years, had reared a family in proud, white-collar poverty, owned his home and was a respected citizen.

Uncle Matthew turned to me next; his eyebrows went up and down swiftly. "Are you sure you locked the safe? Some sneak thief might've followed you up from the bank and waited outside—"

"I tried the handle afterwards," I assured him. "Hadn't we better phone for the sheriff?"

"Not yet," said Uncle Matthew. "Not yet. If you're sure you locked the safe—" Again his glance went questioningly around the circle.

"But somebody might've come in," I argued desperately. "Norma was in your office—the reception room was vacant."

"But I always hear the outer door when it's opened," Rush inter-posed. "It squeaks a little, and the check doesn't work very well, so it closes with a little slam."

"You might not hear it every time," I objected.

"No," admitted Rush gravely, "but I heard Regina come in and leave, and I heard the postman, and the boy who came to collect for the paper, and the insurance salesman and the telegraph messen-ger—"

"What do you do besides listen to the door?" Uncle Matthew de-manded.

A flush spread over Rush's face. "I—I was just—thinking this morning." From his confusion I guessed he had been listening for

Norma's voice and step—to see if she went into Tony's office. "And I was going to say I heard the door just a minute ago," Rush continued, "but I think Cappy was in the reception room then."

"I opened the door and looked out in the hall," I admitted.

"And I was in here," Norma spoke up, "when the insurance man and the newspaper boy and the postman and the messenger boy came, and I know none of them did it."

"Nobody else came in?" Uncle Matthew asked.

"Nobody else," said Rush positively.

Uncle Matthew searched our faces again. "Bless my soul, bless my soul," he muttered. "I can't believe it."

"One of us must've done it," said Tony crisply, putting Uncle Matthew's thoughts into words. "No one else knows the combination. If the safe was locked, one of us must've opened it. I suggest we all be searched before we make the matter public."

"No, no, no, no;" Uncle Matthew decided emphatically. "You're my boys." He had a hand on my shoulder and one on Rush's, but he looked at Tony, too. "You're my boys, and Fenton, here, is my friend. And if one of you is in a jam and took the money, I'd rather not know which one it is. I'm leaving Norma out of it because a girl like Norma couldn't be in a jam."

"You're a good sport," said Norma feelingly.

"I wish you had asked me to lend you the money," Uncle Matthew went on in his deep grave voice. "I'd do almost anything within reason for any of you. I know you boys have the right stuff in you. Tony's been a little wild lately, and Rush hasn't taken as much interest in the business as he should; I don't know what Cappy's been up to at school—but I'm going to call it a loan anyway. And I'm counting on getting that money back, a little at a time if it's easier, so we won't say anything about it to the sheriff or anybody."

"I bet whoever took it appreciates that," Tony declared so earnestly that for the moment I almost suspected him.

But I was instantly ashamed of the thought. Tony couldn't have done it. Nor Rush. Nor Fenton. That left Norma, and I was more ashamed of suspecting her, for I had no reason whatever except that I knew her less well.

"Can you hear the safe door when it is opened?" I asked Rush.

"No; it's too far away, and the door doesn't make any noise."

The safe stood at the opposite end of the reception room from the hall door and about twenty-five feet from Rush's door. If a burglar had robbed the safe, he would have had to walk the entire length of the reception room and pass the doors of the four private offices. He could not hope to escape, had one of these doors been suddenly opened. There were two windows, one on each side of the safe. Both were open, but they overlooked Center Street, the busiest block in our town. It was absurd to imagine anyone's entering there in the day-time without discovery. But I clung tenaciously to the burglar idea.

"I'll ask the patients in Dr. Bowman's office if they saw any strangers around," I suggested.

"But don't say anything about the theft," Uncle Matthew warned.

My inquiry, however, led to nothing except further proof that the robbery had been committed by someone in the office. The patients in the dentist's waiting room had seen everyone who had entered our office during the last hour, and there was not one whose presence had not been accounted for.

I returned to the office feeling rather shaken. Having a good memory, I recalled the serial numbers of those three notes issued by the Chicago bank, and, going to my desk, I jotted them down before I should forget. They were: K 705326, K 727200, and H 596555. But I did not mention the numbers to anyone. I was afraid the thief might be found.

Uncle Matthew made out another check for the pay roll, which I took to the bank and cashed.

IX
"THERE'S THIRTY-THREE STILL DOWN
—GOD HELP 'EM"

The explosion came before I finished filling the pay envelopes. It rumbled under the town, rocking the buildings and rattling windows like an earthquake. We knew what it was. It was the thing every mining town lives in fear of. I flung open the door to Uncle Matthew's office. His long thin hands gripped the edges of his desk, and he leaned forward over the littered top, staring at nothing.

I heard Tony's voice in the reception room, his quick step. "I'm going!" he shouted.

The outer door was flung open.

"Wait a minute, wait a minute!" Uncle Matthew called in a strained voice. He pulled himself heavily from his chair.

Rush brought him his hat.

"Bless my soul, bless my soul," Uncle Matthew muttered feebly, hurrying after Tony, his lean old form bent forward.

I was afraid it would be too much for him—two such shocks in one day—little thinking that the third and worst was yet to follow.

The streets were full of people now. They came pouring from every doorway; all were running towards the shaft of Haunted Mine at the northern edge of town.

Rush and I were left alone in the office. Norma and Fenton had hurried down to the street to learn, if possible, the extent of the disaster. I turned back to my pay envelopes. It occurred to me I had better put the money in the bank vault, since our own safe had proved so mysteriously unsafe. There would be no chance to pay it out to-day. Some of those who had earned the money would never claim it themselves.

"Pat's going to get the upper hand in Genesee—after this," Rush was saying. "He's been fighting us tooth and nail, but I can't believe it's just jealousy and hate, as Uncle Matthew says. I believe Pat's honest and sincere—he really thinks Uncle Matthew is a greedy profiteer and a slave-driver and all that—you can say those things about any successful man. Since the bank failure, Pat's turned Regina and a lot of others against us. And now—this—he'll have the whole town against us." Rush turned to the window restlessly.

"Rush," I exclaimed suddenly, "Do you think Pat had anything to do with this?" The thought rocked me.

"With what? The explosion?" Rush was shocked. "Why you couldn't think Pat would—"

"Wait—" I sprang to my feet. "Pat knows about Tony and Regina—" I dropped my voice—"they've been meeting, Rush." He nodded. "Last night Pat found them here at the office, and then he left town on a business trip—and to-day—this happens. Don't you see any connection?"

Rush turned away. "No, no; I don't believe it!"

"I know Pat was your friend—and still is—or pretends to be. But I'm going to find out what caused this explosion," I declared.

But in the tragedy and the mystery of what followed, I was soon to forget that resolve.

Rush was staring gloomily out of the window. I gathered up my stacks of pay envelopes, tied them together and took them to the bank for safe keeping. Then I hurried out to Haunted Mine.

Several thousand people were crowded about the shaft, from which a column of black smoke arose. No one knew exactly how many men were still down, nor who they were. Most of the workers, though, had been in the hundred-foot level and had escaped.

Women were hunting frantically for husbands and sons. Grimy-faced miners, Davy lamps still burning like fireflies on their caps, pushed through the crowd shouting to loved ones. Relief work was being organized. Volunteers with set, stern faces made their way to the pit mouth.

I found Big Bill, the engineer, anxiously tending the fan.

"It's bad business!" he shouted at me over the whir of the great fan. "But I'm gettin' all I can out of this old engine. My kid's down there—my Billy." He turned away and began oiling the machinery from a gleaming copper can. "It's curious how things happen—some folks gets off lucky and others don't. It was only yesterday Pat Brace was saying he was always glad to get out of Haunted Mine safely."

"Was he here yesterday?"

"Yeah; he's always nosin' around—must think he's an inspector. Says he's representin' somebody that's suin' Mr. North and he wants to know all about the mine. He was down in the workin's pokin' about yesterday—even asked me a lot of questions about the fan—but I guess he didn't get much satisfaction out of me. Hope nothin' goes wrong now," Big Bill finished worriedly.

He stood up, shaking his bushy head and wiping his big freckled hands on some waste. He blew his nose loudly; his eyes were red-rimmed.

"I wish I could go down," he said. "But I got my job here—"

I offered to stay with the fan, but he shook his head.

"Nobody can handle this old buzzer like me. Besides, I'm gettin' old and short of wind. I wouldn't be no good down there. I told them boys to look out for my kid, and they'll bring him up if they can get to him. I wouldn't trust nobody else with this old engine and fan now. I can get more out of 'em than anybody."

From Big Bill I learned that the explosion had been caused by a fire that had started in the two-hundred-foot level—just how no one knew.

"The boys on the first level just had time to get out before the smoke caught 'em. The bug dust from this coal is somethin' fierce—the fire eats it up like gasoline. Some of the fellers had to be dragged out, and others come up lookin' pretty wobbly. There was a few from the second level got out, too—them that was workin' close to the shaft. Two of 'em come up the ventilatin' shaft here."

There was an emergency exit built into the air shaft, though partitioned off from it, like a great brick-walled chimney with a vertical iron ladder.

"They was lucky to be close to it," Big Bill added. "But there's about thirty-three still down, I reckon—God help 'em."

The first rescue squad, six men in gas masks, had just gone down. I pushed my way through the throng up to the edge of the black pit.

From there I could hear the voices of the rescuers echoing up from the darkness. The crowd listened in silence, but no shout of good news came up to us.

The signal to hoist was given. The crowd surged closer as the cage came up. In awed silence, two bodies were carried out on stretchers. Women with children in their arms fought for a glimpse of those limp straight figures. The silence was broken by low, tense voices—and a hoarse sob as someone recognized a still form. The crowd made way for a woman with tears streaming down her white, scared face.

The first squad, making quick dashes into the poisonous air of the pit, soon brought out six other unconscious forms—men who had fallen near the shaft. The bodies were carried on stretchers and doors to the improvised first aid station—there was no more room in the little hospital. I pressed through the anxious, frightened throng to see if Big Bill's son were there, but none was the face I sought.

I saw Dr. Ames, his arm in a sling, trotting about, applying his stethoscope to motionless breasts, directing the relays of men working frantically to pump air into those still lungs—there was only one pulmotor.

I had to return to Big Bill with my bad news. Billy had not been brought up yet, and with each minute, hope grew less.

In the next few hours, eight others were brought up from the black depths, two or three at a time, and among them, Billy, quiet and calm-faced. Dr. Ames shook his head as he examined the still form.

I carried the news to Big Bill. "I'll watch the fan if you want to go," I told him.

But he still refused stubbornly. "I can't do him no good now. But maybe there's some I can help if I get all the speed I can out of this old fan." He drew his greasy blue sleeve across his eyes.

But the chances were becoming smaller and smaller for the rescue of any others from Haunted Mine. Hope seemed to die as the sun went down over Moon Mountain. Most of the crowd dispersed. Yet the rescuers worked on doggedly into the night, making trip after trip into the gas-filled depths and being forced back empty-handed.

Of the sixteen brought out, only the first five had been revived. The other eleven had been too long in the poisonous atmosphere.

Seventeen were still unaccounted for. Relatives and friends waited patiently, hoping against hope, praying for the miracle that might save those still entombed. The only chance now was that they had had time to build a bulkhead against the smoke and the after-damp that crept, deadly and invisible, through the black drifts.

I saw Regina standing alone on the outskirts of the crowd. When I went up to her, she gripped my arm impulsively.

"Oh, Cappy, isn't it terrible?"

There was something in her voice that made me think she might suspect Pat. "Gina, where has Pat gone?" I asked suddenly.

She pulled the collar of her coat up around her—a gray woolly coat. In the dusk her hands were like white moths fluttering over the gray collar.

"I told you he's gone to the city to get some evidence," she answered slowly as if repeating a lesson.

Tony rushed up then, coatless, grimy with dirt and smoke, his face flushed, his hair tousled. Beads of moisture stood out on his forehead. He wiped his face with the sleeve of his sweater—a slipover sweater with zigzag green stripes—and smiled at Regina—a tired smile.

"Tony, what have you been doing? How much longer are you going to stay here?" Regina asked.

"As long as there's any chance. We've got the drill ready. If the men are alive, we'll drill a hole to them. We're ready to start working the minute we find out where they are."

"Can't you be spared a little while? You ought to have something to eat and get a few minutes rest while you can. You may have to work all night. Come home with me, and I'll give you a warm supper."

Tony hesitated only a moment. Then, turning to me: "You take charge of my crew, Cappy. I'll be at Regina's. If the rescuers reach the men, start drilling, and dig like hell!"

He was gone with Regina in her gray car. But in half an hour, he was back again. There was nothing we could do, though. Hour after hour passed in vain attempts to reach the entombed men. Tony went down several times, but, like the others, was beaten back by the heat and the choking after-damp that seeped into the masks

Norma came with her mother and her little sisters. It was she who cried out when Tony volunteered for his last desperate attempt.

X
"MY WHITE BEARD WAS GONE"

At dawn I went home, wretched and stunned. There were lights downstairs. I heard the voices of neighbor women in the living room and Aunt Addie's quiet sobbing. I went in the side door and up the back stairs to my room. I could not face anyone yet.

I couldn't realize that Tony was gone. That fearless, eager, questing spirit of his must go marching on. Tony couldn't be crushed out of existence! I opened my windows. The stars, just vanishing in the pale early light, seemed to add their mystery—the mystery of infinite space—to that of life and death. Life without Tony was hard to imagine. I had depended on him and patterned myself after him as most boys do after their fathers. I wondered if the hopelessness of his love for Regina had driven him to such recklessness—if he had deliberately sacrificed his life. But Tony would not have admitted himself beaten so easily—that was not his nature. And his love was not hopeless, for Regina returned it. I felt as if I ought to go to Regina now, but I was too wretched to attempt to comfort anyone.

I found a package of cigarettes on the dresser and was about to light one when I noticed my make-up box—the little kit of theatrical grease paint I had bought for the play—was lying open there. The tops had been removed from some of the jars, some of the contents used; one of the pencils had vanished entirely. The little mirror, conveniently fitted inside the lid, had been pried from its metal frame and carried away.

These trivialities made no impression on me at the time. They flitted across the tragic background of my consciousness and aroused no more than a mild wonder if Hilda had been suddenly overcome by temptation and vanity. I snapped shut the lid of the black tin box and shoved it back in the drawer. It was then I noticed my white beard was gone. That would not have tempted Hilda. I was certain it had been there this morning. For a moment I was annoyed—I had been put to some trouble and expense to secure that beard—until it occurred to me that without Tony, there would be no play. In such small matters does death make itself felt most keenly.

In the mirror I saw the door to Tony's room—our rooms adjoined—and for a long minute I remained motionless staring at the reflection, half-expecting to see the door open and Tony standing there, half dressed perhaps, and with shaving lather muffling his face, as I had seen him so often in the early morning. So strong was the spell, I listened a moment breathlessly for Tony's step in there, for a whistle or a snatch of song rising above the splash of water in the bathroom, as I had heard it so often at this hour. So vivid was the illusion that Tony must be on the other side of the wall that I crossed the room hurriedly and flung open the door.

The first pale rays of sunlight fell across the smooth empty bed. The spell had vanished.

And yet the room seemed full of Tony's presence—the snowshoes crossed on the wall, the great shot gun, the slender rifle, the skin of the bobcat killed with that gun head down over the mantel, staring at me with ferocious glass eyes; and the two deer heads, one on each side—how proud Tony had been when he brought home that big one, his first, four years ago. The skis in one corner with the bag of golf clubs—the bookshelves full of adventure, pirate and mystery stories, histories and travel books. . . . Looking at these things, I felt suddenly older than Tony—Tony who would never grow old now. The room was too full of memories. I closed the door.

I lay down without undressing and buried my face in the cool smoothness of the pillow. As I did, my hand touched something chill, metallic. It was a pair of scissors lying at the edge of the pillow. Aunt Addie's stork scissors. I knew them well enough. The blades of the scissors made the long beak of the stork. I wondered how Aunt Addie had happened to leave them here. They belonged in her sewing basket—she was an orderly soul. She might have been mending some of my clothes when the explosion came, I reflected, and in the excitement had gathered up the other things in her basket and left the scissors. In such small problems did my mind seek relief.

I traced the woven pattern of the bedspread and counted the number of threads in stripes and figures. And because my glance was focused on these minute objects, I discovered something that otherwise would have escaped notice—a long white hair. I picked it up. It was too white for Aunt Addie's, I thought. Then, searching, I discovered another. They were soft and silky, but as I examined them carefully, I concluded they were floss—not hair. They must have fallen from the false beard, I decided. And in wondering about the beard, I finally dropped asleep.

It was nearly noon when I awoke. I went to Aunt Addie's room. She was sitting by the window, her plain face distorted by crying. She was extracting what comfort she could from the newspapers' praise of Tony.

"Hand me the scissors, Cappy," she requested in a choked voice. "I want to cut out this article about Tony."

"You left your scissors in my room." I started for the door.

"I didn't leave them in your room." Aunt Addie was gently positive. "They're in my sewing basket."

I went to my room and returned with the scissors. Aunt Addie looked up surprised and slightly annoyed.

"I don't know how they got in your room. I had them in here yesterday morning. When the explosion came, Hilda and I went to the mine, and there was nobody in the house after that—unless Rush came home while we were gone."

It was on the tip of my tongue to tell Aunt Addie about the make-up box and the beard, but something—I don't know what—kept me quiet.

I went downstairs. Rush and Uncle Matthew were in the library. Neither, I think, had had any sleep. Rush was smoking one cigarette after another. The fire at the mine was worse, he said, and there was no hope of bringing out Tony's body. Uncle Matthew looked so ill I was worried. He sat hunched over in his chair; his lips moved soundlessly.

"You must go upstairs and get some sleep," I told him.

He glanced up with dull, vacant eyes, then seemed to pull himself together. He rose stiffly and moved towards the door, shaking his head. I heard him mutter: "Nothing but trouble, trouble. . . . Lord, let me have peace. . . ." His lips continued to form words, but no sound came. He climbed the stairs slowly.

Rush was walking up and down the room with quick nervous strides.

"Have you been to the mine?" I asked.

"No."

Rush was never any good in a crisis, I reflected, though for that matter, I had done little enough, myself.

"What have you been doing?" I asked.

"Just walking around."

"Where?"

"I don't know." He turned abruptly, facing me and running his fingers through his hair. "Cappy, you remember that old prophecy that Haunted Mine would some day be a grave for its owner? It's come true, hasn't it?"

"Uncle Matthew is the owner," I pointed out.

"Well, Tony would have owned it—or a fourth of it. Uncle Matthew intends leaving it to us. I made his will. Haunted Mine goes to Aunt Addie and the three of us—or would have—one fourth each. It's that prophecy come true."

"Bunk," I remarked. "Anything would come true if you twist it to suit yourself." Then my thoughts reverted to the mystery of my make-up and the beard. "Were you prowling in my room last night?"

"No; I didn't come home till an hour ago. After I heard about Tony, there didn't seem much use coming home."

"Where were you before that?" I persisted.

"Well, if you must know," said Rush jerkily, "I was taking care of a woman's kids. She had five and was trying to carry two of them and run to the mine because her husband was down. She was afraid to leave them alone because the oldest wasn't more than eight. So I took the whole gang back home and fed and tended them."

And I had thought Rush was no good in a crisis.

"About one o'clock this morning the woman came home to tell me about Tony," Rush went on. "Her husband was still down, she said, and there was no chance. But I thought there might be some mistake about Tony. I started running towards the mine, but I met Big Bill—and he told me. They'd shut off the fan and boarded over the shafts. After that—I don't know where I went. I wish I hadn't quarreled with Tony—it's not a nice thing to remember." He stared moodily at the floor.

"But it was only once." I couldn't tell him now that Norma's childish pique was responsible for everything—it would only make him feel worse.

After a moment Rush said huskily. "You don't suppose Tony did it—stayed down, I mean—purposely, do you?"

"Of course not," I defended stoutly. "Why do you say that?"

Rush looked ashamed "Well, Tony's been making rather a hash of things lately. And then—this theft. . . . I can't figure it out." Rush did not look at me. He lighted one cigarette from the butt of another. Automatically he held out his case, but I refused—Rush's cigarettes were too mild. "It's not very loyal, I know," he mumbled apologetically, "but I thought maybe Tony was in some sort of jam we didn't know about."

"It couldn't be that bad," I argued, though the suggestion was tightening its grip on my mind. "Tony would've come to us first."

"But eight thousand dollars—" said Rush wretchedly.

"I'll never believe Tony took it," I declared staunchly.

We did not mention the theft again, but the mystery of it was constantly with us.

XI
"TONY'S GHOST WAS AT THE WHEEL"

Tuesday evening I climbed the hill to Regina's house. I had not seen her since the night of the disaster.

Once I stopped to look back at Haunted Mine, grim and lonely in the early dusk. For the first time since the disaster, the anxious and the curious had deserted the scene. Only Big Bill was there as night watchman now. Smoke tendrils still writhed upward through the boards across the shaft. Uncle Matthew would not consent yet to sealing the mine—he was still hopeful that the fire would burn itself out after destroying some of the timbers, now that the draft had been shut off. But, from the odor, I knew that smoke came from burning coal, not wood. The covering over the shafts would have to be made air tight with cement, and even then the coal might smolder for years.

Grief and tragedy had settled over the town like gray clouds and blanketing snow. Funeral services had been held this morning for the eleven whose bodies were recovered, and to-night there was to be a memorial service for those who might rest forever in Haunted Mine.

I found Regina on the porch. And Rush was there, too. They had been talking of Tony, I knew.

"Don't give up hope yet," Regina was saying. "I feel that Tony *can't* be dead." She covered her face with both hands.

Rush nodded solemnly. "I know—but there's no use pretending."

Regina looked up and saw me. She started nervously. "Oh, I almost thought you were Tony!" Her voice was a little breathless. "It's getting dark, isn't it? I must see about Minnie—she ought to be through ironing by now."

Regina sprang up and vanished in the darkness of the house. We heard her voice as she spoke to old Minnie, the Negro laundress.

"You needn't stay to finish the ironing, Minnie. You've done enough."

And old Minnie's soft, mellow accents: "You ain't goin' to stay heah all night by yo'self, Miss Gina? Wouldn't you like fo' me to stay heah with you?"

"No, Minnie; thank you. I'm not afraid." Regina was firm.

Then Minnie, coaxing and obstinate: "You oughtn't to stay heah in dis house by yo'self, Miss Gina."

We didn't hear the rest of the conversation. Regina came out presently.

"Minnie seems to think I need a chaperon," she said lightly.

To make conversation, I asked: "Hasn't Pat come back yet?"

"Not yet."

"You'd better come to our house."

"No, no; don't ask me."

"Why not?" I insisted.

"It would remind me too much of Tony. It's bad enough to have you two here."

Minnie came around the corner of the house, an old woman who walked with her body bent forward as do those who have worked very hard. Shabby black skirts flapped about her ankles. Tufts of woolly hair straggled from under an incongruous gold metal hat perched on top of her head. She turned her sullen black face towards us reproachfully and went on down the walk without a word.

We were silent a moment, then Regina said tensely: "I wish you'd go home—both of you. I can't sit here and talk to you without thinking of Tony."

We were not hurt by her abruptness, but I was worried because it was unlike Regina to avoid people—especially Rush and me.

"Why don't you go to your father's house?" I suggested.

"I don't want to see anyone. I think I'll go to bed. I haven't slept much—since. . . ." Regina bit back the words.

She stood in the doorway while Rush and I went down the walk. Then I heard the door closed softly.

Rush said: "I'm going for a walk."

"You'll wear yourself out."

"That's what I want to do."

The quarrel with Tony was still troubling him.

"Don't go by the mine," I said. "There's no one about now but Big Bill—it won't do any good to go near the place."

"I shan't—never fear."

He swung off along the Hill Road away from town as if he could escape from his thoughts. I watched him vanish in the dusk. Still I stood there a moment, not knowing where to go and dreading to go home. In spite of my advice to Rush, I could not keep my eyes from the scene of the tragedy in the valley below, though only the gaunt outlines of the tip house, and the smokestacks were visible now in the deepening twilight. The hills behind were misty and violet. I was sorry for Big Bill alone down there with his thoughts and the ghosts of the past.

I turned reluctantly towards home. Then across Regina's lawn, I saw the maltese cat playing with something white. When I came near him, he tried to scamper through the hedge, but he was tangled up in something—like the kitten with the spool of thread in the advertisement. I made a grab for him, and my hand came away with some wisps of white floss. It looked like part of my beard.

The cat was lost now in the shadows of the hedge, but, dragging the white strands over the grass, I coaxed him out again, and soon disentangled from his claws the remainder of the cottony hair. I crammed the stuff in my pocket, and, puzzling over the incident, walked on down the hill.

As I reached the avenue at the foot of the sloping street, the bent figure of old Minnie stepped out from the shadow of one of the big elms. Her black little shoe-button eyes squinted up at me.

"Mist' Cappy, what's the mattah with Miss Gina?"

"She's upset about Tony, of course," I answered a little impatiently.

"No, sah; 'tain't jus' that—it's sumpin' else."

"What then?"

"I don' know—but I knows dere's sumpin' wrong. I knows."

She shook her head like an old crone, and her stiff, knotted fingers clutched at my arm as I started to move on. Minnie had done our laundry, too, for years—she was the best laundress in town—and she assumed the privileges of an old friend in prying into our personal affairs. Her flat, broad face was warped by lines of perplexity now, and her voice sank to a worried whisper.

"She's been talkin' to herself, Mist' Cappy. I went upstairs once, and I heard her just talkin' away to herself and nobody else around 'tall."

"What was she saying?"

"Couldn't heah nothin' she said. But she sho' actin' funny. Sumpin' botherin' her, Mist' Cappy. Can't you make her tell what it is?"

"It's Tony's death," I repeated, though not so convincingly.

Minnie shook her head. The preposterous spangled hat gleamed faintly. "She act to me jus' lak she seen a ghost, Mist' Cappy."

"Nonsense," I said stiffly.

"She's 'fraid of sumpin'—you'll see—she's 'fraid of sump-in'." The whites of Minnie's eyes glistened in the dark.

"Don't you worry, Minnie. Miss Regina has plenty of friends to go to if she's afraid or in trouble."

I passed on, but the memory of Minnie's anxious old black face worried me, though, with Tony dead, I could imagine nothing for Regina to fear, even from Pat. I loitered through the side streets, like Rush, dreading to go home. I stopped at a drug store for a magazine and a package of cigarettes, and talked for a while with a school friend.

It was after nine when I reached home. The house was dark and empty—Uncle Matthew, Aunt Addie and Hilda had gone to the memorial services. They had expected me to go, too, but I would not torture myself so, even to please them.

In my room I drew out the wad of white floss and held it under the light. I saw now, by the length of the strands and by the straight edges of some of the tufts, that the hair undoubtedly had been cut from the false beard. I could not understand how it had come to be at Regina's house.

A withered rose petal was tangled in the floss, and a bit of fluffy grayish lint such as accumulates under beds. I picked it out carefully, together with a piece of broken broomstraw. The rose petal might have been picked up under the hedge, but not the lint and the broomstraw.

I remembered that Regina kept a trash box on the back porch. I had seen her emptying a dustpan into it one day, and once, I, myself, had dropped in the pieces of a plate I had broken. The cat must have got it out of there. I thought of going back and searching the box for loose strands to make sure, but put the idea aside when I thought how ridiculous I should feel if Regina should find me there exploring her trash box at night. I couldn't very well tell her I suspected her of destroying my false beard.

Undoubtedly, there was some simple explanation of the affair, but it continued to elude me. Regina might have borrowed the beard for some reason, and then forgot, after the disaster, to mention it to me. But if she had taken it before the explosion, Aunt Addie or Hilda would know it; and I had already asked both casually if they had seen the beard. Aunt Addie had answered with a perfunctory: "No, dear," without even looking up from the letter she was writing.

And Hilda, plodding heavily across the kitchen, had turned a pink steamy face towards me with: "I don't know you got a beard. I t'ank it is no time to joke now," china-blue eyes regarding me suspiciously.

I tried to put the problem aside and interest myself in the magazine I had bought. But nothing could hold my attention. I went downstairs to look for a book. The clock on the landing, I remember, was striking ten as I passed it.

Before I reached the foot of the steps, the side door was flung open—then slammed. I heard someone breathing heavily. I hurried into the rear hall, switching on the lights.

Rush stood there, leaning back against the door, his face like paper, his eyes wide and staring. He held his hat crushed in one hand; his breath came in short gasps, and his whole body was trembling.

"Rush, what's the matter?"

He grasped my arm. "Where's Tony's car? Tell me—where's Tony's car?" he demanded in a high-pitched voice.

"In the garage," I said, "You know it hasn't been used—"

"I saw it!" Rush interrupted. "I saw it, I tell you! It passed me on the Hill Road. And Tony was driving!"

I was alarmed for Rush's reason. "Pull yourself together, old man." I gripped his shoulders firmly. "Your imagination has been playing you tricks. It was just an illusion—a car like Tony's perhaps—nothing uncanny about that."

"It was Tony's car!" Rush insisted, still panting. "I saw the license number. And Tony's ghost was at the wheel!"

"Rush, you're mad!"

"Listen! I'd walked on past Happy House—miles and miles. Coming back, nearly to town, I saw the headlights coming towards me. I stepped to one side—there at the curve where the pines are so thick." Rush ran his fingers through his hair. "As it came nearer, I saw it was Tony's car—I glanced at the license plate. When it passed me, I saw Tony at the wheel!" Rush jerked his head back challengingly. "I saw him as plainly as I see you. He was going to Happy House."

"But you couldn't have seen him," I pleaded. "It was an illusion. The car is still in the garage. Come on—I'll show you."

He followed me out. The double garage had been built into one end of the old red brick stables. Both pairs of doors were open. Naturally Uncle Matthew's car was out—he had not yet come home. But it surprised me that the other doors should be open, too. I heard Rush's quick irregular breathing just behind me.

I peered into the yawning blackness beyond the doors, but could see nothing. With a hand that trembled slightly, I struck a match. The garage was empty. Tony's car was gone. In the flickering yellow flare of the match, Rush and I stared at each other.

XII
"A SIGN FROM THE DEAD"

Ezra, the gardener, slept over the garage. I opened the door at the foot of the stairs and called to him. He must have been asleep. Presently I heard his drowsy voice.

"Eh, eh? Who is it? What's the matter?"

A light was turned on, and he came to the head of the steps struggling into an overcoat, below which his old-fashioned nightshirt and thin bow legs were mercilessly exposed. He was an old miner, no longer able to work underground because of rheumatism. Uncle Matthew, partly out of pity, had found employment for him here. A disreputable old character was Ezra Rugg with an upstanding fringe of gray hair, red-rimmed eyes, a red blob of a nose and a chin bristling with a week's growth of beard.

When he recognized Rush and me he grinned, showing yellow stumps of teeth.

"Oh, it's you. Did you want a sip of somethin' to cheer you up? Jus' come on up."

I ignored the invitation. "Tony's car is gone," I said in a voice that I tried to make matter-of-fact. "Do you know who took it out?"

Ezra said: "I thought it was one of you kids."

"How did you know it was gone?"

"I heard it," said Ezra querulously. "You don't reckon it was stole, do you?"

"Oh—no," I answered uncertainly. "But—what time was it taken out?"

"I reckon it was around nine o'clock—mebbe a little before."

"Did you see—the person who took it out?"

"No; I never looked—I was in bed." Ezra hobbled down the steps. "If it was stole, we'd best phone for the sheriff."

"Not yet." I was too bewildered to take any definite action.

"Well, if you or Rush didn't take it, it must be stole," Ezra argued contentiously. He never accorded anyone the respect of a "mister" or "sir", except Uncle Matthew, and that only to his face, I think.

"Maybe Uncle Matthew sent someone for it," I suggested, clutching desperately at any sane explanation. "If his car broke down, he'd send someone for Tony's."

"Ain't but six blocks to the church," Ezra reminded me. "Besides it's been more'n an hour ago, and he ain't home yet."

"Don't say anything about it to Uncle Matthew when he comes," I told Ezra.

"He can see for hisself the car ain't there," Ezra pointed out.

"I'll put Uncle Matthew's car away."

Ezra was suspicious now. "What's goin' on, I'd like to know? What's all this mystery about?"

"There's no mystery," I denied rather sharply. "Uncle Matthew may have lent the car to someone. If it's stolen, the sheriff couldn't do anything about it till to-morrow anyway. Go back to bed and forget about it."

"Wisht you'd thought of that before you woke me up," Ezra grumbled as he climbed the stairs again.

Rush and I went back to the house in silence. When we were inside, Rush said:

"You see it was Tony."

"It couldn't have been," I argued, more to convince myself than Rush. "When you recognised Tony's car, you imagined Tony at the wheel—that's all. You were mistaken—it was dark."

"I'd know Tony anywhere," Rush insisted obstinately. "He passed within four feet of me."

"But things like that don't happen."

"Then why don't you report the car as stolen?" Rush answered. "You know Uncle Matthew didn't lend it to anybody. You think maybe Tony will bring it back."

A car turned into the drive then, and the sound of the motor, following so quickly on Rush's words, gave me a start. But it was Uncle

Matthew's sedan I saw when I flung open the door. He stopped at the front steps to let Aunt Addie and Hilda out.

"I'll put the car away," I offered.

Uncle Matthew crawled out from behind the wheel. He looked very tired.

"I want to take out Tony's car," I told him.

"Go ahead," he nodded, "It's yours and Rush's now."

He had not lent the car then, I reflected, as I turned the sedan into the yawning black doorway.

There was a light in Rush's windows now, I noticed, as I locked the garage. I was thankful he had gone upstairs, for I did not want to admit to him that I was going to Happy House. I don't know what I expected to find, but I could not rest worrying about Tony's ghost driving the tan coupé over the Hill Road.

I set out on foot—it was but two miles, and my watch showed only ten-thirty now. Several cars passed me on the road, but none was a tan coupé.

It was a cloudy, windy night. The Hill Road, skirting the edge of the pine wood, was dark and lonely. The tree tops moaned in the wind with that unearthly, droning sound that only pines can make. A fiery moon, veiled in smoky clouds, peeped over the black pine tops, a moon red as flames, a sullen smoldering moon.

The lane that turned from the main highway and rounded the shoulder of a little hill, was overgrown with grass and tall weeds. Tony had had this road cut through the underbrush and dragged, but it had never been graveled or surfaced. Once I stumbled through a dried mudhole left from the last rain.

I struck a match to look for wheel tracks and discovered, not one, but several. They overlapped each other, and to my untrained eye, made only so many little round ruts, indistinct in the weed-grown clay. But even by the dim flare of the match, I could tell that some were recently made, when the earth was soft, but dry, and these had obliterated the earlier prints which might have been plainer. But the edge of one track had been spared. And there, cut crisply in the dried clay for a foot or two, was the print of a nonskid tire. I struck another match and bent over the track. It showed a row of triangles pointing outward. The tires on Tony's car had treads like that. The sight of that print gave me a queer feeling. Then the match burned my fingers and I dropped it.

But there was nothing mysterious about the track, I told myself. It had been made days ago when the ground there was soft and muddy. It had rained last, I remembered, on Thursday. Tony had been to Happy House since then. I felt rather guilty as if I had uncovered a secret not meant for me. I had not suspected Tony of making sentimental pilgrimages to the place. I wondered if he and Regina had been here together, or if Tony had come alone Friday night after Pat had found him and Regina at the office. The track must have been made Friday night, I reasoned. Tony had been at home Thursday night, and the disaster occurred Saturday.

Happy House seemed ineffably lonely, ironically sad, a monument to broken romance. Its unpainted clapboards loomed ghostly white in the moonlight that slanted into the little clearing on the hillside. The shingles had weathered to a silver gray. Behind it the gloomy pines marched up the hill and stood sentinel against the cloudy sky. No sound or whisper of life broke the silence; there was only the soft, continuous wailing of the wind. In the dim light the unusual piles of sand and gravel were like white graves.

And there was that empty shell of a house, abandoned before it was ever lived in, its vacant windows staring hopelessly.

I walked around the house, telling myself I had come on a wild goose chase, that Rush had suffered only a fit of nerves. And there before me was Tony's coupé. There was no mistaking that coffee-and-cream color. I could see only the rear. A queer prickly sensation crossed the back of my neck as though a cold draft had blown over me.

To walk around to the front and look inside was all I could manage. I am not given to nerves; I have never believed in spirits or super-natural things; I haven't the imagination Rush has, and yet I fully expected to be confronted by some unreal, other-world vision of Tony behind the wheel of the coupé.

The seat was empty.

I opened the door. The car was substantial enough. The cold feel of the metal brought back my materialism—and my courage. The car was empty and deserted. I didn't try to figure it out then. I climbed into the seat, switched on the lights, stepped on the starter—everything was in working order.

But on the way home I began to wonder if anyone else had seen what Rush had. Old Minnie's concern for Regina recurred to me. I passed Regina's house, but the windows were dark, and I decided not to waken her at this hour. Then I thought of Big Bill alone and probably anxious for company, and turned the car towards Haunted Mine.

There was a light in the boiler house—an oil lamp, for our power plant was shut down now that the mine was closed. At the sound of the car Big Bill came to the door.

"Just dropped by to keep you company," I announced casually.

He held the door open, and I went inside the little office where Big Bill sat and read when he was not making his rounds. The wind caught the door and closed it with a slam, whipping the oil light into smoky flames and sending grotesque shadows dancing up the bare walls.

"Glad you come," said Big Bill shakily, and not till then did I notice the grayness of his face.

"What's happened?"

Big Bill sat down heavily, his thick hairy hands resting on his knees, his hat pulled low over his eyes.

"Something's sorter got my goat," he confessed without looking at me. He took a plug of tobacco from his pocket and bit off a chew. His big hands trembled slightly.

"Have you seen—something?" I asked anxiously.

He shook his head. "No; I heard it. I was sittin' here while ago—about half past nine, I reckon it was—when I heard Billy playin' his harmonica."

"Billy?"

"He played *Auld Lang Syne*. I couldn't tell just where the sound come from—it was always way off somewheres. I went out and tried to find it. I must've followed it a mile. Then I lost it. I heard it last night, too—seemed like it come from Moon Mountain then. But when I started to climb up the hill, it stopped."

"What did you expect to find?" I asked.

"I don't know. I was just settin' here wonderin' what had become of Billy—where he was now, you know." Big Bill spoke with difficulty as if he were ashamed of such thoughts. "I was just thinkin' how fine it would be if we could get some sort of word or a sign from the dead—how it would sorter ease our minds if we knew they were still livin' somewheres and things was all right with 'em—so it caught me sorter uneasy like—that harmonica—and that tune."

"But it might have been anybody," I argued. "Lots of people can play a harmonica."

"But who'd want to pull a trick like that on me? I ain't got no enemies."

It was true. Everyone liked Big Bill. "Maybe you imagined it," I suggested.

And Big Bill answered stolidly: "I don't never imagine things."

I didn't tell him about Tony's car. He was in a mood to believe anything. Somehow I didn't want a rumor spread about Tony's ghost, and I didn't think Tony would want it. If Tony had come back, he had his own reasons, and it was not to give a show or to frighten people— that would be not quite sporting even in a ghost.

The wind whistled about the boiler house and the empty mine buildings, and occasionally a draft caught the flame of the lamp and made it flicker weirdly. We talked of other things. Big Bill told me the fire and the gas were no better in Haunted Mine.

"If it was just the smoke, the boys could go down and put the fire out, maybe—wall it off, anyway. But masks ain't much good against fire-damp. And as long as you got fire-damp, you're liable to have explosions, too. I caught a mouse in a trap last night—it was just caught by one foot—and I thought I'd see how bad the gas was. I lifted one of the planks off from the shaft, and I put the mouse in a bucket and let it down—used that old hand windlass, and wound it up again as fast as I could, but the mouse was stone dead before I got him out. The mine's got to be sealed up tight before that fire will ever die out."

Big Bill did not speak again of the mysterious music. His practical, commonplace talk did both of us good, though I could not forget about Rush's story.

Before I reached home the rain had begun to spatter down in big drops, and I was thankful that those tire prints would be washed out as well as any tracks I might have left at Happy House.

After I drove Tony's car into the garage, something prompted me to examine the interior. The switchboard light revealed nothing out of the ordinary. I brought a light on an extension cord and held it inside the coupé. The dark brown leather upholstery showed faint smears as if it had been wiped with a wet rag. I was standing by the right door of the car, and as I lifted the light, I observed a dark splotch on the upper part of the back. I touched it and it came away in my hand. Holding it under the light, I realized, to my horror, it was a small clot of dried blood.

I carried it to the lavatory and washed it down the drain. The pinkish tinge of the water whirling over it almost sickened me. But I took a sponge and a cloth and washed the leather upholstery thoroughly.

Rush was waiting in my room—he had heard the car on the drive—but I told him nothing except that I had found the coupé at Happy House.

That clot of blood frightened me. I tortured my mind for any explanation of it and of the unearthly vision Rush had seen, but, though I lay awake till dawn, I could find no plausible reasons for these things. When I dropped into a doze, horrible fancies and dreams floated through my mind, and I awoke damp and shivering to continue my bewildered groping into this growing maze of mystery.

XIII
"ONE OF THE STOLEN NOTES"

Wednesday morning I went to Regina's house. Her father answered my ring.

Mr. Townsend was a neat gray man. He had gray hair, gray eyes, gray mustache and gray clothes, and somehow managed to appear dignified and well dressed in the most shabby of garments. Perhaps the rimless nose glasses gave him a fastidious look. The gray eyes were wide set, his forehead was broad and high; and his face, in spite of financial difficulties, calm and untroubled. For all his gray hair, he looked young to be Regina's father. He had little interest in accumulating money, and, since the chicken ranch gave him more leisure for his beloved books and yielded a meager living, he seemed resigned to his fate.

I was surprised to see him at Regina's so early.

"Is anything wrong?" I asked.

He had a letter in his hand. "Regina's gone," he said. "I've been worried about her. And this morning—I don't know why—I felt impelled to come up here. But I'm too late." He handed me the letter.

Regina had written:

> Dear Popsy:
> I've an idea you'll be the one to find this. I'm going to the city to meet Pat. I can't bear to be here when Tony is brought out of Haunted Mine. How much he meant to me, you'll never know. But now that it's over, I'm going to Pat to see if we can't patch things up and be good friends at least. I've hurt him terribly, I know,

but I'll do what I can to make it up to him now. Pat knew when I married him it was Tony I loved and that I was driven to do it through spite and revenge. And I think Pat married me for the same reason—through malice for Tony. No wonder we've made such a mess of things.

Perhaps it will be better if we go away somewhere and start all over again. I'm going to persuade Pat to if I can. I can't come back here where everything reminds me of Tony. I want to get away from the past and everyone I've ever known—yes; even you, Popsy, and Mother, too—for a while. It's the only chance Pat and I have of making a fresh start.

Don't try to find us, please, and don't worry about us. I've a feeling Pat and I will make a go of it yet. But till I'm absolutely certain, I shan't come home and you probably won't hear from me—it's better not to write as long as I'm so unhappy and uncertain. But I won't be beaten like this by life, and when you do hear from me, you'll know I'm happy or at least making a good beginning. I'm going to start life over.

Your girl,
Gina.

Mr. Townsend removed his nose glasses and wiped them and his eyes of a suspicion of moisture. "It isn't like Regina," he said. "She didn't even stop to tell us goodbye."

"I think it's very like her," I objected. "She was afraid if she confided in you, you'd dissuade her. And I think she's right—it's the only chance for her and Pat. But I doubt if she can persuade Pat to the idea—he won't want to leave Genesee now that he's made a good start here."

"You think not?" Mr. Townsend seemed hopeful.

"But I hope she can," I told him. "If Pat comes back here, his hatred for Uncle Matthew and us is going to ruin his life as well as Regina's."

Mr. Townsend nodded thoughtfully. "It isn't natural for a young man like Pat to be so embittered by something that happened before he can remember—and something which Pat himself admits was justifiable and entirely legal. He has a jealous, envious nature, I'm afraid."

"All the more reason he should get away from here and forget about us if he can. I hope Regina succeeds with her plan."

Mr. Townsend seemed relieved. "It's always helpful to obtain another's viewpoint—our own is so utterly selfish." He folded Regina's letter and put it in his pocket. "It's going to be a shock for her mother. Gina should have said goodbye. She went in the car—at least the Tiger's gone—she should have come by the house a few minutes."

"Regina will come out all right—don't you worry," I assured him encouragingly. "I've an idea she can do almost anything with Pat if she wants to. You'll soon hear from them in Miami or Los Angeles or some romantic place—you'll see."

I was rather pleased with my cheerful prophecy until I told Rush about it. Rush set down his coffee cup—he was having a late breakfast all alone when I got home—and frowned up at the ceiling. At last he said:

"I don't believe it."

"Believe what?"

"That starting-life-over stuff. It doesn't sound natural. Nothing will ever change Pat, and Regina ought to know it by now. Besides, she doesn't love him enough to cut herself off from her family and all her friends like that—and hurt her parents. Some women might do it—for adventure or change—but Regina would do it only for the man she loves."

"Bunk," I commented. "Regina wrote the letter herself."

"I suppose that was the best reason she could think of—besides the real one," Rush decided slowly. "But I think she was afraid of something."

Rush and I looked at each other. We did not mention the strange occurrence of last night, but the thought was uppermost in both our minds. It was only because of our strained nerves that a thought so utterly mad had suggested itself—that Regina should run away because of some supernatural manifestation. I knew there must be some reasonable explanation.

"I think Pat made her write that letter," I ventured. "He may have some hypnotic influence over her. Norma says his eyes look like a hypnotist's. It sounds fantastic, I know," I added as Rush raised his eyebrows, "but after all, there is such a thing as hypnotism."

Rush burst the bubble of that theory with: "But why would Pat want to leave—just when he's got the upper hand? After this disaster, and with Tony gone, Pat will have everything his own way here. Nothing could persuade him to leave. Something has happened to Regina." Rush pushed back his chair and strode over to the window. "I wish she had told us."

I remembered how unnerved Regina had been when she came home that night after the rehearsal and told me she had taken Pat to the train. There must have been a scene between Pat and Tony—I was sure of that. Pat must've threatened Tony's life. But Tony had escaped unharmed, though Pat had a revolver. Regina might have saved Tony. But it seemed queer Pat had left town so suddenly after finding Tony and Regina together. And where had Tony been that night between twelve and one? The same thought must have occurred to Rush, for he asked:

"I wonder if Tony went to the mine to watch the graveyard shift Friday night?"

"He didn't go at eleven," I answered. "I phoned the shift boss because I was worried. Pat was looking for Tony then—to shoot him. And instead, it was Dr. Ames, who—" I was brought to my feet by a thought that flashed across the confused background of my mind with the sudden revealing glare of lightning. "What kind of car is that coupé of Dr. Ames'?"

My excited tone brought Rush around. "A Pearson. Why?"

"It's just like Tony's except it's red, isn't it? Don't you see, Rush? Don't you see why Pat left town? He was looking for Tony and Regina that night—"

Rush's dark eyes opened wider. "You mean—Pat shot Dr. Ames?"

"That's the only explanation. Pat knew Tony usually checked up on the shifts—probably thought Tony would be leaving about then. But on the way to the mine Pat saw Dr. Ames' coupé—he couldn't see it was red at night because he had his headlights off. Dr. Ames said the car was running without lights. Pat thought Dr. Ames and Miss Dunlap were Tony and Regina."

Rush nodded. "That's why Pat left town that night. He didn't know but what he'd killed Dr. Ames. It's a wonder he didn't."

"Pat must've seen his mistake after that first shot. There are lights at the mine gate, you know. Pat waited till the car was slowing down to turn, so he could see to aim. Then he saw the car was red."

"And after that," Rush paced the room restlessly, "Pat must've found Regina and told her he was leaving town." Rush paused abruptly, frowning. "But there isn't another motor in town that sounds just like the Tiger even when the cut-out's closed. Miss Dunlap wouldn't notice, probably, but it's queer Dr. Ames wouldn't recognize the Tiger if it was that close to him."

"It is queer. I'm going to ask him." I started for the door.

But Rush stopped me with: "You can't do that without telling about Tony and Regina."

I turned back, feeling as if I had almost betrayed Tony.

"We mustn't tell anybody," Rush went on. "Not even the Townsends. They'd be more worried if they knew Pat had done that. And it would only make things harder for Regina if Pat were arrested. I suppose Regina is trying to protect him through loyalty."

At that moment the dining room door was pushed ajar, and Hilda's broad peasant face appeared in the opening. One red-knuckled hand grasped the knob.

"The washlady is here," she announced in her flat slow accents. "She wants her money."

I found a note in my pocketbook and followed Hilda into the kitchen. Old Minnie was waiting; beside her on the table, a basket of laundry still exuding the warm smell of the iron.

"Howdy." Her greeting was rather sullen because last night I had made light of her fears.

I gave her the money. She fumbled in her ragged beaded bag for change, but her stiff old fingers could not find the coins among the conglomeration of trash she carried. She finally had to empty the bag out on the table, mumbling all the while. She bent over the heap, pawing aside bits of ribbon, cheap jewelry, a package of turnip seed, a green silk handkerchief, a worn picture of a movie star and some colored post cards, and at last uncovering the desired pieces of silver.

My glance had fallen on a crumpled ten-dollar note, and, out of habit, I observed the name of the bank and the serial number. The bank was the same as that of the forged notes I sought, and the serial number ended in 555. It was, I thought, one of the notes stolen from our office safe.

"Where did you get all this money?" I asked lightly, picking it up.

"Miss Gina gave it to me las' night," Minnie replied, cramming her heterogeneous possessions into the bag. "She done owed me for two-three weeks' washin'."

"Haven't you any more like it?" I tried to make my tone teasing. "Is this the only one? A rich woman like you with a gold hat—"

"Mo'n some white folks got," returned Minnie crossly, thrusting out her thick lips.

Her beady black eyes rested on Hilda and me alike with suspicion, and I handed back the note; but I had managed surreptitiously to exchange it for one of my own.

"You needn't worry about Miss Regina any more, Minnie. She's gone to the city to meet her husband."

"Huh, what I tell you? Sumpin' botherin' her." Old Minnie's stiff fingers picked a bead or two from her shedding bag, and her eyes rolled sideways in her head like little black marbles. "She was scairt to stay in dat house, Mist' Cappy—she was plumb scairt."

My smile angered Minnie, and she hobbled towards the door with an indignant swish of her long black skirts.

When I compared the serial number of the note with those I had jotted down immediately after the robbery, I found it the same as the third. But how had Regina come to have some of the money stolen from Uncle Matthew's safe?

When I told Rush, he said: "Tony stole it. He was going to run away with Regina."

I couldn't believe that—Tony a thief! "Tony might've planned to run away with Regina, but he wouldn't steal!" I defended indignantly.

"Then who stole it? Regina?"

"Of course not!"

Rush and I were silent. I could think of no argument in Tony's favor. I admitted to myself that any stranger presented with the facts would believe Tony guilty. It looked as though he had passed the money to Regina when she left the office that morning, then after Tony's death Regina had become afraid of an investigation and had fled, taking the money with her. A stranger might believe that. But I knew Tony. And I knew Regina. I couldn't believe it.

XIV
"TONY MAY BE ALIVE"

Rush was gone all morning. When he came home, he avoided me. He was gloomy and irritable, but I could not blame him. The thought of Tony's body sealed up and probably lost forever in the underground maze of Haunted Mine had left all of us unnerved. Uncle Matthew had given the order that morning for the shafts to be sealed over.

The next day Uncle Matthew went to the office as usual, as did the rest of us. But there was little to do until the mine could be opened again. The theft had made us self-conscious and suspicious. Everyone dreaded being left alone with that safe. Tony's death was still fresh in our minds. The office was a dismal place those first days.

I had officially assumed Tony's duties, though I could make no plans yet. But I sat at Tony's desk and wondered what thoughts had run through his head as he sat there. In one of the drawers I came across a little account book filled with cabalistic figures and initials of which I could make nothing. They probably concerned his winnings and losings at poker, I decided. But on one page the initials, "N. E." caught my eye; and underneath on one side, the figures, "85", and on the other, in a column, "5, 2, 3, 1, 5, 1, 3, 2.50."

That last entry indicated that the figures represented money. I wondered if the initials stood for Norma Elliott, if Tony had been lending her money. And I wondered, not for the first time, how Norma managed to dress so well on her salary and still contribute anything to the family income. Had Tony been captivated by her smartness, her petite daintiness, her cameo-like beauty, which made Regina—Regina with her fly-away hair, her little tilted nose, her still faintly visible freckles—seem by comparison provincial and merely pretty?

My suspicion was strengthened by the information Fenton volunteered. He and I were alone in the office during the noon hour one day. I looked up from my desk to see him standing there regarding me over the top of his spectacles, his forehead creased in little worried wrinkles. I offered him a chair, but he remained standing.

"There's something I think it's my duty to tell you, Mr. Sheridan," be began in a low voice, glancing about apprehensively. "I don't like to worry Mr. North about it—or your brother—but I think that—ah—in justice to myself, I must tell. I know—I am aware that some suspicion must rest on me since the—ah—the robbery."

"You know we all trust you implicitly," I murmured politely.

Fenton rested his ink-stained fingers on the desk top and leaned forward. "Thank you, Mr. Sheridan. But Miss Elliott and I are the only two outsiders in the office, and I, for one—ah—feel my position keenly. And that is the only reason I am disclosing this—" He hesitated a long moment, then cleared his throat and went on: "About two months ago I went down to the train to see my wife's brother off on the midnight express. And about three blocks before we got to the station, we passed Miss Elliott. She was alone and standing in the doorway of a picture show—the Lyric. The theater was closed and dark, and I—ah—wondered what she was doing there at that hour. I said, 'Good evening,' but she turned away and—ah—pretended to be interested in the pictures displayed in front there."

"Are you sure it was Norma?"

"I wouldn't mention it unless I was absolutely certain," Fenton assured me with injured dignity. "I saw my brother-in-law off on the train, and when I returned about fifteen minutes later, I observed a stranger walking ahead of me—at least he was no one I knew and he glanced about the street like a stranger. I had an idea he had come in on the train, though he had no baggage with him. Then I saw Miss Elliott waiting on the sidewalk for him. She threw her arms around his neck and kissed him—ah—affectionately. They didn't see me. I was nearly half a block behind. And I walked slowly, thinking they might go on ahead, not wanting to embarrass Miss Elliott. But they stayed there talking. When I passed the theater, they were standing in the entrance, and I thought I saw Miss Elliott take something out of her bag which looked like a roll of bills and pass it to the man.

That's all I saw. I didn't get a look at the man's face—he had his back towards me. But if Miss Elliott is—ah—in trouble, it looks—ah—I hope you don't think I've done wrong in telling you?" Fenton finished apologetically.

"Not at all," I assured him, rather coolly, I am afraid.

I wanted proof of my brother's innocence, yet it seemed unfair to shift all the blame on Norma. I couldn't bring myself to tell Uncle Matthew or Rush. Instead, I decided to ask Norma to explain. There might be some innocent interpretation, though I had summoned all the reasons I could think of for a girl's meeting a man at that hour—a secret love affair, a secret marriage, blackmail—and had found none excusable in view of her engagement to Rush.

Late in the afternoon I called Norma to take a letter. Then, closing the door of the office, I asked:

"Who was the man you met in front of the Lyric at midnight two months ago?"

Norma paused with her pencil in the air. She looked up at me from the corners of her eyes, a teasing smile curving her lips.

"What's it to you, Mr. Sheridan?" impudently.

"I'm serious," I said, standing before her. "Someone saw you giving this man some money. And—since the robbery—we're all more or less under suspicion—"

Her amber eyes flashed. "If that's the way you feel, why don't you get a detective? I'd like to have this mess straightened up as much as anybody."

"Then why don't you explain—?"

"I don't see how what I did two months ago has anything to do with the robbery. And since I'm not going to marry Rush, I think you've got a lot of nerve to ask me." Norma drew herself up to her full five feet and glared at me. "If you want to believe anything that old Fenton tells you, go ahead and believe it. You know he can't see three feet in front of his nose. He wouldn't know me from—from Regina."

But Norma's own words proved Fenton was right—I had not said it was Fenton who saw her.

"Did Tony give you some money?" I persisted.

"No; he didn't. What do you think I am, anyway, Henry Sheridan?" When she called me Henry I knew she was really angry "If you're going to keep on making insinuations—" there was a catch in her voice—"and calling me a thief and a gold digger and a wild woman, I won't work here any more!" With a toss of her short curls, she was gone, slamming the door.

I felt rather ashamed of myself. Women have a way of putting a man in the wrong even when he is right, I reflected sourly. At least I had the satisfaction of knowing I was right.

Rush and Norma were still frigidly formal with each other, and as long as matters stood so, I decided to say nothing to Rush. It wasn't fair to suspect Norma of any connection with the robbery when all the evidence I had pointed to Regina. I would have given much just then to ask Regina how she had come by that ten-dollar note.

But no word had been had from Regina yet, her father told us when Rush and I met him on the street Saturday morning.

"If we only knew Gina was all right," Mr. Townsend said, "we wouldn't worry. But Mother is afraid she might have been kidnapped or forced to write that letter so we wouldn't try to find her. Mother thinks I ought to ask the police to look for her or employ a private detective."

"I wouldn't do that yet," Rush advised. "Wait a while. Regina's probably having enough trouble with Pat without being ragged by police and detectives. Give her a chance to try out her plan first." This from Rush, who had utterly disbelieved Regina's motive.

"But it doesn't seem necessary for her to keep us worried," Mr. Townsend objected. "She could surely write a few lines—it doesn't seem like Regina—"

"I expect you'll hear from her soon," Rush predicted confidently.

"I've considered inserting an advertisement," Mr. Townsend said thoughtfully.

"Regina would never read the agony column," Rush returned. "And she wouldn't like the publicity. Some of her friends would be sure to see it. If I were you, I wouldn't make such a mystery over her being gone—for Regina's sake. It'll just make people curious about her and Pat, and that much harder for her if they come back."

Mr. Townsend nodded. "You may be right. But the uncertainty—"

"Just make up your mind to wait till a certain date," Rush advised. "And if you don't hear from her by then—"

"I'll wait another week," Mr. Townsend acceded. "But if I don't hear by then, I'll have to do something. I'm afraid Regina may be in trouble—though I don't know what it could be. She wouldn't come home after Pat left, and she seemed to avoid me the last few days she was here." There was a puzzled look in Mr. Townsend's gray eyes. "She acted almost as if she didn't want me to come to see her even. And she looked—frightened—I thought, though I may have imagined it."

That evening, when I asked Rush why he had changed his opinion about Regina's letter, he said: "It was plain, from that note, that Regina doesn't want to be found. And if she doesn't, she probably has a good reason."

My mind reverted to the ten-dollar note. "You don't think Regina has the money? It's absurd—Regina wouldn't—"

Rush shrugged. He pretended to be absorbed in the book he held open before him, but I could tell by the fixity of his eyes he was not reading. The hand that held his cigarette trembled slightly. Rush was not looking well. There were circles under his eyes, and he was unusually pale. He was worrying about something. He started when I leaned over and laid a hand on his knee.

"What's on your mind?" I asked. And as he hesitated: "Come on—out with it."

Rush glanced over his shoulder. We had the living room to ourselves, but across the hall we could see Aunt Addie and Uncle Matthew in the library with the checkerboard between them. I rose and drew shut the folding doors.

"It's about Tony—" Rush began.

"You haven't seen—anything else?"

Rush shook his head. "I had a queer dream the other night. I dreamed Tony was alive and had run away with Regina."

"That's not a queer dream," I told him. "You've been worrying about Regina's being gone—"

"But do you think it could be true?" Rush interrupted in an odd strained voice.

"True?" For a moment I thought he was a little mad.

Rush leaned forward, his fingers gripping the chair arms. "Do you think it really was Tony I saw—not a ghost? Do you think Tony may be alive? Do you think he could have got out of the mine?" As he met my unbelieving stare, Rush went on rapidly, jerkily: "Wait a minute! Regina's gone, hasn't she. And she doesn't want anyone to know where she is."

"That's because of Pat," I argued "Pat's afraid Dr. Ames knows who shot him. Regina is trying to save Pat."

"I don't believe Regina is with Pat," said Rush, his head flinging back in that quick nervous way he had when he was excited. "Why would Regina go to him? She's loyal, I know, but I don't think she would protect him if she knew what he'd done. And how did she get the pay roll money? She had the money that was stolen from the safe—or some of it anyway. Pat couldn't have taken that. But Tony could. He and Regina would need money if they were going to run away, wouldn't they? They'd have to go to some foreign country, I expect, because Pat would probably kill them if he could. And when was that money stolen? The day after Pat left town. They wanted a few days' start before Pat could find out."

"But Tony—" I began bewilderedly.

"Wait a minute. Tony could have gotten out of the mine if he didn't go towards the fire—if he went directly to the ventilating shaft—it isn't sixty yards from the main shaft. There's an emergency exit there, you know, and it's walled off separate from the main shaft. It wouldn't take him two minutes to reach it—he could manage that no matter how bad the gas was. He could almost hold his breath that long. Once he reached it, he'd be safe—there's a good tight door at the bottom. He could wait there the rest of the night. But he wouldn't have had to wait that long. The fan was shut off about an hour after Tony went down, and Big Bill left the fan house—I met him, you remember, and he told me about it. If there was no one in the fan house, Tony could come up without being seen. He probably got away while it was still dark and after most of the crowd had left. Anyway, I don't believe Tony's dead!" Rush finished defiantly.

He took a quick turn about the room, then dropped down at the piano and began to play some weird, melancholy Russian piece,

I hardly dared think about what he had said. Almost anything can be argued when there is no absolute certainty. It is so easy to argue oneself into false hope. And yet—Tony knew all the intricate maze of

Haunted Mine. He could have found his way blindfolded through the crosscuts and the doors between the two shafts.

"But why would Tony go to all that trouble? Why would he take so much risk? Why would he want us to believe him dead? Why wouldn't he simply run away with Regina?"

"I don't know," Rush confessed, distressed. He leaned his head over on one hand and picked out some chords with the other. "I can't understand—" He didn't want to talk about it.

"Unless Tony wanted Pat to believe him dead," I offered. "Tony wouldn't be so afraid of Pat as that."

"No. And Tony wouldn't sneak away."

"No; he wouldn't," Rush agreed. "But I saw him! If I didn't, who was driving that car?"

And I had found the car later with blood on the upholstery. I couldn't tell Rush that.

"You know," Rush continued meditatively, "I believe Tony was hiding in Regina's house—that's the reason she didn't want us to stay. They left together that night."

And old Minnie had heard Regina talking to herself. Everything seemed to fit in with Rush's theory—everything except Tony's character. Tony was not a coward—nor a sneak. If he were going to run away with Regina, he would do it openly, defiantly, proudly—if I knew Tony.

XV
"TONY'S REVOLVER HAD BEEN FIRED"

I had already decided to go back to Happy House Sunday morning. That would be my first opportunity to get away without attracting attention to my absence—except in the evening, and I wanted daylight to examine Happy House. My talk with Rush had made me only more anxious. Sunday I rose early and slipped out of the house before the others were awake.

Happy House, with its unpainted, silvered shingles and clapboards, seemed peaceful enough in the clear early sunlight. The first thing I noticed when I entered the bare, unfinished living room was that the floor had been recently swept. The dust and the dead leaves that had blown through the empty windows had been cleared out. An old broom stood in a corner.

Ashes on the hearth and charred, half-burnt logs marked the remains of what must have been a roaring wood fire. And in one corner of the fireplace, a blackened coffee pot rested on two stones. I lifted the lid. Cold wet coffee grounds emitted a musty odor. A long forked stick, charred and greasy at the end, looked as if it had been used for broiling meat, and on the mantel little heaps of red paraffin drippings remained from the burning of small colored candles. Three had apparently burned down to nothing, but the fourth had been uprooted from its foundation of drippings.

Someone had been camping or picnicking in the unfinished house. And even this brief occupancy seemed to have given the house a little character or soul or whatever is lacking in houses that have never been lived in. But there was nothing to show who the people were. The other rooms apparently had not been entered. The visitor might have been a tramp, but he would not have swept the hearth and left the place so tidy. If campers had taken possession, they would have left empty bottles and tin cans about, and the other rooms would have shown signs of tenancy. A crowd of picnickers would have left the same litter. Besides, the coffee pot would not hold enough for a crowd. It was very tiny. The grounds in the bottom would not have made more than two or three cups. It looked as if there had been only a pair of lovers.

And who, more than Regina and Tony, would have been attracted to the place? I was a little ashamed of prying into their secret and was about to leave the house, feeling like an intruder, when a cigarette stub at the edge of the hearth caught my eye. I picked it up. It was cork tipped, and the name stamped on it was "Vaquero". That was the kind Rush smoked. Tony did not like them—he declared they were too mild and tasteless. And Regina did not smoke. I dropped the stub in my pocket.

Other people, of course, used that brand, I reflected. But the cigarette was less than half smoked—and Rush had a habit of flinging them down like that when he was nervous. I looked about for others and wandered around the house outside. I found no more, but I discovered something else.

The sand pile had been disturbed recently. The packed, hard, crust-like surface, already giving root to a few straggling weeds, had been shoveled away on one side. A short piece of clapboard had apparently been used for a shovel. I picked it up and dug into the soft sand.

Before I had gone far, I dropped the board in horror. I had come upon a rusty, coagulated mass of sand—and dried blood. I could go no farther. I raked the loose clean sand back over the dark splotch, and then took a turn about the clearing to see if anybody had been watching.

But I might have been a hundred miles from civilization. No one was in sight; no human sound disturbed the Sunday calm. I sat down on the steps and lighted a cigarette and tried to think out the awful discovery I had just made. But I could conjecture no reason for it.

The events of the past eight days left me in confusion. Other people apparently suspected no mystery and no connection in the events. But other people did not know the strange circumstances Rush and I had stumbled on. There must, I thought, be some thread of connection running through these happenings, but I could not find it. I pinched out my own cigarette and dropped it in my pocket—I wanted to leave no trace of my presence there.

I began to search the clearing for other evidence of what had happened. I noticed a rough stone the size of a plate that looked as if it had been recently uprooted. Even the rain had not washed the crevices clean of the stiff clay. It was lying in a small cavity several inches deep, and I saw that the stone had been merely turned upside down in its original resting place. I lifted it. There was nothing underneath except slimy little gray bugs running from the light. I turned it over, and it settled into the hollow where it had lain so long, its irregular outline fitting perfectly into the hard-packed clay. But as I did, the color of the rock caught my eye. There was a big rusty stain on it. Hastily, I turned it over again and stamped the earth around it, so it would not be apparent it had been moved. It had been turned over to hide that dark splotch, and so had been protected from the rain which might have washed it clean.

Even while I took these precautions I wondered if Tony had escaped from Haunted Mine only to be murdered, and if I were helping his murderer to escape. But some instinct warned me to reveal nothing until I was more sure of the situation. The proof would be there later if I should want it.

I discovered now that dead leaves had been piled around the upturned stone, but the wind had uncovered it. The brown leaves seemed to make a sort of path across the clearing from the edge of the wood to the sand pile. I had not noticed it before on account of the weeds, but when I stood here I could see that the weeds had been broken down in a narrow swath. The dead leaves had blown to one side and caught in the grass. There were pine needles here, too, and leaf mold, though I found none anywhere else in the clearing. The path had not been trampled. It would hardly have been noticed except for that trail of brown leaves, last year's sodden decaying leaves, too moldy to have lain long in the sunny open clearing. The leaves and pine needles might have been scattered there to hide something—something that the rain had washed clean.

The vision that rose before my mind sent a chill of horror through me. I could see a body dragged over that trail—a limp heavy form dragged with difficulty by another dark figure. I could not see the faces of those two. They were only shadows. But in the trail they left, rusty splotches stained the weeds and grass. I was glad the rain had washed that path clean.

I went on to the edge of the wood, drawn by a dreadful fascination. Properly, it could hardly be called a wood; it was only a copse or a thicket, a fairly dense growth of brush dignified by a few tall pines and rising to a rocky ridge which separated Happy House from the main highway. The road Tony had built circled around that ridge, which was about fifty feet high and fifty yards wide. But a path had been cut through the thicket over the ridge to the highway. It had never been used, but the swath through the undergrowth was still visible from the clearing. And the trail of dead leaves seemed to lead towards that path.

I climbed the rough pass. There was nothing here but dead leaves and pine needles underfoot. I could see no trace of those shadowy figures I had imagined. But the wind blowing over the ridge rustled the dry leaves and reminded me that any sign or tracks would soon be lost in the shifting leaves. The pine needles and leaf mold underneath formed a carpet too springy and elastic to retain a footprint.

The brush reached out thorny fingers that caught my clothes and held me. I freed myself and pressed on, trying to avoid the briars. Then, as I pushed aside one insistent branch, I discovered, caught on a thorn almost at my fingertips, a tangle of bright thread. I loosened the little knot. There were three long silk threads, rose in color, shaded from light to dark. Regina's rose shawl had fringe shaded like that. I pocketed the threads and went on slowly, keeping my eyes open for other signs.

A few steps farther as I drew near the top of the little hill, another bit of color caught my glance. Clinging to a green leaf was a streak of red paraffin, dropped evidently, from a burning candle. I broke off the leaf and took it with me.

And then I came to a spot where the bare earth showed through in little patches. The leaves and pine needles had been scraped away and then scattered again loosely over a spot two or three feet square.

The shifting leaves had almost concealed the signs of disturbance; but under those loose dry leaves was no springy mattress of pine needles and leaf mold, only the dark damp ground. Stooping, I brushed the leaves away carefully. The soft earth still showed irregular raking marks as if dead branches had been used in turning over the mold. But I could discover nothing else. I avoided stepping on the bare earth and replaced the leaves as well as I could.

In doing so, I noticed a number of burnt matches—matches that had been burned down to the last quarter inch as if someone had been depending on them for light. The tiny stumps of uncharred wood were still fresh and white. They had not lain there very long, though they might have been there before the rain—probably had, I decided, since all the burnt ends had been broken off. Most of the matches were the large size—kitchen matches. But a few were the small size that come in penny boxes for smokers.

Before I finished brushing back the leaves, I came upon the guttered stub of the little red candle, burnt down to a half-inch hollow shell. The matches evidently had been used after the candle had given out.

It looked as though someone had been hunting for something. I had probably chanced upon nothing more dreadful than traces of a search for a lost coin or a ring, I thought with relief. And perhaps a dog had buried a rabbit or a chicken in the sand pile—I was seeking desperately for some innocent explanation. But a dog would not have turned that stone over to hide the stain. I gathered up matches and candle and slipped them in my pocket.

I followed the rough path on over the ridge and down to the edge of the paved highway. The hill was steeper on this side, and the trail slanted down the slope in a series of zigzags. The undergrowth was thick enough to prevent my being seen by passing cars. Near the foot of the path I almost stumbled over something glittering in a patch of sunlight—a nickel-plated revolver. It was Tony's. There could be no mistake. His initials were scratched on the handle. I turned the cylinder. One cartridge had been fired.

I put it in my pocket, and, glancing around hurriedly, stepped out into the road. I did not go back to Happy House. It seemed now to hold some awful secret. I would not have dared just then to investigate that sand pile further. I was almost afraid for my own safety. I walked rapidly towards home, anxious to tell Rush of my discoveries.

I believed now that Rush had really seen Tony on the Hill Road. Ghosts do not drive cars nor leave revolvers about. But if Tony was alive, what had happened that evening he went to Happy House? What would Rush say when I told him Tony's revolver had been fired?

But when I reached home, Aunt Addie told me Rush had left. Aunt Addie was in the yard cutting sweet peas. She snipped the stems precisely with her garden shears.

"You just missed telling Rush goodbye," she said.

"Where's he gone?" My surprise must have shown in my tone.

"To the city. Don't you know?" Aunt Addie looked at me, mildly puzzled. "Rush said you'd understand." Her calm gray eyes rested on me questioningly.

"Oh—oh, yes; I remember now," I replied in some confusion, instinctively protecting Rush yet feeling rather guilty about deceiving Aunt Addie.

"I tried to get Rush to wait till to-morrow," she continued, "but he said it was necessary for him to be in the city to-day."

I hurried upstairs to see if Rush had left a note for me. But there was nothing in my room or his. I felt, somehow, that he had gone to look for Tony, so certain had he been last night that Tony was alive.

I returned Tony's revolver to the middle drawer of his desk where he usually kept it. Nothing had been disturbed yet in his room, and I felt sure it had not been missed.

The matches and the cigarette stub I dropped into my paper basket. The sight of that cork tip of Rush's seemed to take on a new and dreadful meaning. What had Rush been doing at Happy House? Had his quarrel with Tony gone deeper than I suspected? Had Tony ever met Norma at Happy House? Had Rush taken Tony's gun—? I put aside the suggestion as too horrible. But I returned to Tony's room and wiped the revolver off careful in case there should be fingerprints on it.

XVI
"REGINA MAY HAVE BEEN MURDERED"

Horrible fancies took root now in my imagination. If Tony had escaped from Haunted Mine he had planned to disappear. But who had been killed at Happy House? I could find no explanation for my discoveries but murder. I wondered if I should go to the sheriff with my story or go back and dig farther into the sand pile by myself. But I was afraid to do either—afraid of what hideous thing might come to light.

My distrust of Norma grew until I was almost convinced she had stolen the pay roll or persuaded Tony to do it for her. Those figures in Tony's notebook seemed to indicate some secret between them. I considered every possibility—even that Tony might have planned to run away with Norma instead of Regina, and that Rush had surprised them together that night he came in pale and breathless with his story of seeing Tony's car on the Hill Road. But Rush would not have been carrying a revolver about unless he suspected something, and he surely had had no inkling before that Tony was alive. Did Regina know something? Had she, in jealousy, warned Rush? They had been talking of Tony that Tuesday evening on Regina's porch. But Rush had gone directly from there to the Hill Road. He could not have had the revolver with him then. But he could have circled about and gone home before I did, secured the revolver and left again. I did not go home till after nine that evening. It might have been Rush who took Tony's car out then. Was his story of seeing Tony trumped up only to hide his nervousness? Had Rush run away because he guessed I had gone to Happy House? I could not believe it, and yet the possibility tortured me.

But there was the fringe from Regina's shawl tangled on the thorns. Perhaps Regina had found Tony with Norma that evening. It seemed impossible her jealousy could go to the length of murder—yet such things had happened. Women, seemingly as innocent as Regina, had killed their lovers.

Or perhaps Pat had come home and discovered Tony and Regina at Happy House. But it was Tony's revolver that had been fired. And I could not believe Tony a murderer.

When the days went by and no word came from either Rush or Regina, Norma's quick jealousy flared up.

"Rush has gone to meet Regina," she declared. "That's why they don't write. They're afraid somebody will check up on them." Norma jabbed her pencil at her notebook and broke the point.

"You ought to be ashamed of yourself," I reproved. "You've no reason to suspect Regina."

"Haven't I?" she flashed. "Why has she been coming here to the office?" Norma jumped up and thrust her pencil into the sharpener. "And Rush was at her house the evening she left. Minnie, the wash-woman, told me so."

"That's nothing. I was there, too. Rush and I left together."

"And where did Rush go when you left? Did he go home with you?" Norma whirled the sharpener viciously.

"No."

"Then how do you know he didn't go back to Regina's?"

That was the night Rush had seen Tony at the wheel of the tan coupé. I couldn't tell Norma about that, nor that I had tormented myself imagining that Rush had gone to Happy House with Tony's revolver. Neither could I tell her of the little things I had seen which made me so certain it was Tony Regina loved.

"Regina was engaged to Tony, not Rush," I reminded Norma.

"People change," Norma retorted in her self-sure way. "Tony had got all over that."

"How do you know?" I asked quickly.

She did not answer, but drew little circles and flowers on the cover of her notebook.

"You were rather fond of Tony, yourself, weren't you?" I persisted.

"Well, anybody would be," she admitted with a little defiant toss of her bright head. "He was quite loveable."

"More than Rush?"

Then Norma cut me off with: "I thought you wanted me to take a letter."

On Saturday, Regina's father came into the office looking unusually alert and spruce.

"I had a letter from Gina," he announced, beaming. "She said she'd write when she was certain of herself." He felt in his pocket and drew out an envelope which he handed to me. "She and Pat are in New York. She doesn't know just where they're going next. But Gina seems to be happy—and—she's planning to come back here."

Mr. Townsend smoothed his close-clipped little gray mustache and adjusted his nose glasses more securely; his gray eyes shone with happiness.

I opened the letter and read in Regina's scrawling hand:

Thursday.

Dear Popsy:

Pat doesn't know I'm writing you. But I want you to know I haven't made a mistake. Pat is so thoughtful and considerate, and I believe we are as happy as anyone can expect to be. The mistake most people make is in believing love is everything. But love is not so important as honesty and truth. Given honesty and kindness, love will grow. So please do not worry about me.

We are going to the Follies to-night, and Pat has bought me a new evening wrap. To-morrow we are going to strap our suitcases to the Tiger and seek new adventures. I've no idea where we'll go—we are just like gypsies. It's a wonderful carefree way to live, and I wish it could last forever. I rather dread coming back to Genesee. People are so snoopy.

It's very kind of you to take so much interest in me, but I am perfectly capable of managing my own affairs and feel sure everything is turning out for the best.

Sincerely,
Regina.

I skimmed through the letter again, puzzled.

"What I don't understand," said Mr. Townsend, "is that last paragraph. It's a queer thing for a girl to write her father—'very kind to take so much interest—' What does she mean? And she doesn't mention her mother."

It was a queer letter—almost defiant. I couldn't understand it either—until I noticed that the "h" and the "r" in Thursday seemed to be in a slightly darker shade of ink. Looking closer, I discovered the "r" was written over an "e", and the "h" was crowded in between the capital and the "u". Tuesday had been changed very cleverly to Thursday. But why?

I looked at the salutation and discovered two shades of ink there. The curve of the capital "P", the little "p" and the "s" were in a slightly —very slightly darker—blue. I took the letter over to the window, and, examining it closely, I could see where the new lines were joined on to the old. That curve in the capital changed a "T" to a "P". A straight line had changed the first half of an "n" to a "p", and a little crook had changed the second half to an "s". The letter had been written originally to Tony!

Looked at in that light, it was not a queer letter at all. It must have been written soon after her marriage while she and Pat were on their honeymoon. Tony had probably told Regina she was making a mistake in marrying Pat—and this was her rebellious answer. All her talk of honesty was understandable, too—it was a thrust at Tony for his share in her father's failure. Her show of happiness was not convincing. It was not the kind of letter a young bride ought to write. Her love for Tony was visible between the lines.

But who had changed it and sent it to her father? I looked at the envelope—it had been postmarked in New York on Thursday—but the handwriting, though it looked like Regina's, seemed a little stiff as if it had been written slowly and with effort. Some of the straight lines were a little trembly; some of the curves had been gone over twice. I had no doubt an expert would declare it a forgery and a poor one. The ink on the envelope was a shade darker, too, than that of the letter.

"What do you think of it?" Mr. Townsend asked, a little anxiously now, since I had been so long examining the writing.

I hesitated, dreading to destroy his peace of mind. "There's no doubt Regina wrote it," I assured him.

I could not understand why the letter had been sent. If Regina had run away with Tony and wanted to make her father believe she was with Pat, she could have written another letter. I could think of only one reason for the sending of that old letter—Regina's death.

Fear held my tongue silent. I couldn't tell Mr. Townsend that Regina may have been murdered and her body buried in the sand at Happy House.

The sender of that letter knew Mr. Townsend would turn the matter over to the police if Regina's absence remained unexplained. But how had anyone but Tony come to have that letter? Tony must have saved it. There was a drawer in his desk that was locked, I knew. But who would have thought to look there? No one except Rush. And why would Rush want to deceive Mr. Townsend? The thought that Rush might have had something to do with it was vaguely reassuring. But my uneasiness seemed to have communicated itself mysteriously to Mr. Townsend.

"Do you think Gina wrote it of her own free will?" he asked now, little worried wrinkles appearing around his eyes. "Do you think she may have been forced to write it?"

"No," I answered truthfully. "It does sound a little strange, but people so often think one thing and write another, or leave out some little explanation that would make everything clear. Can't you think of anything Regina might be referring to in that last paragraph?"

Mr. Townsend frowned thoughtfully. "Well—yes," he admitted reluctantly, "I did suggest a few weeks ago that she should come home and leave Pat—she seemed so unhappy. I suppose Gina must've resented my interference, though she didn't seem to at the time."

"Then that explains everything," I said with false cheerfulness. "Regina has too much pride to want any help or sympathy. She didn't want even you to know her marriage was such a wretched failure. But she and Pat will make a go of it yet."

One lie seemed to commit me to another. I would have given much just then to talk the whole thing over with Rush, but the thought that Rush had avoided me lately and had not taken me wholly into his confidence left me uncertain and worried. Rush must know something about Tony he had not told me, since he had gone to hunt for him—I could think of no other reason for Rush's absence. But the letter seemed to indicate he had failed in his search. If Rush had sent the letter he had probably done it through kindness, to relieve Mr. Townsend's anxiety, though it seemed to me a mistaken kindness and not like Rush, who had never tried to varnish over disagreeable truths. If Rush had not sent the note, I dreaded to think what it meant.

When I reached home I hurried up to Tony's room. The lock of the small right hand drawer of his desk had been pried open, and recently, too, to judge from the fresh, bright scratches around the brass keyhole. I pulled out the drawer. It was filled with letters—Regina's letters. Tony had kept them all, even little notes on ruled paper in a round, childish hand, passed across the aisle at school, I had no doubt.

Now I was more certain than ever that Rush had mailed the letter to Mr. Townsend. If anyone else had robbed Tony's drawer he would have taken all the letters; only some member of the household could examine them at leisure and pick out one that could be used again. If Rush had discovered something which had sent him in search of Tony and Regina, he must have discovered it from these letters. Perhaps he had been ashamed to tell me he had read them. But so great was my anxiety now that I hesitated only a moment. Surely, if ever anyone was justified in such a course, I was, but the sight of those words never meant for my eyes, made me feel guilty of some actual crime.

I skipped over those schoolgirl notes and those written while Tony was at college and read only those written since her marriage. There were only a few, and all were apparently recent, though none was dated; the notes I had seen her drop on Tony's desk probably. They were poignant with regret and remorse. Her first proud defiance, so pitifully transparent, in that note Mr. Townsend had showed me, had long since been crushed. Some of her phrases gripped me with their suggestion of tragedy.

Oh, Tony, can one never go back? Can a mistake never be undone? Must we go on paying forever? Can nothing

ever give us back the happiness we have lost? Do you
remember when we were building Happy House?

I wondered why Regina did not divorce Pat and have it over with.
She could never be happy with him while love for Tony swayed her
whole being. But Regina had already answered my question in one of
her notes. It was dated simply "Wednesday", and I believe was written the Wednesday before the disaster at Haunted Mine.

Tony, my own: (she had written)
I'm afraid of Pat. He is acting so strangely. I don't dare
mention divorce again. When I spoke to him about it
he declared I want to divorce him and marry you because he is poor and you are rich—or will be. I never
saw him so furious. He told me he would ruin you and
your family—make beggars of you. I don't know what
he thinks he can do, but he has some scheme, I feel
sure—he seems so excited.

When I tried to question him, he said, "Just wait.
You stick by me, Gina, and you'll have all the money
you want. Our turn is coming. And it won't be long
till you can move into Matthew North's old red brick
mansion if that's what you want. God, I'd like to live
in that house and see all that gang looking through the
iron fence from the outside as I used to. And by God, I
will yet!" He simply raved all yesterday evening, Tony.

But nothing he could do like that would stop me
from marrying you, darling. What I'm afraid of is that
he would try to do you some harm. He has a revolver,
a dreadful, heavy black thing. I don't know where he
got it. I saw him looking at it the other day—I think he
was loading it. After he left the house, I hunted for it
and found it in his chest of drawers. It was loaded and
oiled. I must warn you, dear—please be careful—for
my sake.

We must try not to see each other alone for a
while. I'll see you whenever I can, though, and even

if we cannot talk together, you'll know every time my
eyes meet yours that I'm loving you so much my heart
is almost bursting.

Gina.

I was afraid now that Pat had killed Regina, too. And, more
dreadful, still, if he had taken her away with him, we might never
know her fate.

XVII
"WAS REGINA'S COMPANION DEAD?"

For me the long days that followed seemed endless as a nightmare. Often I was tempted to unburden my dreadful imaginings to Uncle Matthew, but he seemed so broken and feeble I did not dare add to his worries. I could not rest unless I was prying into the mystery that seemed to have engulfed my life like a dense black cloud from which there was no escape, yet every discovery I made only deepened the awful darkness. At times I feared for my own sanity. Everyone else seemed so completely unaware of any mystery. Even Rush's continued absence was attributed to grief over Tony's death.

"He hates to come home, poor boy, now that Tony's gone," Aunt Addie said. "Perhaps it's better for him to stay away a while, but he should write. I wish I could get Matthew to leave. He isn't sleeping well at night, and he won't see a doctor."

On Tuesday evening, two weeks after Regina's disappearance, I took Tony's car and set out in search of her, telling Uncle Matthew and Aunt Addie I was going to the city for a day or two. Regina, I knew, had left at night, driving the Tiger, which in spite of its sedate gray coat was still a racing car and easily recognized. Whatever her destination, she had probably gone to the city first, I reasoned, since all the other roads led only up the valley and farther into the hills; and if she had stopped anywhere on the way, that car would be remembered. But even if I got trace of her, it would be difficult to find her in the city. I knew some of her friends, but it would be useless to inquire if she were stopping with them. However, I could make the rounds of the public garages at night in search of the Tiger and possibly trace her in that way without asking questions. Beyond that, I had no plans.

Fortunately, I found a trace of the Tiger before I had gone fifty miles. I had stopped at every filling station and garage that was open along the way. It was tedious traveling, and discouraging, too, for I had not, so far, discovered the slightest indication that Regina had passed that way, though I not only hinted, but asked openly for information. I dared not, for Regina's sake, arouse suspicion by pressing my questions too determinedly. I had stopped at first for gas, buying only a gallon or two at a time, and when my tank was full to running over, I stopped for air and water, draining out the radiator and letting the air from a tire whenever the lights of a filling station or garage came in sight. Naturally, my progress had been slow.

It was nearly midnight when I came to the Roxbury Garage, which seemed to be the only lighted place in the village of Roxbury. I stopped in a dark spot and disconnected the generator wire. I had learned by now that requests for water and air did not loosen men's tongues. Some little trouble necessitating service and a small fee gave more time and opportunity to talk than mere buying of gas.

I drove into the Roxbury Garage and stopped with the engine running. I had to sound my horn half a dozen times before a sleepy night man in khaki overalls came out of the office. He was a moon-faced, stupid-looking youth, with heavy, drooping eyelids. He greeted me with an affable, but simple, smile that trailed off into a yawn.

"What kin do f'r you?" he mumbled.

"Generator trouble—it's not charging."

"Huh?" He yawned again.

I went into detail, thinking I was wasting time here; but, as I soon discovered, the youth was friendly and talkative enough when he was fully awake. A cigarette helped arouse him.

"Been working here long?" I asked conversationally.

"'Bout six months," drowsily.

"Many people come through here at night?"

"Yes; we gets some queer 'uns." He lifted the hood and rested one elbow on the door of the car lazily. "Yes; I get to see a heap of strangers here. Uhhuh; lots of excitement sometimes." He regarded the generator dully.

"And women drive everywhere now, just like men," I continued casually. "I know a girl who drove through here a week or two ago by herself. She drives a big gray racing car—a Ditzenberg—it made some records on the track years ago."

"Yeh; I reckon I seen that car," the youth announced, pausing to scratch the back of his neck with the pliers. "Did it have a little baby buggy top and a big spotlight on the running board?"

I nodded, afraid my voice would sound too eager.

"Uhhuh; I remember. She come through here about this time of night, or maybe a little earlier. It was raining that night." He turned back to the generator. He had by now discovered the loose connection and a turn of the pliers tightened it.

I was glad he could not see the surprise and pleasure that must have shown in my face. When I spoke I tried to make my voice solicitous and casual:

"I hope she wasn't having trouble with the car?"

"Nope—not much. Lemme see—" He leaned on the open door of the car again and puffed thoughtfully at his cigarette, his thick-lidded eyes half closed. "Seems like it was the fan belt. Yeh; that's what it was. The fan belt was broke. Put a new one on for her, I did. The engine had got het up awful because she hadn't even tried to wire up that busted belt. You'd think even a girl 'ud know enough to do that, wouldn't you? She said she had to stop once or twice and let the engine cool off, too. She couldn't a drove much farther either without ruinin' the whole works."

"She probably didn't want to get out of the car in the rain—and when she was alone, too," I suggested.

"She had her grandfather with her," said the mechanic. He let the hood fall with a clatter and fastened it down, grunting.

"Grandfather?" I echoed.

"Yeh; old bird with white whiskers."

"Oh—oh, yes; of course." I nodded, pretending to understand. So thankful was I to learn that Regina was alive that I gave little thought at first to her companion.

"Yeh; neither one of 'em seemed to know what was the matter with the car." The mechanic's mouth was stretched in a broad silent laugh. "The girl thought maybe it needed water."

"Didn't her grandfather know?" I asked, wanting only to keep the mechanic talking.

"Him? He was asleep, I guess. He just sat there like a dummy. The curtains was up on account of the rain so I didn't get a good look at him."

"How do you know it was her grandfather?" I demanded, letting curiosity get the better of my caution.

But the moon-faced mechanic attributed my eagerness to jealousy. He lowered one heavy eyelid in a knowing wink. "Maybe he wasn't—maybe she just told me that because she liked my looks."

"Did she tell you he was her grandfather?"

"Well, now—" the mechanic used the pliers on his head thoughtfully—"she says for me to hurry because her grandfather was tired. And I reckon he was. He just sat there with his whiskers on his chest and didn't say nothin'."

"Were they going on to the city that night?" I asked.

"I reckon so. The girl asked how the road was and if there was any detours."

"She was a pretty girl, wasn't she?" I pursued, still wondering if it could be Regina. "Fair skin, light hair, tilted nose, little mouth, pointed chin?"

"Yeh; she was sorter pug-nosed," the mechanic agreed listlessly. "And she looked kinda peaked."

It must have been Regina. I asked a few more questions about the car to make sure. But Regina had no grandfather. Not until I was a mile away from the Roxbury Garage and headed towards the city again, did it occur to me that in the white whiskers I had got trace of my missing beard—I had almost forgotten such a thing ever existed. Now I began seriously to consider its disappearance and Regina's strange companion.

The night Regina drove to the city was the night Rush had seen Tony on the Hill Road and I had found the tan coupé with blood on the upholstery. Tony might have obtained the beard and the make-up from my room—he knew I had bought them. But so did everyone else who was taking part in the play—I had exhibited the things at one rehearsal. Tony knew where to find Aunt Addie's scissors to cut the beard short; but anyone else, hunting about in a strange house for a pair of scissors, would naturally look in a sewing basket.

Tony had left the mine with Regina the evening of the disaster, I remembered now. He might have gone home and obtained the things then—there was no one in the house at that time. But there was no one at home all afternoon; anyone might have entered and searched at leisure.

Why would Tony want the beard and the make-up then? To escape from the mine, of course. The answer was inevitable. There had been a crowd about the main shaft and the grounds for days. Tony had waited till Big Bill left the fan house to come up from the ventilating shaft. Rush and I thought Tony had taken a chance on escaping unnoticed in the dark. But he had not depended on luck. The disguise had enabled him to walk through the grounds or even the town unrecognized.

Tony alive! The words pounded through me with my pulse beats. Tony alive! For the first time I allowed myself so much certainty.

I remembered Tony's reluctance in soiling his hands with small repairs on the car. Tony would not have got out in the rain to fix the fan belt as long as the car would run. Pat would have stopped to fix it no matter how great his hurry or how heavy the rain. Pat was a natural mechanic. To run a car under such conditions would have been intolerable to him. Not while he was able to lift a hand would Pat Brace have permitted his beloved racing car to heat like that.

The form which my thoughts had taken, commonplace enough under ordinary circumstances, now suddenly startled me—"not while he was able to lift a hand—" The mechanic said the bearded man had sat as if he were asleep. The curtains were up. Regina was in a hurry. Was her companion ill—injured—*dead?*

Just when I was convinced that Tony lived, hope was crushed out by new fear. Tony—or someone—must have been killed at Happy House. No merely wounded person would have been buried in the sand pile. But why had Regina carried his body away?

Regina could not have lifted a dead body into the car alone—ordinarily. But fear sometimes lends unnatural strength. Could Regina have killed Tony? The fear tightened like fingers about my throat. I despised myself for even imagining such things. Yet I was in such a state of mind I could not free myself from its horrible grip. I was ready to suspect anyone. Regina had shown how complete was her love for Tony. What if Tony's love were something less than that? What if Tony had not been so firm and unchanging as I liked to think? Suppose Regina had found Tony at Happy House with some-one else—say, Norma—?

Revolted, I succeeded at last in putting the idea from me. Yet I was only beginning to realize how little we know of the secret thoughts and passions that sway those around us. The brief glimpses I had had into those concealed places of consciousness sometimes called hearts, strange and mysterious as the hidden depths of the ocean, amazed and frightened me with their awful possibilities.

For two days I stayed in the city searching for a glimpse of Regina or Tony or Pat or Rush; but soon I realized the hopelessness of my task. I had no idea where to find any of them, no knowledge, even, whether they were here or in New York or hiding in some out-of-the-way village. Rush, too, I imagined was following illusive conjectures in the hope of finding Tony alive.

I returned home, thinking some news might have come in my absence; but there was nothing, and everyone in Genesee still believed Tony dead in the fiery tunnels of Haunted Mine.

XVIII
"A MYSTERIOUS VISITOR HAD
SEARCHED REGINA'S HOUSE"

On Saturday morning, three weeks after the theft of the pay roll and the disaster at the mine, Uncle Matthew held a sort of conference at the office about opening the mine again. No warmth could be felt through the concrete over the shafts, and it looked as if the fire had died down. I was for opening the shafts at once, my anxiety to know Tony's fate overriding my judgment. But the foreman and the engineers believed it was too early to risk it and might only give the fire a fresh start. It was decided to wait two more weeks.

When the others were gone and Uncle Matthew and I were alone in his office, I broached the subject of the theft.

"Has none of the money been paid back yet?" I asked.

He shook his head. His gray hair was long and untidy now. His eyes, with the heavy pouches underneath, looked watery and red. The disaster and Tony's death had aged him pitifully.

"Are you still determined to keep the matter secret?" I continued.

"If I can," he answered wearily. "Titus, at the bank, asked me the other day why we drew out the pay roll twice. I told him I intended to send Rush to the city to buy some bonds. But he knew I was lying. He knows I wouldn't be fool enough to send the cash, and I wouldn't want the exact sum of the pay roll anyway. But Titus won't ask again—I let him understand it was none of his business. But he'll talk, I expect."

"Have you any idea who did it?" I ventured to ask. "Is that why you won't have it investigated?"

"I've no idea—except that it must've been someone in the office. And if it was—" He broke off abruptly and looked at me very hard

135

from under his black shaggy brows. "You don't think I'm a hard man, do you, Cappy? I've been good to you boys, haven't I?" His voice trembled slightly.

"Our father couldn't have done more," I assured him truthfully.

"Thank you, Cappy. And—no matter what people say about me—" his words were barely audible—"will you remember that?"

"Of course, Uncle Matthew. But no one would ever call you a hard man."

He shook his head. "I am hard—to my enemies. But I've been in some hard places, too. I've been forced to do things I didn't want to do."

"You're thinking about that deal that caused the bank to fail," I said. And though I had blamed him, myself, at the time, I was touched by his evident regret. "You mustn't worry about that any more—it's over and done with."

"The past is always with us," he muttered.

"You're feeling responsible for the break between Tony and Regina—but you couldn't foresee that." I tried to comfort him. "It was only a mad impulse that caused Regina to marry Pat."

"I've done the best I could for you boys. I'd stand by you in trouble—that's why I'm keeping it quiet about the pay roll—and I hope you'll do as much for me—if it's ever necessary."

I patted him on the shoulder, and turned to look out the window. It was not often Uncle Matthew spoke so intimately, and I felt rather awkward as one does on such occasions. After a moment, I asked:

"Did it ever occur to you that Pat might have stolen the money?"

"Pat?" Uncle Matthew was plainly surprised.

"He doesn't like us, you know. He'd do almost anything to ruin us."

"How do you know that?" Uncle Matthew asked rather sharply.

I couldn't tell him I had read Regina's letter to Tony. "Everybody knows that," I answered. "It's only a surmise about the theft, of course. But Pat might have found out the combination in some way."

"How?"

"Hypnotized Rush, perhaps," I offered lightly, remembering Norma's remark about Pat's eyes.

"Pat didn't do it," Uncle Matthew said abruptly.

I had a feeling that he knew more about the theft than he was willing to tell. He must have suspected Tony. And I wondered again if Tony could have been in some predicament I knew nothing about that would cause him to counterfeit his own death. He surely would not have gone to such lengths to avoid Pat's vengeance.

That afternoon I asked Regina's father for the key to her house. I told him I wanted to borrow a book, but what I really wanted was to search for some clue to Tony's fate.

The old stone cottage looked shabby and deserted in the bright afternoon sun. The shades were drawn; the grass had grown high; the old-fashioned daisies and corn flowers needed water; the tall holly-hocks were beginning to turn brown. I let myself into the house. The closed rooms were warm and musty. I raised the shades and opened some of the windows to air it out. One of the dining room windows was not fastened—it lacked an inch or more of being closed.

When I lifted the sash, I noticed a fresh splinter of wood on the sill, and soon discovered it had been gouged from the bottom of the window on the outside with some sharp heavy instrument, possibly a tire tool. I looked at the catch. It was loose. Someone had found a window where the catch was not quite secure and forced it open. The screen was unhooked, and there was a small torn place in the wire where something had been inserted to lift the hook.

My first thought was of burglars. I looked in the buffet at once, but the silver had not been disturbed. I went upstairs to Regina's room and found several pieces of jewelry in a tray on the dresser, inexpensive things, but good enough to attract any ordinary burglar.

I was about to conclude there had been no burglar, that the window had been forced by Pat and Regina sometime when they had forgotten the key, though it seemed strange it should be the only one unlocked now; then I wandered into Pat's room and discovered something curious, not in itself, but in connection with the open window. The bedspread was wrinkled and awry; the covers looked as if they had been thrown on the bed. Regina would never make a bed like that, nor any other woman. It had much the appearance of my own bed when I attempted the deceiving task of making it; I could never attain that finical precision demanded by Aunt Addie and Hilda.

I wondered if Pat had been at home. It looked as if he had spent a night or more in his own house without letting anyone know of his presence. But when I turned the covers down, I found sheets and pillowcases fresh and unwrinkled. No one had slept on that smooth linen since it had come from under Minnie's iron. Then why had the bed been left so disorderly?

I glanced about the room for other signs of Pat's presence and discovered everywhere the same lack of order—it could hardly be termed disorder. The clothes in the closet were carelessly hung. Those on hangers drooped slovenly one-sided and full of wrinkles; others were thrown over the rod anyhow while the hangers lay on the floor. The dresser and the chest of drawers lacked their usual neatness. The scarves hung crookedly; the toilet articles were jumbled together anyhow; the drawers were not closed tightly, and folds of clothing protruded through the cracks. I looked inside the drawers and found everything tumbled and wadded in heaps. It would not have been unusual in some houses, but both Regina and Pat were orderly. Even when things were occasionally neglected, there was never such thorough untidiness. Even the rug was awry and wrinkled. If Pat had come home and gone through his things hurriedly, he would not have left the rug twisted—it could have got like that only by being moved, for the furniture rested on it. Somebody must have searched the room and searched it thoroughly. I could find no other explanation.

Regina's room was in its accustomed order. I wondered where she kept the rose shawl. The tangle of silk thread I had pulled off the briar was still in my pocket, and I wanted to make sure it had come from Regina's shawl—one can so often be deceived in colors. I looked in the cedar chest, taking care not to tumble things about. The rose shawl was there. I spread it out on the bed and laid the tangle of silk thread on the fringe—it was the same. And with a little trouble, I found the cluster of short ends where the knot had been broken off.

Then something else attracted my attention—a two-inch streak of red wax ending in a thick little drop. I lifted it off with my fingernail and scraped the silk clean as well as I could. Regina must have carried that little red candle into the wood. But here in her house and among her things, I could not believe Regina guilty of any wrong. I could almost feel her presence here, and she was still the same childhood pal and playmate I had always known. My nightmare suspicions had vanished, and I would have done as much then to protect Regina as if she were my sister. I folded the shawl and laid it back.

I glanced into the guest room; nothing there apparently had been touched. But downstairs, now that I observed closely, I discovered signs of disturbance. The books on the living room shelves presented irregular wavy rows. Some were turned upside down. The pictures hung slightly askew; the lampshades were tilted at drunken angles; the candlesticks and vases on the mantel had lost their precise alignment; the pillows on the couch were all in a heap, their fancy tops turned down; the rugs were not in their accustomed places—the one in the doorway was too wide for the space and was turned up at one side. Regina would never have left things like that. Yet nothing was obviously disarranged. The room had seemed in order when I first entered. Whoever had made the search had gone to some trouble to replace things and had probably thought no one would notice the difference. But Regina, I think, would have discovered it the minute she entered the room. I could not imagine what had been the object of the search.

My own search so far had yielded no hint of Tony's fate. Shamelessly, I opened Regina's desk. I found not a scrap of Tony's writing, but, from the disorder, I surmised the other prowler had been there ahead of me. I could think of no other place to search. My investigation of the little house seemed complete. But as I was about to leave, my glance fell on the small closet under the stairs. I opened the door. A collection of umbrellas, overshoes and raincoats was all I saw. I struck a match and discovered in the dark angle under the steps a wooden box full of Christmas decorations. I pulled it out, and there, under the gaudy tinsel and red paper bells and strings of tiny electric bulbs, I found a handful of red candles. I compared them with the candle-end I had picked up in the thicket and found them the same shade and size—or as nearly the same size as could be determined from the melted stump. I gathered the candles up and stuffed them in my pocket—I did not want anyone else to compare them with the little heaps of red wax on the mantel at Happy House.

I closed the windows and drew the shades again. The massive, old-fashioned furniture that had been Pat's mother's was dimly outlined in the shadows. Its heavy respectability seemed vaguely depressing as if it were defying me to discover the secrets it shared with the old stone cottage.

As I went down the hill I stopped at the nearest neighbor's—the Mrs. Barnes, with whom Aunt Addie had sat up a few weeks before. The little old woman was almost recovered now from her illness and was sitting in a big rocking chair on the front porch with a quilt wrapped around her. She was a tiny wrinkled creature with sharp features, bright bird-like eyes and a caved-in, toothless mouth. I stopped to ask how she was feeling, though I knew it would be hard to get away again.

"Well, if it ain't little Henry Sheridan!" She greeted me in the same words and the same shrill tones I remembered from childhood. "My, but you're getting to be a big boy!"

I bent over from my five feet, eleven, and took her frail bony little hand in mine. I do not know whether her hand trembled or whether its gentle movement was intended for a shake.

"Yes; I'm getting real spry again." She looked up at me with her head on one side, bird-like. "Where've you been, Henry?"

I told her I had been to Regina's and mentioned the open window, hoping she might have observed something. "I didn't miss anything," I added. "I suppose the burglar was frightened away before he got in."

"You say Pat and Regina ain't been there for pretty near two weeks?" she quavered excitedly. "Why, it ain't been more than a week ago, I know, I seen a light up there. It was nearly midnight, too. You know I don't sleep so good since this spell I had here awhile back, and sometimes I lay awake most all night. I can see the windows on this side of Regina's house real plain from my bed even through the trees. I remember thinking it was a funny sort of light—it came and went. The shades was down, but I could see the light through them, sorter dim. Do you reckon it was one of them burglar's flashlights?"

I told her it was probably Regina's father hunting for something with matches or a candle, and that he had had the electric lights turned off since Regina left. I stressed the fact that nothing had been stolen. Mrs. Barnes seemed disappointed, but I did not want the news spread that a mysterious visitor had searched Regina's house.

To Mr. Townsend I said nothing except that I had found a window unlocked but nothing missing.

XIX
"TONY HAD BEEN SHOT"

Five weeks after the disaster at Haunted Mine, the shafts were opened again, and after the ventilating fan had been going several hours, two rabbits in a cage were let down into the pit. They were brought up at the end of five minutes—alive. Again they were let down, and after half an hour were still alive, though plainly suffering from the effects of gas. It was deemed safe, however, for men to venture into the mine, though only for short periods.

I went down with the first group. We descended to the second level. The cage was left waiting for us in case we should run into danger.

Our Davys made a yellow haze of light around us in the blackness. The air was still odorous of smoke and burnt wood. The timbers around the foot of the shaft were scorched and charred. The flames had reached even to the stables, and the lamp room. As we entered the gangway, we stumbled over the charred body of one of the mules, cut from the traces as his driver fled.

We had not penetrated a hundred yards before our way was barred by a cave-in, caused evidently by the last explosion. The half-burnt timbers had given way, and great boulders had fallen into the drift. The passage was not entirely blocked, for the draft whistled through the dark holes, but no one could attempt to crawl under the great rocks.

The sight of those piled-up stones and crushed timbers so near the shaft left me with a queer sinking feeling—fear that Tony might have been caught in that cave-in and that all my elaborate conjectures about his escape were based on nothing more substantial than fancy and desperate hope.

We turned back and entered one of the crosscuts through the double doors that formed a sort of lock like that in a canal to prevent the draft from taking a short cut through the workings. We had to go carefully because the cave-ins had changed the course of the air and we might run into a pocket of gas in an unventilated crosscut.

In one of the farthest corners of the workings, we found an abandoned winze partly blocked with a hastily flung up bulkhead of timbers torn away from the walls and great blocks of coal. One of the men held his Davy over the partition and by its yellow gleam we saw the blackened forms of the seventeen entombed miners sprawled in the attitudes in which death had taken them. They had died quickly. One knelt by the half-built barricade as if he had been trying even while he sank to his knees to wall off the insidious, invisible death, rolling through the black drifts. Another had fallen across the beam he was carrying. The flames had not reached the bodies, but the thick clouds of smoke that had filled the mine had poured over them.

We took only one brief glance and turned away. But that was enough to show me Tony was not among them.

By now our heads were reeling in the foul air, and we fought our way back to the cage and gave the signal, four quick rings, to hoist away.

That afternoon the bodies of the seventeen were brought out of the mine. Every corner of the workings was explored for Tony's body, but no trace was found of him. I, myself, made several trips down, and once I took the short cut through the double doors to the ventilating shaft, the course I thought Tony must have taken if he escaped from the mine. But I found no sign of his presence there.

I began to fear Tony's fate would remain a mystery until the big cave-in was cleared away. And even then it might still be uncertain, for the roof had come down in a dozen other places. Some of the working rooms along the face of the seam were half filled with fallen coal and rock.

With two companions I was waiting at the foot of the shaft for the cage to be lowered—it had gone up with the last of the bodies—when one of the men leaned over the pit at the bottom of the shaft. I saw him start, a curious expression on his face. He held his Davy over the dark hole.

I stepped close to him. My own light added its feeble ray. In the shadows below was a huddled form. My heart felt squeezed out and soggy like a mass of putty when I saw that green striped sweater. In spite of smoke and flames those zigzag stripes were still recognizable.

Then the descending cage cut off my view. I turned away, feeling sick. Someone shouted up for the cage to be hoisted a little way. It rose, creaking. Three men climbed down into the pit under the cage.

I remember the grip of fingers on my arm, and my companion, a rough, hardened old miner, growling: "Best look away. It ain't a nice sight to think about afterwards." And I was thankful to him—Fritz Muller, I think his name was—for I would not have liked to admit how weak I really felt.

But I heard them passing up the lifeless scorched thing that had been Tony. The cage came down. When I looked around again, my gaze fastened itself with something like hypnotic fascination on the long dark form the men had laid on the floor of the cage. It seemed so abnormally long, as a dead body always does. The clothing was little more than burnt rags. The flames had swept over him there in their course up the huge chimney of the shaft. I saw one of the men spread a clean blue handkerchief over the face. With an effort I averted my eyes as I stepped into the cage.

The ascent seemed interminable. I remember only that the man next to me was carrying a smoke-blackened gas mask—the one Tony had worn. I stared at it, and at the big signet ring on the man's grimy hand. And to this day the sight of a big signet ring sometimes gives me a queer sinking feeling.

Uncle Matthew was waiting at the surface. He was not so hard hit as I; but then he had expected nothing else, while I had argued myself into believing Tony alive. I realized now how slight was the foundation of my hopes.

Then a new horror gripped me. It must have been our impatience which had cost Tony his life. I remembered how Uncle Matthew had ordered the cage hoisted for fear Tony had reached it too weak to signal. And during that brief period Tony must have stumbled into the pit at the bottom. The fall of eight or ten feet had probably stunned him. And already weak from the poisonous air, he had failed to rise. The ascending cage had prevented us from hearing his fall.

The same thought must have passed through Uncle Matthew's mind, for when I told him where the body had been found, he mumbled: "If I'd only waited—everything goes wrong. . . ." His voice died away to a hoarse whisper. "It must be a curse. . . ."

As we turned towards the car, Fritz Muller touched my arm again. He put something into my hand. It was Tony's watch and fountain pen.

"Found them things on him," Fritz Muller explained gruffly.

That afternoon late Dr. Ames called at our house. Uncle Matthew, Aunt Addie and I were in the library. Dr. Ames' usually smiling face was grave and worried, an expression that sat strangely on his pink round countenance. He looked, with his bald head, his blond eyebrows and his fat rosy cheeks, like a perplexed old baby on the verge of crying. He sat on the edge of his chair, his puffy little hands on his knees which just showed under the balloon-like expanse of his waistcoat. He looked at Uncle Matthew very hard and cleared his throat.

"You know, don't you, I'm the coroner here," he blurted out.

Uncle Matthew looked up suddenly from the inkwell he had been fidgeting with. "Yes."

"Mark Powell phoned me a while ago—asked me to come over to his place." Powell was the undertaker. "The fact is—Tony was shot."

"Tony?" Uncle Matthew's trembling hand upset the inkwell.

Aunt Addie sat primly erect in her chair, staring at Dr. Ames as if she were frozen. She still held a needle poised over her embroidery hoops.

"How could he have been shot?" she demanded at last.

Dr. Ames brows puckered up. "Don't know—don't know. But—" his pudgy little fingers brought something out of his waistcoat pocket—"there's the bullet—a thirty-eight. Got it out with a probe." No one looked at it, and he slipped it back in his pocket. "Have to hold an autopsy and an inquest."

I sat still, wondering whether or not I should tell of my discoveries. Tony's revolver was a thirty-eight.

"How was he shot?" I asked.

"Through the back. The bullet entered the fourth intercostal space and penetrated the right ventricle."

"He couldn't have shot himself?"

"Through the back?" Dr. Ames frowned. "No, no. The bullet took a straight course—straight—through the body. A man couldn't fire a shot straight into his back. The bullet would go sideways—to the left if he was right handed. Besides—there were no powder burns on the back. The front of the body was burned some by the fire, but the back was protected—no burns. Why did you think—? You didn't find a gun by him?"

"No; I didn't look," I answered. "But if there'd been one, I'm sure the men would've seen it. But I don't understand how he could have been shot in the mine."

"Bless my soul, bless my soul!" Uncle Matthew exclaimed suddenly.

I looked around. Aunt Addie had fallen back in her chair in a faint. The sight of her white upturned face and her glassy eyes gave me a start. Her embroidery hoops and the strip of tan linen slid slowly off her lap to the floor.

"Tut, tut!" muttered Dr. Ames, "should've known better than to talk before her." Then turning to me: "Fetch my bag—in the hall."

A whiff of ammonia brought Aunt Addie around. Hilda and I helped her upstairs to her room.

It was worse to know that Tony had been murdered than that he had died. And yet, in spite of the strangeness and the seeming impossibility of it, I was not altogether surprised. It was the one shock for which I was prepared.

Uncle Matthew looked done in. Dr. Ames was still with him when I went down to the library again.

"I'll give you a sleeping powder," Dr. Ames was saying.

Uncle Matthew seemed not to hear. He sat bent forward in his big arm chair, his long thin fingers clutching the arms.

"Murder—murder. . . ." His bloodless lips formed the words almost silently. He looked up at Dr. Ames bewilderedly. "But how could Tony be murdered? He died in the mine."

"Don't worry about that now," Dr. Ames told him.

"Tony was all right before—he was all right when he went down in the mine, wasn't he?" Uncle Matthew looked from Dr. Ames to me questioningly. "There was no one else in the mine," he mumbled. I think the shock had left him dazed.

"Here, take this." Dr. Ames had stirred up the powder in a glass of water. "You'd better go upstairs and lie down."

Uncle Matthew shook his head stubbornly. "I'll stay here. I'm getting too old to be climbing stairs a dozen times a day."

"Lie down on the couch then," Dr. Ames advised as he turned to leave.

From the hall he signaled me with a jerk of his head. I followed him out. He opened his fountain pen and dashed off a few unintelligible scrawls on a prescription slip.

"For your uncle," he said. "Sleeping powders. Strain's been too much for him—heart's not too strong."

He took my arm and drew me out on the porch, closing the door behind us.

"Now tell me," he began with an uneasy glance towards the library windows, "could anyone else have got into the mine that night?"

"I don't think so. There's a ladder down the ventilating shaft, but Big Bill was running the fan. He refused to leave it until it was shut down—I know, because I urged him to. No one could have gone down there or come up without being seen by him. That's the only entrance except the main shaft, and you know what a crowd was there."

"Nobody could've gone down after the fan was shut off?"

"There wouldn't have been any need then—that was an hour after Tony went down—Tony couldn't have lived that long. The oxygen tanks are good for only half an hour."

Dr. Ames wiped his face and his bald head with his handkerchief, then blew his nose loudly. "It's beyond me. Somebody might've fired down the shaft after he was lying at the bottom," he pondered. Then: "But the cage would be in the way." He shook his head, puzzled.

"Nobody could fire down the shaft without being seen anyway," I objected. "There were people around all the time for several days."

"Maybe the autopsy will show something. Must find out whether he died of gas or the bullet. Was he still wearing the gas mask?"

"I don't know. But the men brought the mask out. I saw it."

"Must have it for the inquest. Bring it, will you, just as it is."

He bustled down the walk with brisk little steps.

I was almost certain he would find Tony had died from the wound, not from gas. I was on the verge of hurrying after him and telling him my discoveries when, as if by telepathy, he turned on his heel and came back.

"Tony have any enemies?" he asked abruptly.

"You ought to know as much about that as I do—I've been away the last three years," I reminded him.

I couldn't tell him I suspected Pat without telling that Tony had been meeting Regina at Happy House—that made the whole affair so sordid. I couldn't reduce Tony to that tabloid level even to avenge his death. Shot through the back by a jealous husband—if that had been Tony's fate, it was better his death should remain a mystery.

"Wasn't Pat Brace still jealous of Tony?" Dr. Ames inquired shrewdly.

"Why do you ask that?"

"Thought maybe it was Pat took a shot at me the other night because I got a car like Tony's."

"Pat?" I echoed dumbly. "But why—"

"Sounded like that racing car of his behind me when it turned up the hill." Dr. Ames pulled the long lobe of his ear thoughtfully. "Didn't like to accuse Pat before. He didn't have anything against me. Might be other cars in the country like that, too. Thought maybe I was mistaken. Couldn't prove anything anyway. But with Tony shot—and Pat gone—things looked different. Maybe that slug I got was meant for Tony. Haven't heard from Pat, have you?"

"No."

"Townsend said Regina wrote from New York, but didn't send any address. Looks bad for Pat. When's Rush coming back?"

"I don't know."

"What about that quarrel he had with Tony?" Dr. Ames went on. "Heard they made quite a scene at the Opera House the other night."

"It didn't amount to anything," I assured him quickly.

"H'mmm," Dr. Ames cleared his throat. "Heard you lost some money at the office few weeks ago?" His tone was questioning.

"Who told you that?"

"Fellow at the bank. Said your uncle was trying to keep it quiet. I don't want to butt in, but—a lot of things may come up at the inquest. Where's Rush now?"

I felt the warm blood flooding up under my cheeks at the suspicion that had crept into his tone. "In the city," I said.

"Like to have him here for the inquest," said Dr. Ames off-handedly.

But I knew it was a warning, a friendly warning. And I did not know how to reach Rush. What if he did not come home? And now that he would learn from the papers that Tony was really dead, he might stay away till the first shock should wear off. Rush was always something of a recluse.

I was thankful now, as I watched Dr. Ames drive away in the dusk, that I had not told him Tony had probably been killed by his own gun and that Rush had come in one night pale and breathless declaring he had seen Tony on the Hill Road.

XX
"THEY'RE SAYING RUSH KILLED TONY"

The inquest was set for Tuesday. That morning at dawn I was awakened by a rain of gravel flung against my windowpane. I looked out. Norma was standing in the drive below, hands thrust in the pockets of her green sweater. With a little imperious backward jerk of her head, she beckoned for me to come down, then walked away.

I dressed hurriedly. From the front steps I caught a glimpse of the green sweater through the trees. Norma was sauntering leisurely towards home. I soon caught up with her. She caught my arm. Her face was troubled and earnest.

"Cappy, where's Rush?"

"I don't know," I confessed.

"Why doesn't he come home?"

"I don't know."

She stopped and leaned back against the bole of one of the big elms, hands in her sweater pockets, feet in green and white sport shoes, thrust out before her. She studied the tips of her oxfords reflectively.

"Do you know what people are saying about Rush?" Her voice dropped to a whisper. "They're saying Rush killed Tony."

Instinctively, I glanced around, but the leafy tunnels of street and sidewalk were deserted and peaceful in the pale early sunlight. I managed an uneasy smile.

"It's absurd, of course. Rush will explain everything when he comes home."

"But it's all my fault for ragging Rush. I just wanted to see how much he cared. Glory, I wish I hadn't done it. I didn't know these hillbillies could be such gossips. Give me a smoke." She took a cigarette from my package and lighted it defiantly. "You know what they're saying, Cappy? They're saying I vamped Rush into stealing the pay roll to run away with me, and Tony knew it and threatened to tell because he didn't want Rush marrying me, so Rush hired somebody to go down in the mine and kill Tony—that's what they're saying."

"But it's utterly impossible," I protested miserably. "No one could have gone down. Big Bill was at the other shaft all the time."

Norma nodded. "That's it—they say Big Bill did it. Someone saw him talking to Rush that night after the disaster. They walked down the street together. And Rush looked like a ghost, they say."

The memory of a conversation with Rush flitted back to me.

"It was Big Bill who told Rush of Tony's death. Rush just happened to meet him. Everyone knows Big Bill wouldn't harm a fly."

"I know he wouldn't. But it's so weird about Tony, people are ready to believe anything. They say Big Bill is getting cuckoo talking about ghosts. . . ."

"It's because he lost his son. Billy meant everything to him."

"But people say it's his conscience. And with Rush gone and all. . . . Why doesn't he come home, Cappy?"

"Rush always goes poking off by himself when things go wrong."

"I don't blame him," said Norma fiercely. "I'd get away too, if I could. People in this town are horrid. They know about everything. How did they find out about the theft, and why do they blame me? They've got it all figured out that one of you boys stole the money and that's why your uncle's keeping it quiet. But they aren't quite sure whether it was Tony or Rush," her tone was bitter. "I guess they think I'd run away with either one for that much. Oh, I know they're talking about me. One old cat stopped my little sister on the street yesterday and asked her who bought my clothes for me."

"Your clothes look more expensive than any girl's in town," I pointed out.

"And I'm only a poor widow's daughter!" she mocked.

"You can't blame people for talking when you're seen meeting a strange man at midnight and refuse to explain. This theft and Tony's death have made everybody suspicious."

Norma was silent. After a moment she asked quietly: "Do you think Rush knew?"

"I expect so."

"He didn't ask me about it."

"He wouldn't. Rush is too proud and sensitive to ask about anything you wouldn't tell of your own accord."

"I didn't want Rush to know," she said softly, digging one toe into the grass. "But, since you think I'm so dizzy—that was my father I met."

"Your father?"

"Mother's always let you think she's a widow, but she isn't. She left my father five years ago because—well—he was bootlegging. Not regularly—just on the side." The color rose faintly in Norma's cheeks. She kept her eyes on the toes of the green and white oxfords. "But he's not such a bad sort—really. And—he's my father. Mother won't take any money from him. She's too proud. But I'm not. When he's flush he sends me some. Mother knows it. But she doesn't know I meet him sometimes. I've spent Sunday with him in the city several times. And Mother doesn't know I let him have some money when he was in a tight place. He wanted a hundred. And I only had fifteen. I had to borrow eighty-five from Tony. But he was a good sport. He let me have it without asking any questions or looking righteous either. I paid part of it back, a little at a time."

So that was the explanation of that little row of figures. "I wish you'd tell Rush," I said.

"I will if I ever see him again. I didn't want him to be ashamed of me—because of that. But why doesn't Rush come back? Can't you phone or wire him?"

"I haven't any idea where he is."

"I wish we could get word to him. Some reporters have come from the city for the inquest. I'm afraid they'll put it in the papers that Rush is suspected. People are talking so."

Norma was right. The papers that morning played up Rush's mysterious disappearance and the theory that he might have arranged Tony's death either through jealousy or because Tony knew about the theft. It was all very adroitly done. No open accusations. Only veiled insinuations that were even more damning.

The inquest was held at Powell's mortuary because the body had been taken there from the mine. The inquiry didn't last long. It was merely a legal formality, because no one knew how or why Tony had met his death, except that he died from the bullet and not from gas. The autopsy had shown that as I expected. With Rush still absent. I couldn't tell even the little I knew.

We sat in two rows along the walls of Mark Powell's office, the six men called for the jury on one side, the witnesses and two reporters on the other, with pudgy little Dr. Ames behind the desk at the end, and beside him, Sheriff MacFarland, grim, frowning, arms folded and chin on his chest.

Uncle Matthew and Big Bill were taken into a rear room to identify the body. The jury went too. But I could not bring myself to look at that form vaguely outlined under a long white sheet that I glimpsed while the door was open.

The jurors filed back, walking awkwardly on tiptoes. They sat on the straight little chairs, holding their hats and looking uncomfortable and worried. Big Bill had to assist Uncle Matthew to his chair. The sight had been almost too much for him, I was afraid. Mark Powell brought him a glass of water, and his hand shook so he spilled a little on his coat.

Fritz Muller, who had discovered the body, was there, and one of the miners who had brought it up. Dr. Ames asked few questions. There was no need; everyone had heard the story a dozen times before.

I had brought the oxygen helmet Tony had worn. The tank was two-thirds full. From that, it was concluded Tony had been killed before he was in the mine ten minutes. Dr. Ames said that death had come instantly. But Tony could not have fallen into the pit ten minutes after his descent because the cage was at the bottom then. And if his body had been thrown there while the cage was up, the murderer must have waited almost half an hour in the mine, which would have been almost certain death even with a gas mask, and for no conceivable purpose.

These circumstances, brought out for the first time at the inquest, left the jury bewildered and almost ready to believe some supernatural agency responsible for Tony's death. But they only confirmed my growing belief that Tony had been murdered at Happy House, and his body let down the shaft sometime later, for, when the rescue work was abandoned, the cage had been hoisted to the top of the tip house to save it from the fire, and for several days only rough boards had covered the shaft. But the body had not been thrown down the shaft. No bones had been broken. I remembered that Big Bill had used an old hand windlass to lower a mouse. A bucket large enough to hold a man's body was already attached to the rope. Everything had been in readiness for the murderer's scheme, and Tony, himself, had aided it by planning to disappear. Tony had planned a counterfeit death, and it had been turned into grim reality.

But when had the body been lowered? Someone had been at the mine night and day. Big Bill would have known. For a moment, I almost suspected Big Bill. Then I remembered how he had been lured away by the sound of the harmonica. Everyone knew of Big Bill's love for his son, and of Billy's fondness for the harmonica. It had been a simple matter to get Big Bill away from the mine.

The murderer had expected the fire to obliterate all signs of the wound, but the flames had swept over the body lightly, and since it had been lying face up, the back was protected. But for that chance, we might never have known Tony had been murdered. Everything else had played into the murderer's hands. Someone who hated Tony had found him alive when supposedly dead, and had made Tony's playacting serve his purpose. Tony's motive, I could not understand, but everything else was clearing up, and in my own mind, I was confident the murderer was Pat Brace.

And yet, I could prove little or nothing. Everything was conjecture. It must have been Pat with Regina that night she had driven into the Roxbury Garage; and, since he had not repaired the fan belt himself and had sat so still and quiet, I concluded that he had been wounded, and Regina was taking him to the city to a doctor. That explained her sudden departure, and explained, too, the finding of Tony's revolver with one empty cartridge.

But Tony must have fired first, since the bullet through his heart had killed him instantly. Or almost instantly. He had certainly fallen with the shot, Dr. Ames said, and had died in a very few seconds. I did not like the thought that Tony had fired first. I could not believe it. But Pat, perhaps, had fired one shot wild before that. Tony had been shot through the back, though, and he surely would not turn his back after shots had been exchanged.

These thoughts passed through my mind during the inquest. But with Rush still absent, I could say nothing, for all my evidence might be turned against Rush instead of Pat.

Big Bill was asked about the ventilating shaft. He said the opening was closed by a trap door in the fan house, and no one could have passed through it without attracting his attention. He did not leave his post from the time of the disaster till nearly one the following morning when all hope of rescue was given up and the fan shut down. Two miners had escaped from that shaft immediately after the first explosion, but no one else had used the shaft during that time. Of that Big Bill was certain.

Uncle Matthew and I testified that no one had gone down the main shaft after Tony and that no one who had remained in the mine could have been alive when Tony went down. Also that Tony was not in the habit of carrying a gun, and that, to the best of our belief, he had never contemplated suicide. The miners who brought up the body testified that no gun was found near it. The verdict, of course, was "murdered by a person or persons unknown". And the jury seemed thankful to get it over.

Rush's name had not been mentioned, and for that, I was grateful, but I could see that suspicion was growing against him. I heard two of the jurors whispering something about a quarrel.

And then, just as we were ready to leave, the door was thrown open, and Rush stood there.

"I saw the papers," he said, "so I came back."

Dr. Ames looked up, surprised. "Glad you did. Anything you can tell us about your brother's death?"

"No."

Rush stood there looking us over gravely. He seemed to think it unnecessary to modify the statement.

"H'mmm," Dr. Ames cleared his throat, uncertain how to proceed. "Where've you been?"

"In the city."

"Why did you go?"

"It was too depressing at home without Tony."

"H'mmm. Guess that's all—unless anybody else has a question." Dr. Ames glanced inquiringly at the jurors.

They fumbled with their hats and shook their heads. I knew they were thinking that Rush had probably come home only through fear of being caught, but no one dared Put his thoughts into words.

When they were gone, Rush said: "I want to see the body."

"Don't—" I urged.

But Rush's lips were set tight, and I knew he was determined to go through with it.

Mark Powell opened the door to the rear room. Rush walked in with his head up stiffly. I glimpsed the sheeted form again. A few minutes later Rush came out looking pale and rather sick.

XXI
"TWO DETECTIVES ARRIVED"

That night I told Rush everything I had discovered or imagined. He was still unnerved from the ordeal of the afternoon and had gone upstairs early. I heard him walking about in his room before I went in. When I opened the door, he sat down and picked up a book and pretended to be reading. I knew he didn't want to talk to me, but I had to tell someone.

It was hard to put into words some of the things I had seen and feared. Rush didn't help me. He sat there frowning at the floor and fidgeting with the cord of his dressing gown, his features thrown sharply into relief by the reading light on the table beside him, the sensitive curves of his mouth drawn into firm hard lines. At last he could be still no longer. He took a turn about the room, coming back to the table to jerk out a cigarette and light it. He offered no comment until I said:

"I found one of your cigarette stubs."

"I was there," he flung at me over his shoulder.

"When?"

"The day after—after that night I saw Tony." The words came jerkily.

"Did you know all I've been telling you?"

"No. I didn't go snooping around. But I went in the house and guessed that Regina and Tony had been there."

"Why did you send that letter from Regina?"

Rush wheeled about. "You knew that?"

"Yes. But I haven't told anybody. Mr. Townsend is satisfied. Why did you want to deceive him?"

Rush pulled the cord of his dressing gown tighter. He didn't like that word "deceive".

"I wanted to protect Tony and Regina," he explained impatiently. "I didn't want detectives sent after them and the whole affair dragged through the newspapers. After I saw Tony on the Hill Road, I had an idea he and Regina had run away, and she wouldn't write because Pat might find them."

"But you knew Pat would give it away—that Regina hadn't been with him."

"I thought about that. But all I wanted was to give Tony and Regina a little more time. I thought they'd probably planned to go to some foreign country. Tony was always talking about the opportunities for a mining man in South America. And, you know, he seemed to appreciate what Uncle Matthew said about considering the money a loan. I thought if the police started looking for Tony and Regina, they might be stopped before they could enter a foreign country. But if they just had a few months for Tony to find work and get settled down, they'd probably be safe. There might be a search for Regina, I thought. Everyone would know she had run away from Pat, but no one would guess she was with Tony because Tony was supposed to be dead."

"That was what Tony planned, I imagine. But why—why? Why did he want us to believe him dead?"

Rush shook his head.

"Regina must've told the truth after all about going to meet Pat," I argued. "Then why doesn't she write?"

"I don't know." Rush answered shortly. He turned away from me.

"Don't you see?" I went on excitedly, seizing his arm. "It was Pat who killed Tony! Pat came back and found them together that night after Tony took his car from the garage. There was blood on the upholstery when I brought it back. Pat must've been waiting there at Happy House for Tony. But Pat was hurt too, I think, because Regina was driving when they stopped at Roxbury. Don't you think we'd better go to the sheriff or Dr. Ames with the whole story?"

Rush flung back his head. "No! Don't do that! Not yet!" He jerked his arm away.

"Why not?"

Rush didn't answer. His attitude surprised and angered me.

"You aren't still thinking of Pat—trying to protect him, after he's murdered Tony? Don't you want to see justice done?"

"It would be better forgotten—all forgotten," Rush said sternly. "Nothing can give back a life."

"Pat has hypnotized you," I declared heatedly. "He always did have an unnatural influence over you."

Rush flung himself into a chair and buried his face in his hands. When he spoke his voice sounded muffled and strange: "It isn't for Pat's sake, but Tony's."

"But it isn't right. We're making ourselves accessories or whatever you call it. I only waited for you to come home because—" I broke off, then added: "If you knew what people are saying—they're suspecting you, Rush—"

He nodded. "I know. I saw the papers. It doesn't matter if they suspect me."

I tried to argue with him, but it was useless.

"You know how it always is in a case like this," Rush said. "Pat would get all the sympathy and Tony all the blame, in spite of the fact it was Tony who loved Regina most and longest and Pat who came between them. Just because a few words had made Pat legally her husband, people would think that gave him a right to kill Tony if he found them together. You know that belief is one of the foundations of American society—" his tone was bitter—"if a man loses his wife, he loses his honor and only murder can restore it."

"You were ready to fight about Norma," I reminded him.

"And I've been sorry ever since. If I hadn't been so crazy mad at Tony, I'd have—" he broke off abruptly. "I wouldn't be under suspicion now. But no matter what people say, promise me you won't tell about—your theory."

At first I refused. But Rush said:

"Wait till we see Regina anyway. Think what it would mean for her—a murder trial and all the publicity. It would ruin her whole life. I've been trying to find her, but I couldn't. She's hiding somewhere, of course. Do you want Regina arrested and brought back and her love for Tony turned into a degrading, shameful thing? Would Tony want that?"

I gave Rush my word I would not reveal my discoveries. And while I listened to him, it seemed the only just thing to do. Had it not

been for that promise I would have told everything the following day
when two detectives arrived from the city to help the sheriff investigate Tony's death. MacFarland had asked for aid because the inquest
had left him utterly at sea.

They drove up to our house in the detectives' car—Detective Captain Thornberry, Detective Quinn and Sheriff MacFarland. Two reporters were with them, but Captain Thornberry made them wait in
the car. I was grateful for that.

Captain Thornberry was a young man with a high bald forehead,
an unlined face, wide-set serious blue eyes, small unsmiling mouth,
and a short chin with a dimple in it. And in spite of the chin and the
dimple, he looked like a detective. Perhaps it was because he talked
little and seemed never to smile. The other detective was a sharp-
nosed blond young man whose duties seemed to be principally those
of chauffeur and secretary to the captain.

"Captain Thornberry here," Sheriff MacFarland jerked his thumb
towards the detective, "wants to ask a few questions. He's going to try
and clear up Tony's death."

The sheriff's tone was slightly contemptuous, partly because of
his own failure, and partly, I surmised, because of disappointment
in the detective's appearance. MacFarland, himself, was six feet two,
with a protruding lower jaw and deep stern lines about his mouth.

Thornberry said: "I'd like to see all the family." He had a surpris-
ingly mild voice. "Servants, too."

He made us all rather nervous, sitting there looking us over as we
came into the room, as if we were actors on a stage. The sharp-nosed
blond man sat at a table in the corner with pencil and notebook before him. Sheriff MacFarland lounged against the wall by the door,
arms folded, glowering around as if he expected one of us to make a
dash for freedom.

I, for one, felt ready to confess almost anything. Rush was pale
and nervous, and even Aunt Addie had lost something of her usual
calm. There were tired little wrinkles about her eyes and mouth I
had never noticed before. As for Uncle Matthew, it seemed cruel to
torture him with further repetition of the tragedy. His dark eyes were
sunk deep in their sockets, and the skin beneath hung in little empty
sacs. Hilda was stolid and defiant, her china-blue eyes narrowed

obstinately. Only Ezra Rugg seemed unmoved. His nose was a little redder than usual, and his squinted, red-rimmed eyes were bright with interest.

Captain Thornberry referred to his notes. "There was a theft at your office, Mr. North, on Saturday, July 15th," he began in a business-like manner. "Why did you not report it?"

Uncle Matthew explained in a low quavering voice.

"And whom do you suspect?"

Uncle Matthew shook his head helplessly.

Captain Thornberry had found out a great many things during the few hours he had been in Genesee. He knew even that Rush and Tony had quarreled. He got the whole story out of us piecemeal, though I said as little as possible, and Rush sat staring out of the window and answered only in monosyllables.

"Was Anthony Sheridan in love with anybody?" Thornberry asked.

"I think not," I lied.

"Wasn't that unusual in a young man his age?"

"Tony liked to go with different girls."

"Had he ever been married or engaged?" Thornberry persisted in his crisp manner.

I had to tell him—he would have found out anyway. Probably he already knew.

"Did he see this—Mrs. Brace often?" Thornberry had a habit of picking our names up with "this" or "that" as if he did not like to touch them.

I hesitated, and in that second, Ezra, who till now had maintained a respectful silence, piped up in his shrill old voice:

"He was out somewheres at all hours of the night, Tony was. A regular stepper, he was."

Captain Thornberry regarded Ezra with interest. "Did he go to see Mrs. Brace?"

"Sometimes—all of us did," I explained hurriedly. "We're all good friends. We grew up together."

"Yeh; that's right." Ezra's little round head with its bristling, up-standing fringe of gray hair, bobbed up and down emphatically. "She thought so much of Tony she went and left town right after he was killed, she did. Yes, sir; and I wouldn't be surprised if that husband of hers didn't know something about it, too," Ezra added darkly.

I could have choked him—after I had warned him, too, not to say very much. But he was so eager to attract attention I knew there would be no stopping him now.

"Do you suspect Mr. Brace of killing Anthony Sheridan?" Thornberry asked gravely.

Ezra blinked. "I ain't sayin' nothin' about that. I ain't sayin' I suspicion nobody. But there's been some queer goings on I could tell about," he muttered threateningly.

"Let's hear them," invited Thornberry pleasantly. He sat back in his chair, placing the fingertips of his two hands together and regarding Ezra expectantly.

Ezra cast a sullen sidelong glance at me. "I was told not to," he muttered.

"By whom?"

"Him." Ezra jerked his thumb at me.

Thornberry eyed me speculatively through half-closed lids. I felt myself growing red.

"I am sure Mr. Sheridan wants his brother's death cleared up." Thornberry's voice was smooth as ice. "You've no objection," he asked me politely, "to this—Mr. Rugg's telling me anything he thinks relevant to the investigation?"

I shook my head. "But he doesn't know anything that matters," I managed to say. "He'll talk all day about nothing if you give him the chance—that's why I told him to keep quiet."

"Really?" Thornberry commented softly, but his tone sent the blood surging into my head.

Ezra seemed to swell up with importance. "Tony's car was took out one night," he began, leaning towards Thornberry confidentially with a smile that displayed his yellow stumps of teeth. "I heard it took out, but I didn't see who taken it. And the kids wouldn't let me call the sheriff." He repeated most of our conversation of that night, and finished by telling of my bringing the car back. "It was pretty near midnight, I reckon, and I heard the water runnin' down in the garage. And bein' sorter worried about the coop bein' gone, I went piece ways down the steps and peeped into the garage. And there was

Tony's coop, and Cappy washin' off the seat." Ezra sat back, blinking his little red eyes.

Thornberry's brows lifted slightly. His eyes, turned on me, were like little cakes of blue ice. "Why did you wash the seat?"

"There was blood on it," I whispered.

"Where did you find the car?"

I told him.

"Why did you go there for it?"

Rush turned about quickly, his head flung back. "Because I saw the car on the Hill Road. And I thought Tony was at the wheel."

"Why didn't you want this told?" inquired Thornberry.

"Because it was after Tony's death," Rush said. "I've always had a reputation for being queer. I don't want to add to it by seeing ghosts."

Thornberry was silent a moment. Then he asked: "Who had the key to the car?"

It was the first time I had thought of that. "Tony always carried it," I told him.

"Was the car usually locked when it was left in the garage?"

"Yes."

"And the key was in it when you found it at—this place you call Happy House?"

"Yes."

"The same key your brother used? Not a makeshift one filed to fit?"

"I'm sure it's the same." I took the key from my pocket and handed it to him.

He looked at it and nodded. "Evidently the one that came with the car. There was no similar key found on the body when it was brought out of the mine?"

"No; I don't believe there were any keys at all. One of the men gave me Tony's watch and fountain pen—that was all. I didn't think about keys."

"Anthony Sheridan carried a key ring, didn't he?"

"Yes."

Thornberry placed the tips of his well-manicured fingers together and studied them thoughtfully. Presently he said to Rush: "It probably wasn't a ghost you saw. Ghosts don't drive cars away. If Anthony

Sheridan could not have been shot in the mine, he was probably shot outside. Where is this house where the car was found?"

I began to like Captain Thornberry then, though I was to change my opinion several times during the next week. I knew he would go to Happy House and probably discover everything I had—except, of course, the clues I had removed. He might discover more. He did not have those ice-blue eyes and that high forehead for nothing. But he would not find Rush's cigarette stub, nor the fringe from Regina's shawl, nor Tony's revolver. The other things I wanted him to find. It would relieve me of responsibility.

I was not too happy over the promise I had made Rush. The maddening uncertainty surrounding Tony's death was beginning to tell on all our nerves; and at that time, I wanted the mystery cleared up regardless of the price it cost Regina or anyone, much as I disliked the idea of dragging her into it. Though I resented then the policy of secrecy Rush had urged upon me, I was later to realize that, in his place, I would have done the same.

Tony's funeral was held the next day.

XXII
"THE WOODS AND THE HILLS WERE
SEARCHED FOR REGINA'S BODY"

My faith in Captain Thornberry's ability was not misplaced. Before the week was over all Genesee knew that Tony had been killed at Happy House, and police all over the country were hunting for Regina and Pat.

When I saw Regina's name in the headlines and her wistful, heart-shaped face looking out at me from the printed page, I was thankful I had had no part in putting it there. Everyone believed then that Pat had returned unexpectedly, had surprised Tony and Regina at Happy House and killed Tony. It seemed quite plain.

I did not tell that Pat might have been wounded, too, nor that he had been in disguise the night he and Regina fled from Genesee. It seemed likely now that Pat, not Tony, had taken the beard from my room. He would have needed some sort of disguise to go about Genesee unrecognised. But how had he managed to reach our house unseen in broad daylight? Even during the first excitement of the disaster, someone would have noticed and remembered him. And I could find no one who had seen Pat Brace after he left town that Friday night.

If Pat took the beard and the make-up, he might also have taken Tony's revolver. But whether he had used it to kill Tony or had fired it and left it there to form a basis for a plea of self defense, I could not decide. The latter seemed unlikely, since Pat evidently had expected the murder would never be discovered. Neither was it likely that Tony would be carrying the revolver about, even after Regina's warning. The thirty-eight was too large for convenience. Had Tony been really afraid, he would have carried his automatic. He had one, a tiny, blunt-nosed thing that just fitted the palm of the hand. And the automatic was still in its place in the desk. I made sure of that.

Tony had not expected trouble of that sort with Pat—that was what he intended to avoid. Tony intended to make Pat and everyone else believe him dead. And when the excitement had died down Regina would join him somewhere. That conniving, round-about way wasn't like Tony, usually so straightforward. But it seemed the only explanation. He must have had some good reason, something I didn't know about, I thought, to plan to disappear in that way and cause us so much grief.

The supposition that Pat had taken the revolver and had used it to kill Tony seemed the only feasible one. It also cleared up the mystery of Tony's being shot in the back. Tony surely had not fired his own gun, then carelessly turned his back. He had been taken unawares and shot from behind, probably while he was coming along the little path over the ridge. Pat must have been hiding in the thicket. Tony had probably fallen where I had found the leaves cleared away from the trail. The blood-stained leaves and mold had been raked away with a dead branch and scattered about the thicket, and the bare ground covered with other leaves. Tony's lifeless form must have been dragged down the path to the sand pile. And the rain had washed away any tell-tale stains that had been overlooked.

But why had Tony used the path to the house instead of the road? It would have been a little shorter for anyone on foot, but Tony had driven his car to Happy House. He had driven the car into the clearing and behind the house. If Tony had been killed in the wood, why was there blood on the upholstery of the tan coupé?

I had found the car less than two hours after Rush had seen it on the Hill Road. During that interval Tony must have met his death— perhaps while Rush and I were asking Ezra about the car or while I was walking along the Hill Road. I wondered if Tony had been lying dead in the thicket then while I walked about the empty house or if his body had already been buried in the sand pile. I remembered how the sand and gravel piles had looked like white graves in the moonlight. The thought that Tony might have been lying there still warm while I was so near left me feeling all gone, with a lump in the pit of my stomach.

Pat might have been watching me from the thicket when I drove Tony's car away. If I had tried to investigate then, I might have paid for my curiosity with my life.

But why had Regina gone along the path with a candle? It must have been Regina, I reasoned. The candle had dripped on her rose shawl. Had she found Tony's lifeless body? But Regina would not have struck all those matches—she never carried matches. Pat must have done that. But why? The light of one match would have been enough to show that Tony was dead.

But if Tony had not fired his gun, how had Pat happened to be wounded? I felt sure nothing short of a wound would have prevented his repairing that fan belt. Could it have been Regina who fired Tony's gun? Had she shot Pat after he killed Tony?

Pat might have been lying in wait at Happy House; he might have fired as Tony drove up. I was sure the upholstery of Tony's car had been washed before I found it, except for that little stain high up, overlooked in the dark.

After Tony was shot, Regina might have run along the little path and fired at Pat. Yet I could not imagine her doing it; revenge seemed so foreign to Regina's nature. Pat could not have been so severely wounded, since he had carried Tony's body first to the sand pile and then to the mine. If he had been able to do that, why hadn't he fixed the fan belt?

My arguments went around in circles. One moment I was sure Pat had been wounded, the next I was equally sure he couldn't have been. One moment I was sure Tony had been killed with his own gun, the next I was equally sure Pat could not have obtained the revolver.

I would have given much then to know if that fatal bit of lead had come from Tony's thirty-eight. The question could have been readily answered by the rifling marks on the bullet had I turned the revolver over to the officers. But I had promised Rush to say nothing about it, and later, I was to be thankful for that promise. I wondered if Pat's revolver, which Regina mentioned, was a thirty-eight, too, but had no way of finding out. Pat must have taken it with him; I was certain it was not in his house.

The mystery haunted me. At times I thought I knew exactly what had occurred that tragic night. At others I conjured up fantastic, impossible explanations, even going so far as to wonder if Pat had hypnotized Tony into driving to Happy House that Tuesday evening. But it all must have happened between the time Rush saw Tony on the Hill Road and the time I reached Happy House.

I tried to figure out the sequence of events. The car had been taken out of the garage at nine o'clock or shortly before. Rush had seen it about an hour later or a few minutes before ten just beyond the edge of town on the Hill Road. It had been just ten o'clock when Rush reached home, pale and panting. But it was only nine-thirty, Big Bill had said, when he had been lured away from the mine by the sound of the harmonica. Tony was still alive then. It did not seem possible that Pat would lure Big Bill away from the mine before Tony was killed.

Big Bill had followed the sound about a mile. Even allowing for a certain amount of erratic wandering and moments lost in listening, he must have been back at the mine within an hour, or by ten-thirty. Pat could not have played the harmonica then, if he had been waiting at Happy House for Tony. But he might have had an accomplice do that. Tony was not killed till after ten, and his body must have been lowered into the shaft before ten-thirty that same night. Big Bill had not heard the harmonica nor left his post since then; and only during his absence and at night could the feat have been accomplished, for there was always someone about the mine during the day.

But Big Bill had heard the harmonica the night before, I remembered. Pat must have been testing out his plan to see if the sound would draw Big Bill away from the mine.

Everything had been arranged beforehand then. Pat must have known at exactly what time to expect Tony at Happy House, though how he could know that I could not imagine.

But where had Tony been during that hour between the time he took the car from the garage and when Rush saw him on the Hill Road? It looked as if Tony had been at Regina's house during that interval, and as if Regina had been expecting him, since she had sent Rush and me away. But if Tony had been with Regina during that hour, why did he go to Happy House? And how had Regina got there, too? Tony had been alone in the coupé when Rush saw him.

But, putting aside these questions, I returned to the problem of Pat's actions on that fateful evening. There had been just time, before Big Bill's return, for Pat to commit the murder and drive back immediately to the mine. He might have brought the body in Tony's car—that would explain the stain on the upholstery.

But if everything had been planned, why had the body been buried in the sand? It could not have been Tony's body that had lain there, I decided with relief. There had been not a minute to spare between the time Tony had arrived at the house and the time the body was lowered into the mine. Everything must have gone as smoothly as clockwork to be accomplished so quickly. Whose body, then, had lain in the sand? I had traced Pat and Regina as far as Roxbury. They had got away safely. And no one else was missing. Was it possible Pat had murdered his unknown accomplice, some stranger hired for the purpose, buried the body there and later decided to move it? Had the man who played the harmonica been killed to insure his secrecy?

Captain Thornberry, I think, followed much the same line of reasoning I had. He questioned Big Bill, I know, and had definitely placed the time of the murder between ten and ten-thirty that Tuesday evening. Then he must have concluded, as I had, that Tony's body could not have been buried in the sand, for he suddenly startled the town by announcing that Regina had been murdered and her body hidden for a time in the sand. The woods and the hills about Happy House were searched for Regina's body.

The detective's announcement gave me something of a shock in spite of what I had learned at Roxbury. I began to doubt the evidence of the moon-faced mechanic in the garage. And yet he had described the car accurately. There could not be two cars like the Tiger. It was too preposterous to suppose that Pat had killed Regina later, brought her body back to Happy House, and still later moved it again.

I was glad then for the letter Rush had sent Regina's parents. It was all that saved her mother's life, I think. And it rather upset Thornberry's nicely calculated deductions. Thornberry was genuinely disturbed by that letter. He had been so sure that Regina was murdered. He compared the handwriting with other samples from Regina's pen and reluctantly admitted the letter authentic. Regina's father had thrown the envelope away, and Thornberry failed to discover those slight changes in the letter.

His failure gave me a not unpleasant feeling of superiority, but it also undermined my confidence in him and left me fearful that Tony's death and Regina's fate might always remain a haunting mystery. Though the few little marks that changed the whole meaning of that letter had been so readily apparent to me, their discovery was due partly, I realized, to my knowledge of Regina's character and life, which Thornberry could not, of course, possess. I had known instinctively it was not the kind of letter Regina would write to her father but was the kind she might have written to Tony just after her marriage. Sensing this, the rest had been easy.

But I did not undeceive Captain Thornberry. It would have meant incriminating Rush. And it might have killed Regina's mother. That letter was the one bit of hope she clung to while Thornberry and the whole town continued the search for Regina's body. I did not want to believe Regina dead, but I was almost forced to accept Thornberry's theory. It didn't seem possible that Regina would remain silent if she were alive. She must know what her parents were suffering. I could think of nothing to justify her action—if it were voluntary. I felt sure she did not love Pat enough to protect him at such cost, and came to the conclusion that Pat had threatened her or had, in some way, enforced her silence.

But Rush differed. He held me to my promise to reveal nothing, even though the knowledge that Regina had passed through Roxbury that tragic night would mean new hope for her parents.

"Regina has some good reason," he said. "She thinks as much of her parents as you do."

"Pat may be keeping her prisoner somewhere," I argued.

"Regina isn't a child, and she isn't so afraid of Pat that he could compel her to keep quiet. And Pat isn't fool enough to attempt such a thing—he'd know it couldn't last."

"Then she wants to protect Pat," I returned. "And so do you."

"It wouldn't do Tony any good to have Pat hung." Rush's great dark eyes were fixed on me reproachfully. "You wouldn't want to be responsible for a man's being hanged, would you?"

"If a man commits murder, he ought to be hanged," I insisted stubbornly. "It's sentimentalists like you who encourage murder in this country. They don't get away with it so easy in England—twenty-nine murders there last year and twenty-seven hangings. If we'd send a few more to the gallows instead of babbling about the unwritten law and such poppycock, there wouldn't be so many killings."

"Wait a minute!" Rush cried, wheeling about on me. "What if Pat were your brother instead of Tony?"

"Pat? Thank God, he isn't!"

"But what if your brother had done such a thing?" Rush whispered, his hand gripping my arm. "What if I had?"

"You?" I stared at him. I couldn't believe it. His words went through me like a scream in the night.

"I didn't," Rush said soberly. "But if I had, would you want me hung? Would it do any good?"

I couldn't answer. I had been so sure that Pat was guilty. Rush went on talking, but I don't know what he said—something about sparing Regina. Finally I could stand it no longer.

"Rush, if you know anything, tell me. Can't you trust me? I swear I'll never tell. But this uncertainty—"

"I can't tell you anything," he said dully.

Afterwards I realized that sentence might be interpreted in two ways. But at the time I thought he meant only that he knew no more than I.

"Then how can you rest until this is cleared up?" I demanded impatiently.

"I think Regina knows what happened," Rush answered slowly. "And if she wants to keep it secret, we ought to be willing to trust her."

"But what if Pat should kill her—then how would you feel? If he's not in his right mind—if he's kidnaped her—there's no telling what he might do."

Rush looked surprised. After a moment, he said: "But Regina was driving the car when they stopped at Roxbury. That doesn't look as if she were being kidnaped. And if she knew what had happened, she knew it then."

"But if Thornberry knew about it, he might be able to clear up the mystery," I persisted.

Rush silenced me with: "Are you ready to tell him about Tony's revolver, too? How could you be revenged on Pat if he could plead self defense with Tony's revolver and an empty cartridge for evidence? If you're going to demand justice you'll have to tell everything. And if you do, you'll probably get us all arrested. If Thornberry knew I'd sent that letter—"

"I never knew you to try to whitewash things before," I reproved. "You were always the one to want the truth."

"I know. But I'm not sorry I sent that letter. Thornberry's done enough damage—frightening everyone about Regina. There are times when a lie is more truthful than truth."

"A lot of words," I commented irritably. "I'll never stop till I know what happened."

"And till you know for certain, you'd better keep still," Rush advised. "A few facts can be twisted so—"

We were near to quarreling. Rush picked up a newspaper and hid himself behind it. But I stood before him, and pushed the paper down.

"If I can get at the truth, the absolute truth, and prove it, I suppose you'll agree to making it public?"

Rush looked at me queerly. "Yes; if you want to."

XXIII
"MUTINOUSLY, I DEMANDED
A SIGN OF TONY'S EXISTENCE"

In spite of the strange things Rush had said, I still believed Pat guilty. There seemed no doubt he had shot Dr. Ames, by mistaking him for Tony. After that, he must have found Regina and Tony at the office. But how Tony had escaped harm that night I couldn't understand. Perhaps Pat had been afraid another shooting would make it obvious how Dr. Ames had been wounded. Pat could not have been sure then that that first wild shot would not prove fatal, and while he might plead the unwritten law for Tony's murder, he would have no defense for killing Dr. Ames. Pat would not want the two shootings linked together, as they would be if both had occurred the same night. That explanation seemed to make it clear why Tony's life had been spared the night of the rehearsal.

Pat, I decided, had left town to wait for the excitement of that first shooting to subside. Tony and Regina, seeking then to escape from Pat's insane jealousy that would make their happiness forever impossible here, had taken advantage of the mine disaster to simulate Tony's death. After the explosions and the fire, no one would think it strange if the body were never found. And Pat, believing Tony dead, would not be so relentless or vindictive in his search for Regina. And all had gone well till Pat returned and found them together. Everything seemed to point to Pat's guilt. I wondered how Rush could defend him.

But to make sure Pat's departure had been dictated by impulse and fear, and not by business, I asked Uncle Matthew:

"Did Pat say anything about going away when he was here that night looking for Regina?"

"Going away?" Uncle Matthew echoed absently. Lately it seemed difficult for him to grasp a subject.

"Did he tell you he was going to get Tony, or did he just want Regina to take him to the train?"

"He wanted her to take him to the train," Uncle Matthew repeated. He seemed to make an effort to pull himself together, and added: "Yes; Pat said he was going to the city."

"But he must've said something to alarm you," I pointed out. "Because you drove after Pat—followed him. Try to remember."

Uncle Matthew passed a thin veined hand over his eyes as if the effort were too much for him. Instantly, I regretted troubling him. But after a minute, he answered:

"I went to the Opera House to get your Aunt Addie, didn't I?"

"You drove by Regina's house, too," I reminded him.

"Bless my soul, bless my soul, I believe I'd had a mite to drink and didn't want your Aunt Addie to smell it on my breath. Thought I'd better stay out for a while—till she was sound asleep."

But he had just said he had gone for Aunt Addie. The matter wasn't worth arguing though. I remembered, too, that Uncle Matthew had seemed surprised when I came home that night and told him Pat had gone to the city.

I was uncertain again about Pat's motives. But whether he had planned his departure or not, his actions seemed perfectly clear. Only one question troubled me—how had he returned to Genesee unobserved? He could not have come by train or bus without being seen. And Thornberry had found no one who remembered seeing Pat after that Friday. He had probably rented a car in the city, I thought. But if he had, what had become of the car? Pat had driven back with Regina in the Tiger. I was certain of that. He had used my beard for a disguise, but he couldn't have used it when he came into Genesee. He might have employed some other make-up, though nothing short of a beard would disguise the straight lines of Pat's mouth and chin; and even then, anyone who knew him would recognize those straight black brows and the almost black eyes. It would be easy enough though for him to obtain a beard and a wig in the city, and both together might work wonders.

I decided to question the station master. Strangers are not so common in Genesee but the arrival of a bearded black-eyed man might not be remembered.

Homer Cole, who had been ticket agent and station master for twenty years, was not a talkative man. He had a face that looked as if it had been crumpled up like an accordion or as if he had been struck under the chin while his face was still soft. It was as broad as it was long, though he wasn't fat. His nose was caved in at the bridge and pointed at the end, and his mouth almost disappeared under it as if he had no teeth; his chin stuck out and seemed to turn up in a point. But Homer Cole had all his teeth. He had always looked like that. Some people said it was because he kept his mouth shut so tight. And he was so contrary that a wit once declared he sold south bound tickets to Canada—which was true since the nearest junction was to the south.

If I should ask Homer Cole outright if he had seen a bearded man who might have been Pat Brace get off the train, he would reply, "Dunno", or "Don't remember", and stick to it. So I decided to assume my theory was correct and let him contradict me where I was wrong. Homer Cole was truthful, I knew. He let me get all through my story without uttering a word, but by the gleam in his eye, I knew he was only biding his time.

"I know you must've seen this man with a beard whether you paid any attention to him or not," I finished. "But did you notice if he was carrying a black suitcase like Pat's?"

I didn't care about the suitcase; I didn't know whether it was black or not; but if I could get Homer Cole to argue about some unimportant detail like that, I could soon discover if Pat had returned by train, and when.

But Homer Cole leaned across the counter of the ticket window and thrust his funny little face close to mine.

"Think you're a pretty smart detective, don't you, sonny?" When he smiled his nose and chin seemed to meet. "Well, Pat Brace didn't come back on the train. And what's more, he never took no train out of here, neither."

"I don't understand. You mean he didn't leave on the train? Why, Regina drove him down."

Homer Cole's mouth closed with a snap. "Leastways, he didn't buy no ticket."

"He might've been so late he had to get on without a ticket," I suggested.

"He didn't. I see them trains off."

For a moment I was silent. Then it occurred to me that Pat might have only pretended to leave. His only object had been to deceive Regina. He might have been hiding here in town all the time—or at Happy House. Regina had probably left him at the station without waiting to see the train leave.

"Then what was Pat doing down here at the station that night?" I asked Homer Cole. "Was he waiting to meet somebody?"

"I ain't seen Pat Brace for six months," the station master returned. "If he's been out of town, he ain't been on the train."

But Regina had told me Pat had left on the midnight train. She had no reason for deceiving me then. She must have driven him to the station. But if she had left immediately, I argued, Pat could have walked on past the station without entering the building or waiting for the train. That, I decided, was what had happened.

I pondered the problem all the way home. If Pat had not gone to the city, he must have been hiding at Happy House, I reasoned. I could think of no place in town where he could stay and keep his presence a secret. It must have been Pat, then, who had used the red candles and the coffee pot. But there was the candle dripping on Regina's shawl. Had Regina driven Pat to Happy House instead of to the station? But why, then, had Tony gone there? Where had Tony hidden after he escaped from the mine, and why had he not gone away at once? Why had he waited till Tuesday to meet his death at Happy House?

Either Pat or Tony must have been hiding in Regina's house that evening when she sent Rush and me away. She had been nervous, I remembered. And she had told Rush not to give up hope. What else, I wondered, had she told him before I came up the walk?

Even my first theory, of which I had been so sure, that Pat had surprised Tony and Regina at Happy House, seemed doubtful now. I was no longer sure of anything, not even that Tony had escaped from the mine. If he had planned to disappear, it was queer he would risk everything to come back, steal his own car and go to Happy House. There seemed no earthly reason for it. Regina could have met him in the city or anywhere. But if Tony had returned for her, he could have gone to her home. It was not necessary to go to Happy House to meet her, nor to take the coupé. He and Regina might have planned to use that car in their flight, since it was not so conspicuous as the Tiger, but why had Tony not simply picked Regina up at her home? He must have known that Pat was still away; he and Regina had surely exchanged messages or signals of some kind.

A week had passed now since the inquest, and for all the impressive start Captain Thornberry had made, Tony's death was as much a mystery as ever and seemed likely to remain so. I thought of nothing else day or night, and having to keep all my imaginings and conjectures to myself made it doubly hard. If I could only discuss it with someone, I felt some glimmering of truth might show through all this shadowy mass of speculation. But I had given Rush my promise. And Rush, himself, shunned the subject. He even avoided me. I knew he disapproved of my efforts. He wanted the whole investigation dropped. I could not understand his attitude. If it had been anyone but Rush, I would have attributed it to guilt.

Rush went about his ways calmly aloof. He and Norma had patched up their quarrel, and his evenings now were spent with her. He was there on the Tuesday evening the week following the inquest.

It was a warm August night. I had gone to my room early with a book, hoping to distract my thoughts. But the printed words flowed meaninglessly before my eyes, while my mind persistently darted back to the problem of Tony's fate. Further speculation seemed futile, yet I could no more desist than the imprisoned bee buzzing hopelessly against the window pane. I heard the clock on the stairs strike ten, then eleven, eleven-thirty. At last I turned out the light. But I was wide awake.

I lay staring into the darkness, my mind still occupied with memories of Tony. I remembered how he had ridden Rush's bicycle in circles around the lawn with his arms folded and his feet on the handlebars that day we had first seen Pat Brace. I remembered how Tony had blushed up to the roots of his sleek brown hair the first time he had kissed Regina. We had been playing a kissing game at a children's party. Tony was about fourteen then, and wearing his first long trousers. It was the only time I could remember ever seeing him blush. But all the familiar expressions of Tony's face seemed to rise up before me: his one-sided smile, the challenging tilt of his head; I could see the dark line of his hair clipped close at the temples, his brave brown eyes, the curve of his lashes, the warm tan of his cheeks, the firm angle of his chin. The sound of his laugh, the tone of his voice echoed in my ears. At such moments, Tony's presence seemed tantalizingly near. And real.

During the past few weeks I had, for the first time in my life, given any serious thought to the phenomenon of death. I rebelled against death. Tony could not be blotted out! I rolled restlessly in bed. I lifted my clenched hands in the darkness and mutinously demanded some sign of Tony's existence.

The night was warm and still. I rose and drew back the curtains from the already open windows to coax a breath of air into the room. The clock on the stairs began the monotonous tolling of midnight. A pale worn moon floated wafer-thin in a sullen starless sky. The heavy fragrance of the nicotina beneath my window rose sickeningly sweet in the sultry air. Not a leaf seemed to stir in the oppressive warmth. The lawn and the shrubbery were a painted canvas, faintly silvered by the sickly moon.

Then suddenly I found myself staring at a shadowy figure. Tony was standing there in the moonlight. He was looking at me. He was bareheaded. The moon made a little ripple of light across his shining dark head. I saw him as plainly as if we had not buried him in the churchyard last week.

I tried to call to him, but my throat tightened. Unseen fingers choked back my breath. I managed somehow to cry out: "Tony!" My voice sounded strange and hoarse.

I struggled into my dressing gown and ran barefooted into the hall and down the stairs. There was a light in the library. Uncle Matthew stood in the doorway. He looked at me, frowning and displeased, startled no doubt by my cry and my wild appearance.

"Tony—I saw Tony!" I gasped out.

Uncle Matthew caught me by the arm. I was surprised at the strength of his grasp. "You've been dreaming, my boy," he said sternly.

"Tony was standing in the yard looking up at my window! Let me go! I must see—"

"Cappy, Cappy, bless my soul!" His shaggy black brows went up and down excitedly. "You've been taking Tony's death too hard. You mustn't let it prey on your mind like this. You're young, Cappy." He put his arm around my shoulder. "Your life is all ahead of you." He drew me towards the library, but I jerked away from him.

"I saw Tony," I repeated. "It was Tony!" I started towards the side door. "I'll show you!"

"You're not going out like that, Cappy? You're barefooted," Uncle Matthew remonstrated feebly.

I did not listen to him. I flung open the door, expecting to see Tony still standing there in the patch of moonlight. But he had vanished.

The stone steps, cool and damp under my bare feet, chilled me with the shock of reality as if I had just awakened from a very vivid dream. I walked uncertainly across the drive. The lawn stretched out before me, wide and empty. The feel of the sharp gravel and the close-cut stubble of grass, so earthy and commonplace, brought disturbing doubt. I remembered that I had asked for a sign of Tony's existence.

I was uncomfortably aware of Uncle Matthew in the doorway behind me regarding me with troubled eyes.

"Cappy, where are you going?" he asked worriedly. Then coaxed: "Come back, my boy."

I let him take my arm and lead me back into the house.

"You'll need a mite to drink," he said soothingly. In the library he poured me a thimbleful of whisky, muttering all the while: "Bless my soul, bless my soul."

Rush came in then. "What's up?" he asked.

I told him.

"You would laugh at me for seeing things," he said. "Serves you right." His tone was one of disbelief. "If I were you, I'd keep it dark and not go blabbing it about town." With that he stalked out of the room.

"Rush is right," Uncle Matthew agreed. "Just don't think any more about it. There're some mysteries men aren't meant to solve, and death is the biggest one. Men who worry about such things too much generally pay for it. The brain can't stand it. Something snaps—like a violin string that's stretched too tight. But you're young. You'll soon get over it. You'll forget about Tony."

"I don't want to forget!" I cried. The thought shocked me.

"But you will," said Uncle Matthew gently. "That is life."

XXIV
"AUNT ADDIE'S DIAMONDS HAVE DISAPPEARED"

In the morning I was awakened by Rush's voice: "Your friend, Thornberry, is back again for a conference. I think he's going to interview us separately this time. He's getting suspicious. He thinks we're all thieves and murderers. I feel like a bug under a microscope when he looks at me." Rush sat down on the edge of my bed. "Can you show any good reason for not stealing Aunt Addie's diamonds? They've disappeared mysteriously."

I sat up. "Aunt Addie's diamonds?" I echoed.

"They're gone," said Rush listlessly.

"Stolen?"

Rush shrugged. "Missing," he modified.

"Was the safe broken open?"

Rush shook his head. "Thornberry says it's an inside job. So if you have any alibis or excuses, dust them off and polish them up. Thornberry's downstairs waiting to hear them."

"But when did it happen?"

"Nobody knows except the guilty person," Rush answered darkly. "Aunt Addie opened the safe this morning—she was going to let me have that little diamond and emerald ring for Norma. The jewel box was empty. It was the first time Aunt Addie had opened the safe since the disaster. She wore a pin or something to the rehearsal the night before, and when she put it away, everything was all right. So it's been since then. That's all we know. And it's all Thornberry knows, for all his wise air."

"Then it might have happened the same day the safe at the office was robbed?"

Rush nodded soberly. "It narrows it down to one of us pretty well, doesn't it?—you or Tony or me."

"Did Aunt Addie send for Thornberry?"

"Yes. Uncle Matthew was all against it. He wanted to keep it quiet. But you know Aunt Addie. She didn't believe it was one of us, but if it were, we could take the consequences."

"She's right," I agreed. "I'm ready to face the music. I think we ought to lay all our cards down—"

"Are you going to tell Thornberry you were all in a flutter last night because you thought you saw Tony's ghost?" Rush's voice was level and cruel. I had never heard him use that tone before. It frightened me.

"Why don't you want me to tell?" I demanded.

"How much weight do you think your evidence will carry after you come out with a story like that? I don't want you to talk yourself into an insane asylum."

"I think you're afraid I'll tell something," I accused. "What is it you're afraid of?"

Rush did not answer. His head jerked back in that quick impatient way as if he were trying to fling off an annoying thought. He strode over to the door.

"You gave me your word to say nothing," he reminded me, and went out.

Rush's attitude troubled me more than this latest theft. I hated myself for suspecting him. Yet all the time I was dressing, I was thinking that Rush might have taken Tony's revolver. Rush had broken into Tony's desk and gone through Tony's letters for one that would make Regina's parents think she was alive. How did Rush know Regina wouldn't write? How did he know her parents might not receive another letter at the same time contradicting his? I could not forget how shaken and ghastly Rush had looked when he came in the side door that night after seeing Tony on the Hill Road. And only the other day Rush had said what if it had been he instead of Pat. . . .

I hurried downstairs, hoping to escape my thoughts. Aunt Addie came out of the library, chin in the air. She walked stiffly across the hall, her back straight as a poker.

"That detective," she said with frigid calm, "is suggesting that I stole my own diamonds."

"You?"

Aunt Addie inclined her head slightly. "He seems to think I know something about Tony's death, and have used the jewels to bribe someone to keep quiet."

I could not refrain from saying: "You wanted him to investigate, didn't you?"

Aunt Addie gave me a cold stare and passed on into the dining room.

I entered the library. Captain Thornberry glanced up from the notes he was making, his serious blue eyes fixed on me unsmilingly, his small thin mouth set sternly. I tried to compose myself easily in a chair, but I am afraid I only fidgeted.

"Do you know the terms of your uncle's will?" Thornberry began.

"Why—yes," I answered, surprised. "That is—Rush mentioned something about having drawn up a will for him."

"You don't seem very interested?" The detective looked at me through half-closed lids.

He made me feel guilty. "I don't see the connection," I said warmly. "What has this got to do with Tony's death?"

"Exactly." Thornberry touched the tips of his fingers together. "Your uncle has told me that he intended dividing everything equally among you, your brothers and your aunt. Do you know if your aunt resented this arrangement?"

"We never discussed it," I answered shortly.

"But have you noticed any difference in her attitude towards you?"

"No. You aren't suggesting that Aunt Addie killed Tony because of that will?" I demanded warmly. The idea was ridiculous.

"Stranger things have happened," Thornberry murmured evenly. "According to the will, you each receive a third share now, instead of a fourth, in a very valuable mine and other property. If another one of you should die—"

Something cold trailed down my spine. I sprang up. "You can't really think—"

"Steady," said Thornberry softly. "We have to examine a case from all angles. Your aunt knew that Pat Brace wanted Tony out of the way. It's barely possible she may have aided him in some way—given him her diamonds—"

"It's preposterous!" I exclaimed.

He ignored my protest. "Tell me something about this—Mrs. Brace."

I resented his tone. It was as if he had said "the Brace woman."

"What do you want to know?"

"What kind of woman is she?"

"As fine as they're made. And I've known her since she was ten."

"Is she luxury loving or avaricious? Does she worship wealth?"

"No," I answered emphatically.

"Is she vindictive? Would she nurse a grudge?"

"No."

"Did she break off the engagement with your brother, or did he?"

"She did," I answered curtly, wondering what his object was.

"Do you know why?"

"I suppose you've already heard the story," I returned. "Everybody in town knows it."

"Well—yes;" he admitted, unruffled. "But do you think Mrs. Brace would try to revenge her father's failure?"

"By killing Tony?" I managed a scornful smile. "Regina loved him."

"I wonder," Thornberry mused. "Was Mrs. Brace a good actress?"

"Yes," I said, and then could have bitten my tongue.

"Perhaps she was only pretending to love your brother," Thornberry went on in his brittle tone, "for the purpose of obtaining the money and the diamonds. Perhaps she persuaded him to steal these things and meet her at the unfinished house. Then she and her husband killed and robbed him and left."

For a moment I sat stunned. I must have misunderstood; I could not believe my ears. "You don't mean that you think Regina betrayed Tony? Lured him there for the purpose of—"

Thornberry nodded slowly. "From what I have learned of your brother, Anthony Sheridan must have been forced in one way or another to commit those thefts—if he committed them. He might have been blackmailed. He might have done it for a woman."

"But you don't know Regina!" I cried rebelliously. "She'd never do a thing like that—she loved Tony."

"You have said she was a good actress," Thornberry reminded me. "She blamed your uncle and your brother for her father's failure. How do you know how deep-seated her ill will may have been?"

"There was no ill will," I defended.

"There was bound to be if she thought your brother responsible. Love and hate are closely allied, you know. The balance is easily tipped. Now, do you know anything that would support this theory that the murder was planned for the purpose of the theft—any little incident?"

"Nothing," I declared.

But I thought of the candle dripping on Regina's shawl, of the burnt matches I had found. It looked as if the murderer had been hunting for something. I remembered how well planned, how accurately timed, the murderer's actions seemed, and my belief that Pat knew the exact hour to expect Tony at Happy House. The memory of Regina's tears that night at the rehearsal troubled me. She might have urged Tony to run away with her. But if she had, she was sincere, I argued to myself. I couldn't believe Regina had been acting then—laying a trap for Tony. It was incredible. Regina, a murderess! A traitor!

"Anthony Sheridan was lured to Happy House," Thornberry was saying. "On what pretext, I don't know. But it was not necessary for him to go there to meet Mrs. Brace. If they were going to run away together, he could have picked her up at her house—he knew Pat Brace was out of town—or, if they were afraid of being seen by the neighbors, they could have met a little farther along the road. It's the last house at the edge of town, isn't it? But instead, Anthony Sheridan passed by it and drove on two miles to this unfinished cottage. Why did he do that? He might just as easily have met Mrs. Brace in the city and avoided the risk of being seen. And if he wanted everyone to believe him dead, why did he come back for his car?"

"I can't understand. It wasn't like Tony to try to deceive us, anyway."

"Exactly," agreed Thornberry with some satisfaction. "Anthony Sheridan was straightforward and honest, wasn't he?"

"Yes. If he had wanted to run away with Regina, I think he would have done it openly—proudly."

"Exactly." Thornberry's blue eyes studied me keenly. "Hasn't it ever occurred to you as a strange coincidence that your brother should arrange to appear dead just before he was actually killed? I think it was more than a coincidence. I think that Anthony Sheridan was persuaded to do it so that the murder might never be discovered. Tell me, did your brother see Mrs. Brace after the disaster?"

"Regina came to the mine for him—to take him home with her for dinner," I answered in a low voice. I felt as if I were betraying Regina. But Thornberry could find out from someone else—if he had not already.

"Exactly. She might have persuaded him then to go into the mine and—apparently—not come up again."

"But why?" I demanded. "Why would Tony do it?"

"Mrs. Brace might have frightened him—told him her husband would kill both of them."

"Tony wasn't frightened so easily."

"Perhaps she told him it was the only condition on which she would go away with him. She might have said Pat Brace would not bother to hunt for her if he thought Anthony Sheridan was dead. It's quite logical. A man does not mind simply losing his wife so much as losing her to another man. But the important thing is: Mrs. Brace had the opportunity to suggest the plan to your brother. Perhaps she thought he might actually succumb in the attempt and never come out alive, and she and her husband could enjoy the stolen money in security."

"It's queer," I said, "that if the murderers persuaded Tony to do that, they waited three days to kill him." Unconsciously, I had said murderers instead of murderer. I caught myself and added: "Supposing, for the sake of argument, there were two murderers."

"The body could not be put down into the mine till Tuesday," Thornberry pointed out. "It was safer not to kill him till then."

"Tony would never remain hidden that long unless he were drugged—or hypnotized."

"Exactly," agreed Thornberry. "He probably was."

XXV
"DIAMONDS AND MONEY RECOVERED"

The interview with Thornberry left me with small appetite for break-fast. If he were right, if Regina were guilty of such treachery, I felt as if I could never trust anyone again.

"It's a lot of hooey," Rush commented when I told him. "Nobody will believe Regina guilty of that. Thornberry has to make out a case against someone. And he'll have to arrest somebody to keep up his reputation. If he can't find Pat and Regina, he'll probably take one of us. He's already laying a foundation for that theory in digging up that will. I wish the whole thing could be dropped—hushed up."

"But somebody is guilty," I insisted.

"Thornberry has enough evidence against Pat and Regina to hang them—or at least convict them. Would you want to see Regina arrest-ed and tried for murder and sentenced and kept in prison the rest of her life?"

"But I know Regina didn't do it."

"You can't prove she didn't. Just because you believe she is good and gentle and honest, a jury wouldn't acquit her. She might be ac-quitted because she is young and pretty, but—do you realize what a murder trial means? Even if it ends in acquittal, the defendant is always a marked person." Rush ran one hand through his hair. A lock fell down over his forehead. "Thornberry can probably prove I did it—if he wants to. You can get evidence to prove anything, just as you can get figures." Rush rather frightened me as he had when we were little, looking at me with his big serious eyes from under that disheveled lock of hair.

Thornberry returned that afternoon with a request to search Tony's room. I had not prepared for that, and there was no time now to hide Tony's revolver. Aunt Addie gave the permission readily. And I sat in the living room below, listening to Thornberry's footsteps overhead and knowing he would discover everything.

I wished I had burned those letters from Regina. I dreaded to think of their being spread over columns and columns of newspapers, of all Regina's pretty endearing phrases laid bare for housemaids and gossips to relish.

At last I could stand it no longer. I went upstairs. Captain Thornberry was standing in the center of Tony's room with Tony's nickel-plated revolver in his hand.

"Where did you find this?" he asked me.

Taken by surprise, I blurted out: "How did you know?"

"There are some specks of rust on it," he pointed out. "It has evidently lain outdoors for some time, probably in the rain. There are no fingerprints—you must've wiped it off after you brought it home, or your own would show on it. And there is a blade of grass caught in the cylinder which escaped your notice." He showed me the tiny yellow particle about an eighth of an inch long. "It was caught between the cylinder and the barrel," Thornberry explained. "The blade is yellow but not yet brittle. It hasn't been in there longer than a few weeks. I know you've been making some investigations on your own. Where did you pick this up?"

"In the wood near Happy House."

"Don't you know that by withholding this information, you make yourself an accessory to the crime?" he asked sternly. "Whom are you protecting? Some member of the family?"

My mouth felt dry, but with an effort, I answered: "I thought Pat Brace put it there, so he could say he killed Tony in self defense—in case the murder was discovered."

"Why did you think that, when the revolver is the same caliber as the bullet which killed your brother? The most obvious conclusion is that this is the gun actually used."

"Maybe it is. Maybe Pat took it from Tony's room," I argued. "Pat knew where it was."

"That spoils your self defense idea, though, doesn't it? If the murder was committed with this gun, the murderer couldn't expect us to believe that Anthony Sheridan was firing at him."

"Maybe Pat thought it would fix the blame on one of us," I ventured. "But you know, yourself, Pat Brace is guilty, and no one else. He's run away, hasn't he? Why don't you arrest him instead of wasting time trying to pin the crime on one of us? I can prove Pat's guilty!" I blurted out, then stopped abruptly.

Thornberry regarded me seriously, unruffled and unsmiling. "Then why are you trying to protect him?"

"To save Regina from scandal. But if you're going to try to make her out a murderer—I can't stand that. Pat planned to kill Tony—told me he was going to—that night Dr. Ames was shot. Pat had a gun then. I tried to take it away from him. And ten or fifteen minutes later Dr. Ames was shot. And he was driving a car like Tony's out to the mine!"

"So Dr. Ames told me," said Thornberry smoothly. "But I didn't know before about the threat."

The man frightened me. Little by little he was dragging out the secrets I thought so safe. His face seemed cruel now with that high bald forehead, those calculating blue eyes and the little dimpled chin.

"You may as well tell me now," he went on coolly, "if you learned anything important when you traced Pat Brace's car to Roxbury."

Again I asked: "How did you know?"

"The boy in the garage said someone else had inquired. From the description, I thought it was you."

"I learned that Regina was with him," I confessed wretchedly. "I didn't tell because I don't want Regina arrested."

"This Mrs. Brace seems to have vamped all of you pretty thoroughly," the detective remarked.

His tone made me think of what Rush had said about a murder trial. It seemed to put Regina in a class with other women in triangle murders. Though I had come upstairs to prevent Thornberry from reading Regina's letters, I wanted him to read them now—anything to wipe that superior little sneer from his face. I opened the drawer of Tony's desk and lifted them out.

"There are Regina's letters to Tony—all of them, from the time they were twelve or so. She never loved anybody but Tony. If you can read those and still call her a siren and a vamp, you're no detective."

He turned them over interestedly. "You've read them?"

"Yes;" I admitted shamelessly, "I had to know if Tony and Regina were planning to run away. But before you read them," I covered the letters with my hand, "promise me if you're wrong about Regina, you won't turn these letters over to the reporters. If you can read these and still think she's a traitoress and a murderess, that she vamped Tony and killed him for a little money, then you can do what you please with them. But if you believe she was sincere, you'll give them back to me?"

"I can't make a bargain like that," Thornberry refused calmly. "But unless the letters have a direct bearing on the case, I'll have no further interest in them. And even if they have, I've no desire to see them published. The prosecution needs a few surprises."

I began to like Thornberry again. "There's only one you'll want then. Regina warned Tony that Pat had a gun."

"Really?" He picked up the letters. "While I read them, will you see if you can find the suit this button came from." He handed me a large dark gray button evidently from a man's coat.

"Do you think it came from Tony's suit?"

"Possibly."

"But Tony hasn't had a gray suit for years," I suddenly remembered. "He's had tan and brown suits and blue—but no gray."

"Anybody else here have a gray suit?"

"Yes."

"See if that button matches anything in the house, will you? Or if any gray suit is missing."

Thornberry settled himself in a chair by the window and began reading the letters. I left the room, puzzled and feeling that he wanted to be rid of me and had invented the search for that purpose. If it were anything important, he wouldn't take my word for it, I argued. Nevertheless, I went through Uncle Matthew's closet and Rush's and even my own, but without finding a suit with buttons to match the one Thornberry had given me.

When I returned to Tony's room, Thornberry looked up from the letters. "What does this mean about making beggars of your family?" he inquired. "What did Pat mean by those threats?"

I told him that Haunted Mine had once belonged to Pat's father, and that Pat had always been bitter about losing it.

Thornberry nodded thoughtfully. "What did he intend to do?"

"There was nothing he could do—except take some revenge like this. Regina was afraid he was insane. She said so when I talked to her at the rehearsal."

Thornberry folded the letters and handed them back to me. "You may keep all of them. They're no use to me."

"Not even the one about Pat's threats?" I asked surprised.

"No."

"But I thought you wanted evidence against him. I would've given it to you before but for Regina's sake."

"I won't need it now," Thornberry said shortly.

And though I had come upstairs to save the letters from him, I was vaguely worried.

"Did you find any buttons to match?" he asked now.

"No."

"I didn't think you would." He dropped the gray button into his pocket. "Just look in Tony's closet to make sure, will you?"

Wondering, I did as he requested. There was no gray suit, nor sweater, nor anything with gray buttons.

"And you don't think the button came from anything that was ever worn by Tony Sheridan?" Thornberry insisted. "To the best of your belief, it never belonged to him, nor to any member of your family?"

"No."

"Will you just give me a statement to that effect?" was Thornberry's next puzzling request.

I felt somehow that I was being tricked, that I was doing something that could be used against Rush or me. But I could not refuse, and I wrote the brief statement as the detective dictated.

"Now then," said Thornberry briskly, pocketing the paper, "did you see the body in the mine before it was moved?"

"Yes."

"Was it lying on its face or its back?"

"On its back."

"Are you sure?"

"Yes."

"Then can you account for the fact that the back of Anthony Sheridan's sweater was burned more than the front?"

"I don't know. I didn't see it closely. But the fire reached the shaft where the body was."

"The body was lying on a concrete floor comparatively free from coal dust, wasn't it?"

"Yes," I admitted, wondering where Thornberry's questions were leading.

"Then the flames couldn't have burned the clothing from the under side without nearly destroying the body. And the body was not badly burned."

"What does that mean?" I asked.

Thornberry did not answer. In the silence, I heard someone coming up the stairs. The sharp-nosed, blond young detective burst into the room.

"Wire for you, Captain!" he announced breathlessly. "It just came to the hotel. I rushed right over with it."

Thornberry opened the yellow envelope. His cold intellectual face betrayed neither surprise nor triumph as he read. When he finished, he handed the message to me.

It was from his chief in the city. The words slapped me in the face:

REGINA BRACE ARRESTED AT PARK HOTEL HERE STOP DIAMONDS AND MONEY RECOVERED STOP COMPANION ESCAPED STOP BRACE WOMAN REFUSES TO TALK.

> JOHN HATTON
> CHIEF OF POLICE

I felt as if I had plunged suddenly into icy water.

XXVI
"HORROR CREPT UPON ME"

Thornberry left immediately, taking with him Tony's revolver. I went downstairs and told the others.

The news was in the evening papers. And Regina's picture—Regina's innocent heart-shaped face encircled by the two blond half-moons of her hair. Her wide-set eyes looked out at me sadly—pleading, I thought. Her little round mouth was pressed tight. And beneath:

BLOND SIREN ARRESTED IN MURDER CASE

Rush and I looked at each other, dazed, over that paper.

"Regina couldn't be guilty," I said, fighting against the idea.

"I told you, you didn't realize what a murder trial meant," Rush answered. "Even the defendant's best friends can be turned against him and made to believe him guilty."

"But I don't believe Regina's guilty," I returned warmly.

"No; but you're wavering," Rush accused. With that uncanny intuition of his, he had sensed the doubt laying hold on my mind with its creeping tentacles.

Aunt Addie said: "Regina thought she had to be loyal to Pat, poor child. Maybe she's afraid to talk. I expect he threatened her. That man will have to answer for his sins someday." Aunt Addie sat primly straight, holding her embroidery hoops high and driving her needle determinedly through the strip of tan linen. "Your Uncle Matthew has always been too lenient with Pat Brace. But there's no doubt now that he's the cause of all this trouble." Aunt Addie sighed gently.

Uncle Matthew shook his head over the newspaper, muttering: "Bless my soul, bless my soul." He wiped his face with a handkerchief clutched in his trembling old hand.

193

Then I heard him in the pantry and knew he was having a "mite to drink." He went into the library and shut himself up, and I suspected he had taken the bottle with him.

Captain Thornberry returned to the house that evening. I admitted him. He wanted to speak to Uncle Matthew alone, he said. Uncle Matthew, hearing our voices, opened the library doors a little way. Thornberry passed through. The big doors slid shut.

Rush and I waited in the living room. Aunt Addie had gone upstairs with a headache. Rush was unusually restless. His fingers wandered over the piano keys drawing out the queer strains he seemed to find comforting when he was troubled, though they seemed only to intensify my anxiety.

At last I grumbled: "Will you cut that out?"

The piano lid crashed down. Rush flung himself across the room. He lighted a cigarette jerkily.

"That man, Thornberry, has got at the truth," Rush said. His voice sounded queer—choked.

He dropped into a chair and buried his face in his hands.

I went over and closed the living room doors. Then I stood over Rush.

"See here, you've got to tell me. What do you know that I don't? I don't care what it is—tell me. Anything's better than this uncertainty—it's getting on my nerves. I tell you, I can't stand it!" I was conscious that my voice rose to a jangled, strained pitch. I felt as if something inside my brain would snap unless the tension were relieved. "I don't want to believe that Regina killed Tony. I don't want to believe that she and Pat made him steal—"

"Shut up!" Rush snapped. His head jerked back. He flung his cigarette into the fireplace. After a moment he said in a low voice: "You may as well know now. You'll know soon enough." Rush's dark eyes met mine gravely. "Tony isn't dead."

I stopped breathing. "Not—dead?" I whispered, unbelieving, till the memory of Tony standing in the moonlight flashed into my mind. "Then I did see him!" I cried joyfully. "It was Tony!"

"Good God!" said Rush, "don't you realize what it means?"

I didn't at first. Slowly, horror crept upon me. Pulsing waves of fear engulfed me. If Tony was not dead, someone was. Someone dressed in Tony's clothes, and killed with Tony's gun. I shut my eyes as if I could shut out the sight. That blackened form brought out of Haunted Mine, with the clean blue handkerchief over its face. . . . And Tony, only the other night, gazing up at my window. . . .

Rush and I stared at each other. I knew he had told me the truth. But I asked: "How can you be sure?"

"I was afraid—" Rush said. "I couldn't understand—I'd been so sure Tony was alive. When I read in the papers that the body had been brought out of the mine, I couldn't understand. I came home. I asked to see the body, you remember." Rush didn't look at me. He was staring at the floor. "It was scorched—smoked—not burned much. You couldn't tell about the face. People don't look the same when they're dead, anyway. It had been over a month, too, hadn't it? I couldn't have been sure about the face. And Tony and Pat were about the same size and build. But I looked for the scar—that scar on Tony's right thigh where the bulldog bit him. There wasn't any. . . . I knew then. . . ." His voice died away.

I could feel my heart thumping in my throat, choking me. I had to moisten my lips before I could ask: "Was it—Pat?"

Rush nodded.

We were silent a long minute. I heard only the watch in my pocket ticking noisily. Joy and fear tore at me. Tony alive! Tony, a murderer!

"How did you guess?" I asked.

"I was afraid—all along. After I saw Tony on the Hill Road—after the first shock of that—I knew he was alive. I knew something dreadful must've happened. And then I remembered—" Rush's slim fingers writhed together—"I couldn't tell you then—it seemed too horrible to be true. But I remembered that night Pat was here looking for Regina, I heard Uncle Matthew say: 'Put up that gun, Pat. Don't do anything foolish.' And Pat laughed. That was when I was on my way upstairs. I came in the side door, you know. They didn't hear me.

"I knew then Pat must be looking for Tony and Regina. But I didn't go into the library or try to do anything to stop Pat. I'd give anything if I had." Rush ran his hand through his hair. "I've thought of nothing else. I was mad at Tony—crazy mad—that scene at the rehearsal, you know. I was jealous. Tony was always so good-looking, so much more attractive, so sure of himself. I thought he would take Norma away from me—just for fun. I didn't care what happened then. If I hadn't been so mad, the whole thing might have been averted—that's what I've had to remember. I thought then it would serve Tony right if he should get into trouble. I never thought of anything serious—really serious. It's been hell for me—knowing I might have stopped Pat that night—and didn't." Rush strode across the room.

I put my arm about his shoulders. "It would've happened some time, anyway," I said. "Don't think about that. We must think about Tony now. Where is he? Why did he come here the other night?"

Rush shook his head. "I had hoped he was safely out of the country—until you saw him. . . ."

"But the papers said Regina had the money and the diamonds. Why didn't they go away? How can Tony go now without money?"

"I'm afraid he won't try," Rush said slowly. "It isn't like Tony to run away. I'm afraid he'll give himself up now to stand by Regina."

"Why shouldn't he?" I argued, suddenly hopeful. "If Pat went there with a gun, Tony must've fired in self defense."

"Tony wouldn't have a chance in the world. I've seen murder trials—and read them—and studied them." Rush's dark eyes were tragic. "All the sentiment would be against Tony. It's sentiment that counts in murder trials, not law. In triangle murders, anyway. If Pat had killed Tony, Pat would go free. Pat would've fired to save his honor and protect his home." Rush's tone was cruel. "It wouldn't matter how unhappy he'd made Regina or how wrong their marriage was. Tony would be a homewrecker. If Tony goes on trial, nothing can save him."

I turned away wretchedly. Tony, a murderer. Tony on trial for his life. My thoughts could go no further than that. It was too dreadful. There are some thoughts which the mind refuses.

"Pat was in the library a long time after I went upstairs," Rush continued. He seemed relieved to talk now. "I suppose Uncle Matthew was trying to dissuade him or get him to give up his gun. I don't know how Pat guessed they were at Happy House. But I heard him push open the library doors and come out in the hall and say: 'If they're at Happy House, I'll settle things with them.' And then Uncle Matthew said: 'Don't go there to-night, Pat—not to-night. Wait till you're calmer.' Pat went out then and slammed the door. Something in his voice frightened me. I got up and started to follow him. But before I reached the door of my room, I remembered Tony with his arms around Norma. I went back and sat down.

"Uncle Matthew came upstairs. He looked into Tony's room, hoping maybe Tony was there, I suppose. Then he went downstairs again hurriedly. I knew he must be worried. He went out the side door, and in a minute I heard his car on the drive. And still I sat there, not caring what happened to Tony, or trying not to care.

"Aunt Addie came in then. I got undressed and tried to read. But I was thinking all the time about Tony and Pat and Regina, and wondering why Tony didn't come home. I heard Uncle Matthew come back. Aunt Addie went to the top of the stairs and called down: 'You needn't have gone for me, Matthew. Cappy and I walked home.' Uncle Matthew didn't answer for a moment. Then he just mumbled: 'Better go back to bed. I'll be up soon.' I knew he didn't know anything about Tony, or he would've told Aunt Addie.

"When you came upstairs and began asking me about Tony and Pat, I was scared stiff. But the minute Tony came in and I knew he was all right, I began thinking he'd been with Norma, especially after you told me Regina had come home earlier. Somehow I never thought about Pat—only Tony."

I remembered how Tony had come in and gone straight to his room without speaking to us.

"Do you think it happened—that night?" I asked. "The night before the disaster?"

Rush nodded. "I've thought of nothing else. I've tried a thousand times to convince myself that it didn't, but—"

"Then Pat must've been on his way to Happy House when he shot Dr. Ames?"

Rush nodded. "As soon as Pat realized his mistake, he turned off to the Hill Road and went on to Happy House. Regina and Tony were there. Tony must've—"

"I can't believe it!" I cried rebelliously.

"But Regina told you Pat left town that night, didn't she?" Rush pointed out.

"And Homer Cole said Pat didn't leave on the train," I remembered wretchedly. "He wasn't at the station."

"And Regina drove Pat's car home that night?" Rush questioned.

I nodded. My mind slipped back to that midnight hour and Regina slumped down in the seat of the gray racer, Regina shivering even in the warmth of a July night, and drawing the rose shawl closer around her. I knew then she was unnerved, but Pat's threats and her fear for Tony's safety would account for that.

If she had seen Pat killed that evening, it had taken courage and nerve to sit and talk to me and answer my questions as she had. But I had seen her pull herself together and hide her emotions at the rehearsal earlier in the evening.

"Regina wouldn't come home with me that night," I said.

"She was afraid to." Rush's voice was barely audible. "She didn't want to face us in the light—for fear her expression might betray her. You didn't see her in the light, did you?"

"No; we sat on the porch—it was only a few minutes."

"The next day the pay roll was stolen. Oh, I've been over it again and again. Everything fits together perfectly. There's no other explanation." He said it as if he expected me to contradict him. But I couldn't. "They must've decided that night what to do. Regina came to the office the next morning, you remember."

"She was all in, too—nearly fainted. Tony sent me for water, then shut the door in my face."

"Did you talk to Tony that morning?" Rush asked. "He was joking and kidding at breakfast."

Rush nodded. "Tony would."

"And just before Regina came into the office, he said something about my being able to handle the work here."

"You see," said Rush, "he was thinking about leaving."

"He said there were more interesting places to work, too. I thought maybe he was dissatisfied."

"You didn't see Regina leave the office, did you?"

"No."

"Tony took the money from the safe and gave it to her—I'm sure of that."

"Regina had a shopping bag with her that morning," I added.

"Tony knew you always left the pay roll in the safe while you made out the envelopes. They must've intended to go to South America or somewhere—disappear forever, probably. They'd have to have money."

"Why didn't they go then?" I demanded. "They could've been half way around the world by now."

"Don't you see?" Rush's voice sank to a whisper. "Tony was afraid at first that Pat's body might be discovered any minute."

The vision of Tony as that shadow I had imagined dragging that lifeless form through the thicket rose before me. "He must've buried it in the sand pile that night?"

Rush nodded. "The next day the fire broke out in Haunted Mine, and Tony saw his chance."

"It's queer it happened just then," I mused.

"Tony was afraid the body might be discovered. He probably thought of staying down in reality, at first, and ending it all."

"He wouldn't leave Regina to face everything alone," I put in.

"No;" Rush agreed. "I suppose not. But he saw an opportunity to substitute Pat's body for his own, and the chances were the difference would never be discovered. Whatever grief he would cause us would be better, he thought, than our knowing the truth."

"He must've told Regina his plan when she came to the mine to take him home for dinner."

"If Tony's plans had gone through, if everyone believed him dead, there would be no hurry about getting away. They thought Regina's note would prevent any search for her and Pat."

"But why didn't Tony leave while he could go safely?" I insisted. "He couldn't expect ever to come back here."

Rush shook his head. "That's the part I can't understand. He must've had some purpose in coming back here."

"For the diamonds?" I questioned. "Do you think he took them the other night when I saw him on the lawn?"

"He couldn't have entered the house then. Uncle Matthew was downstairs, wasn't he?"

"Yes."

"Besides, Tony had over eight thousand. Why would he risk everything trying to get more? It was risk enough when he took his car out of the garage. But he had to do that to carry Pat's body to the mine."

"Why didn't he use Regina's car?"

"That would connect Regina with it if he were seen, would make her an accessory," Rush explained. "He must've been on his way back to Happy House after—after going to the mine—when I saw him on the Hill Road."

"He took the car out of the garage just before I reached home, I suppose. Maybe he intended to bring it back, but changed his mind when he saw the light in my room."

"Yes; he probably counted on all of us being at the memorial service that night, though you and I didn't go. But it was his best opportunity to get the car out unobserved, and the first night after the disaster there was no crowd around the mine. Big Bill was there alone, you remember."

"But why didn't Tony wait till later? It would've been safer."

"Some of us would be sure to hear him take the car out if we were at home," Rush said. "Besides, it rained that night, you remember. Tony wanted to get it done before the rain so the tracks would be washed out."

"And it was Tony with Regina when she stopped at Roxbury." Tony, wearing my beard for disguise and slumped down in the seat beside Regina, too unnerved by his dreadful task to drive or to fix the fan belt. But why had he come back into danger after he had escaped safely? I was certain now it had been a flesh-and-blood Tony I saw in the moonlight, no ghostly hallucination conjured up out of my morbid fancies.

"When you showed me the ten-dollar note Regina had given Minnie, I began to realize that something terrible had happened, that Tony had meant to disappear forever," Rush continued. "I remembered Pat's words when he left here Friday night. I went out to Happy House that morning—Wednesday, it was. I saw the candles and the coffee pot and knew Regina and Tony had been there—several times, probably. I saw the sand pile had been disturbed. I got a board and dug into it. You know what I found. I didn't go snooping around any more—wasn't fit for anything after that. But I guessed then what had happened. I began to piece it all together—Pat's threat Friday night, his sudden departure, Tony's staying out so late, then the theft next day, Tony's disappearance and seeming death, then my glimpse of him on the Hill Road, your recognising that ten-dollar note, Regina's leaving—I saw it all. And yet I tried to tell myself it was all imagined, that it couldn't be true. I was afraid to speak of it. I tried to forget it.

"When Regina didn't write, my fears were confirmed. I broke into Tony's desk to see if there were any notes that would give me a hint about their plans, where they had gone. But, of course, there were none. It had all happened so suddenly. I had an idea, too, that I might forge a note from Regina to send to her father, but I found one which seemed to suit the situation as it was with only the name changed. I wanted desperately to help Tony and Regina get away, and I was afraid her father might report the matter to the police and Tony would be found and brought back. I went to New York and mailed the letter.

"After that I haunted the docks, thinking I might see them boarding some steamer—until I read in the paper that Tony's body had been found and brought out of the mine. At first I thought I had been mistaken in all my fine theories. It was almost a relief to believe Tony was dead. It hadn't occurred to me that Tony might have substituted Pat's body for his—until I saw it."

Rush slumped into a chair, frowning moodily at the floor.

I remembered now how I had clamored for justice, and Rush had said: "What if your brother had done such a thing?" I remembered how Rush had begged me to keep my discoveries secret. It was only too clear now. Yet I was perversely happy. Tony still lived! Through all that followed, I hugged that thought to me. Tony still lived!

"If only I had hid Tony's revolver!" I cried out.

"I should have thought of it," said Rush. "I knew. But I was so sure the investigation would come to nothing. No one seemed to question Tony's death. It never occurred to me that his room would be searched. But now—Thornberry must know."

XXVII
"THERE ARE WAYS OF MAKING A PRISONER CONFESS"

Thornberry did know. It was apparent to both Rush and me when he called us into the library. Uncle Matthew knew too. He did not look up. He was sitting on the other side of the room, his gaunt hands gripping the chair arms till the knuckles showed blanched. In the merciless light of the chandelier, his emaciated face, with its sunken cheeks and dark eyes, looked ghastly, as though the skull were showing through the wasting flesh.

"Nothing but more trouble, more trouble . . ." he muttered to himself.

Thornberry addressed me first. "Did you see the body at the inquest?"

"No."

Then, turning to Rush, he said: "You did?"

"Yes."

"You identified it as Anthony Sheridan. Why did you do that?"

Rush didn't answer.

"Did they look so much alike?" Thornberry persisted.

"No," said Rush thoughtfully, "but they were about the same size."

"You asked to see the body," Thornberry went on, "though it wasn't necessary, and you looked at it several minutes, though it was not a pleasant sight. You must have had some object. Your uncle has admitted that Anthony Sheridan had a scar on his right thigh. Didn't you look for that?"

"Yes," said Rush wretchedly.

"You knew then it was Pat Brace, not your brother, who had been killed?"

Rush nodded.

"It isn't necessary," said Thornberry sternly, "to ask you why you carried out the deception. You guessed, of course, that your brother had killed Brace and disposed of the body in this way."

Rush did not look up.

"I don't believe it!" I blurted out mutinously, hardly knowing whether I did or not, but ready to defend Tony dead or alive. "Rush must be mistaken about the scar. It wasn't a very deep scar—it might not have showed at all after the body was burned. Uncle Matthew and Dr. Ames and Big Bill identified the body as Tony," I reminded him.

"That is easy to explain," Thornberry returned calmly. "We see largely what we expect to see. These three had no cause to doubt that Anthony Sheridan was dead. But Rush Sheridan must've had some suspicion of the truth, since he asked to see the body. Mr. North says he did not think to look for the scar. This—Big Bill person—knew nothing about it. . . ."

"Dr. Ames knew about it!" I argued triumphantly. "He took the stitches after Tony was hurt."

"I have talked to Dr. Ames," Thornberry returned with his usual dignity. "He told me he had forgotten entirely about the scar. The body, he said, was the right size and build. The eyes were brown, he noticed. In fact, he did not question the identity of the dead man. You have no reason to doubt Dr Ames, have you?"

"No," I admitted, crestfallen, "but that doesn't prove it was Pat."

"Possibly not," Thornberry agreed equably. "But the bullet taken from the body bears rifling marks that prove it was fired from Anthony Sheridan's revolver. I fired another bullet from the gun, and compared the two under the microscope—no room for doubt there—"

"But Pat could've got Tony's gun," I interrupted.

Thornberry ignored my comment. "Neither is there any doubt that a suit of gray clothes, such as Pat Brace was wearing the last time he was seen, was burned at Happy House."

For the first time I recalled that Pat had been wearing a gray suit that Friday evening—my mind must have taken in that detail subconsciously, to remember it now. But I recalled it distinctly, a gray tweed mixture with little flecks of blue and green.

"I discovered a few ashes of woolen material and the one gray button near the edge of the wood," Thornberry continued. "The weeds and brush about the spot were scorched. The clothes had evidently been burnt there, after having been soaked with gasoline or oil, probably. The ashes were scattered, and the buttons carried away or buried somewhere. But the one button was overlooked."

Detective Thornberry had discovered something at Happy House which I had missed, and, as luck would have it, it was the one thing which would reveal Tony's secret.

"I have your statement that the button did not come from the suit of any member of your family—to the best of your belief," the detective reminded me, "and so was not dropped there accidentally. If clothing was burned there, it must've been because it was blood soaked. Furthermore, the clothes found on the body were hardly stained, though a man loses an enormous amount of blood from a wound of that nature. The backs had been burned from the sweater and the other clothing to remedy this discrepancy in case the wound should be discovered, though the murderer undoubtedly expected the effects of the fire to conceal the cause of death. But the flames swept over the body, and, since it was lying on its back, the wound was plainly visible, and the fact that the back had been burned from the sweater highly significant; enough so, taken with the burning of the gray suit, to convince me that the murdered man had been wearing a gray suit at the time of his death instead of a sweater and knickers, and was, therefore, probably not Anthony Sheridan. And now—" Thornberry placed the tips of his fingers together and turned his cold blue gaze on Rush—"just what caused you to think the dead man might be other than Anthony Sheridan?"

Rush squirmed restlessly in his chair. His voice barely audible. "I was so sure it was Tony I saw that night on the Hill Road."

There was a triumphant glitter in Thornberry's eyes. "That was the night your brother moved Brace's body from Happy House to the mine. All quite clear."

He was building up an airtight case against Tony—and with our evidence. I couldn't stand it any longer.

"But if Tony killed Pat, he did it in self defense," I argued warmly. "You know that Pat had a gun that night and shot Dr. Ames by mistake for Tony!"

"I heard Pat threaten to get Tony, too," Rush spoke up.

"Are there any other witnesses for the defense?" Thornberry asked ironically.

The color flared into Rush's face. "Uncle Matthew heard Pat say that, too. Didn't he tell you? It was Uncle Matthew Pat was talking to. I was upstairs. Uncle Matthew was in the library a long time with Pat. I don't know what they were talking about, but I heard Uncle Matthew say: 'Put up that gun, Pat!'" Rush recounted the other circumstances leading up to the threat he had overheard. "And after Pat left, Uncle Matthew got out his car and followed, so I know he was worried," Rush finished.

Uncle Matthew nodded. "That's true—all of it."

"Why didn't you tell me before?" Thornberry questioned.

"I hadn't thought of it—hadn't had time to get things connected up," Uncle Matthew explained. "It was such a surprise—what you just told me. Bless my soul, it doesn't seem real yet." Uncle Matthew shook his head bewilderedly.

"Why didn't you tell me that Pat Brace had made these threats when you thought it was your nephew who was killed?" Thornberry pursued.

"I didn't think Pat really meant them," Uncle Matthew quavered. "I didn't think Pat would do a thing like that. Why, his father and I went to school together. And Pat and Rush were friends."

"You were worried enough to follow Pat Brace when he left here that night," Thornberry pointed out.

"Yes; but after Tony came home that night, I didn't think any more about it. I thought it was just hot-headed talk. People often say things they don't mean."

Captain Thornberry nodded, apparently satisfied. "What did you and Brace say during the time you were in here together?"

"I talked to him and begged him not to do anything foolish."

"What had he heard about his wife and Anthony Sheridan? Why did he come here looking for them? He didn't expect to find them here, did he?"

"He asked me if Tony was at home."

"But when Brace left here, he said he was going to Happy House. How did he know they were there, and if he did, why didn't he go there first?"

Uncle Matthew was silent.

"Did you tell him where they were?" Thornberry persisted.

Uncle Matthew's hands gripped the chair arms tighter. He said hoarsely: "Pat made me. He put that gun to my head. He made me tell."

"How did you know your nephew and Mrs. Brace had gone to Happy House that night?"

"I didn't know it. I guessed it. I knew they had been there before because I saw Tony's car turn off the road there one night when I was out driving. Regina was with him. They didn't know I was behind them. I was just driving around."

"When did this happen?"

"Several months ago."

"Did you follow Pat Brace to Happy House that night?"

"No, no!" Uncle Matthew's voice rose to the breaking point. His shaggy black brows climbed up his forehead and dropped again.

"If you set out to follow Brace, why didn't you go there? You knew he was going there, didn't you?"

"I started to," Uncle Matthew began so slowly and carefully I wondered if he were making up a story to protect Tony. "I started to, but before I turned into the Hill Road, I saw Pat's car coming down. He didn't see me. He turned into the avenue about a block ahead of me. He was going towards town. I thought maybe he was going to drive out to Regina's father's on the other side of town to see if Regina was there. I followed him a little way, enough to make sure I was right. Then I turned back. I went by the Brace house on the hill; it was dark. I decided I'd had all my fears for nothing, so I came back." Uncle Matthew mopped his face with his handkerchief. His old head shook nervously.

Uncle Matthew had told me he had gone for Aunt Addie and had just driven around afterwards, I reflected. It looked as if he had suspected the truth, as Rush had, and was trying to protect Tony. He did not want me to know Pat had gone to Happy House that night.

The detective's narrow blue eyes were fixed on Uncle Matthew coldly. "It's queer that Pat Brace didn't go direct to Happy House when he left here with that intention. And it's queer you turned back after hearing him threaten to kill your nephew."

"It isn't queer about Pat!" I burst out defensively. "When he left here, he met Aunt Addie and me down the avenue. He stopped his car and asked us where Regina was. I could see he was worried and excited, but Aunt Addie didn't seem to notice. She told him Regina had probably gone to her mother's. We'd heard Mrs. Townsend was ill. Naturally, Pat changed his mind and decided to go to the Townsends' first."

"May I use your telephone?" Thornberry inquired.

He went into the hall and called up Mr. Townsend. From Thornberry's side of the conversation, we knew, even before he hung up and told us, that Pat had not stopped at the Townsends' that night. But he must have driven by there, and, seeing the house dark, decided not to arouse Regina's family but go on to Happy House. He had taken the road by the mine, thinking Tony might have gone there to watch the graveyard shift go down, had shot Dr. Ames by mistake, then turned off to the Hill Road and gone on to Happy House.

I told Captain Thornberry all I could remember about that evening—all, that is, except Aunt Addie's little tiff with Uncle Matthew. And when I had finished, Thornberry asked:

"And Mrs. Brace came home alone?" musingly. "At what time?"

"A little after twelve."

"What time did Anthony Sheridan come in?"

"It was after one," I confessed wretchedly.

Thornberry nodded meditatively. "It would take about that long to bury the body."

He said it casually, yet to me, it was as if he had pronounced Tony's doom. And in spite of that, I still experienced a strange, painful kind of happiness—Tony still lived.

"Curious," Thornberry murmured, "that this mine disaster happened so opportunely the next day. But I suppose there is such a thing as coincidence."

He would have liked to accuse Tony of causing that, too, I think.

"Well, the sheriff is bringing Mrs. Brace back to-morrow," Thornberry told us as he was leaving. "I suppose in time she can be persuaded to clear up the whole mystery. There are ways of making a prisoner confess."

His tone, satisfied and slightly contemptuous, sent a shudder through me. I understood now why he hadn't wanted Regina's letter. It was defense material.

XXVIII
"HAUNTED MINE HAS CLAIMED ANOTHER VICTIM"

After the detective had gone, Rush and I still sat in the library, too dazed and distraught to do anything. But Uncle Matthew climbed the stairs wearily, his gaunt old form bent forward as he pulled himself up step by step.

I do not know how long Rush and I sat there. All sorts of wild fancies ran through my mind, childish plans to spirit Regina away at any cost, deeds of violence. At heart, I became a jail breaker, a desperado, a fugitive with Regina and Tony. My mind seemed divided into two parts, a civilized self sitting in judgment on the other and more primitive self, and rejecting the schemes of the savage as hopeless, impracticable and perilous—not that, in my present mood, I gave much thought to the danger. And curiously, I felt no concern for the unlawfulness of the plans. I considered only their chances for success. Much the same thoughts must have been running through Rush's mind, for once he whispered:

"Do you think we could bribe the sheriff?"

"Not MacFarland."

"The jailer?"

"No use."

And after another long silence, Rush asked: "How far is it to the Canadian border?"

"We'd never make it."

And later: "Do you think Regina knows where Tony is?"

I could only shrug.

"What is a third degree like?" I asked. "Is it—as bad as you read about?"

"Worse—though you'd never get an officer to admit it."

Only such jerky scraps of conversation passed between us.

It was Aunt Addie's voice that finally brought us to our feet in alarm.

"Cappy! Rush! Come here!" she cried from the top of the steps. There was terror in her tone. The last word rose almost to a shriek.

The sound of it paralyzed us for a second. Then Rush and I were up the stairs together.

Aunt Addie in her nightgown was bending over the bed where Uncle Matthew lay. She was slapping his hands and calling to him. Uncle Matthew's meager form lay flat and motionless under the sheet, his long thin arms stretched out limply on top of the covers. His face had a clammy, bluish look, and drops of cold moisture stood out on his brow. His breathing was slow and difficult. The hoarse sound of it seemed to fill the room.

"I can't wake him up!" Aunt Addie said. "He took one of those sleeping powders."

Rush went down again to call the doctor.

"What can we do? What can we do?" Aunt Addie cried, tears streaming unnoticed down her cheeks. "Do something, Cappy."

I shook Uncle Matthew and shouted to him. I wrung a towel out in cold water and slapped his face with it. But it was no use.

Dr. Ames came, breathless and bustling.

But Uncle Matthew never regained consciousness. In the gray light of dawn, his face was like a mask against the pillows—a long gaunt mask, wrinkled like parchment, with loose pouches under the eyes, with dark shaggy brows and sunken cheeks. Dr. Ames pulled the sheet over it. But the long spare outline was still distressingly familiar.

"He must've taken more than one," Dr. Ames insisted. "One powder couldn't have hurt him. I told him not to take more than one."

"But he had bad news again last evening," Aunt Addie explained. "It's been too much for him—all this trouble. That detective was here—" Aunt Addie turned away, her face working in a determined effort to control the rising sobs.

"I know, I know," Dr. Ames muttered gruffly. "Don't try to tell me. Saw Thornberry myself—persistent fellow. Lot of crazy ideas. Can't prove anything though. I forgot about a scar on Tony's leg. Can't say whether there was a scar on the body or not. Maybe there was. Didn't look for it."

"But Rush did," I said. "There wasn't any."

Dr. Ames shook his bead bewilderedly.

"It was such a shock to Matthew," Aunt Addie murmured, her plain face swollen by crying. "He was almost overcome. He wouldn't talk about it. I said I'd never believe Tony did it. Matthew just shook his head and didn't answer. He said all he wanted was just to get some rest. Then he went in the bathroom and took the sleeping powder."

"Probably took two," Dr. Ames muttered. "No wonder—no wonder. Might've done it without thinking. Heart was weak. I cautioned him. Had he been taking them regularly?"

"Yes; every night—ever since you gave them to him," Aunt Addie answered. "It's all that kept him going through these terrible days—getting a good night's rest."

"Did you or the boys take any?"

Aunt Addie shook her head. "The strain wasn't so hard on us. The boys are young, and I—well I tried not to think about it. I tried just to keep busy and take care of Matthew and the boys. I've been worried about Matthew, and that kept my mind off—this other trouble. Besides, I never take medicine as long as I can avoid it."

"Quite right, quite right," Dr. Ames murmured. "Where are the sleeping powders kept?"

"In the medicine cabinet," I answered.

Dr. Ames followed me into the bathroom. He took the little square white box from the shelf.

"Should've been twenty-four to start with," he said. "How long has it been since I wrote the prescription?"

"It was the day Tony's body—the body," I substituted, "was found in the mine—a week ago Saturday."

"Did you get it filled the same day?"

"Yes; I took it to the drug store that evening."

"H'mmm, I gave him one Saturday. He wouldn't take any till Sunday night."

"No; he was already asleep when I came home."

"H'mmm, to-day's Thursday." Dr. Ames counted the days off on his fingers. "Eleven nights—shouldn't be more than eleven powders gone."

He laid the little folded papers out on the edge of the lavatory. There were only ten. Uncle Matthew had taken fourteen.

Dr. Ames frowned. He wiped his forehead and his bald head with his handkerchief. His ruddy face was almost pasty.

"Could he have taken two several times?" I asked.

Dr. Ames shook his head. He closed the bathroom door before he spoke. "Not likely. Not likely. There would've been some effect. Your aunt would've noticed something wrong. He would've overslept anyway."

"Did he take four last night? He couldn't have done that accidentally."

Dr. Ames and I looked at each other, and in his troubled eyes, I read the answer to my question.

"Mustn't jump at conclusions," he muttered hastily.

"Could two have killed him?" I asked.

"Can't tell—can't tell. Heart wasn't too strong. I cautioned him. Not but one, I said. That's the trouble giving narcotics. Patients want to doctor themselves. Doctor gets the blame."

Dr. Ames was not looking at me. His glance was fastened on a tiny crumpled ball of paper in the corner at the end of the bathtub. I picked it up and straightened it out. There were four tiny slips of white paper like those the sleeping powders were folded in.

"That couldn't have been there yesterday," I said. "I saw Hilda mopping the bathroom yesterday." Hilda had been on her hands and knees wiping up the floor when I came upstairs to talk to Thornberry.

The door opened then, and Aunt Addie came in.

"Do you think he took two powders, Doctor?" she asked.

Dr. Ames' hand went into his pocket and came out again. He displayed two of the crumpled papers.

"Looks like that's what happened," he said. "He must've done it by mistake—thinking about something else. All this trouble—"

Aunt Addie nodded. "One powder hadn't had much effect lately. He was getting used to them, I suppose. Maybe he didn't think that just two would hurt him."

"Likely, likely," Dr. Ames nodded. "But I cautioned him."

When I followed Dr. Ames out into the hall, he said: "No use worrying your aunt. Better let her think there were only two papers.

Wouldn't do any good to tell her there were four. No use imagining things you can't ever be certain about, anyway," he finished brusquely.

That was the worst of it, I thought—the never being certain. Had grief and shock driven Uncle Matthew to that, or had it been an accident? At any rate, he had wanted us to believe it an accident, and I was glad Dr. Ames had kept his secret. No one would learn it from me—no one except Rush, and Rush had already guessed it.

Rush said, with that far-away look in his eyes: "Haunted Mine has claimed another victim. It's that old prophecy coming true. Remember—not till the body of an owner lies dead. . . ."

"That meant in the mine," I objected.

"Uncle Matthew is as much a victim of Haunted Mine as if he had died in the workings."

"How can you say that? It's Pat Brace who's to blame. It's his jealousy. He hated us, and he turned Regina against Tony and married her for spite. If Tony killed him, he did it to save his own life—or Regina's. It all comes back to Pat Brace and his envy and malice."

"And what caused Pat's envy? Haunted Mine," said Rush gloomily. "I believe there is a curse on the old pit. I don't like to think that you and I are part owners now."

His words left me slightly uneasy, but not so much as did Captain Thornberry's a little later. The detective came as soon as he heard of Uncle Matthew's death.

"I'm very sorry. It's most regrettable," he began, and I thought his words were intended for sympathy until he added: "He was an important witness. Tell me just how it occurred."

I told him everything except the finding of the crumpled slips of paper in the bathroom. Aunt Addie told him about that, though, of course, she said there were only two, and showed him the two Dr. Ames had given her.

Thornberry regarded Aunt Addie through half-closed lids. "Only two?"

"He shouldn't have taken but one," explained Aunt Addie, seemingly unconscious of the suspicion in the detective's voice.

"It's queer that only two should cause death," Thornberry remarked. "Narcotics are not usually given in such large doses. I should have said it would take three or four anyway—possibly more."

"Matthew's heart was weak," Aunt Addie said. "Dr. Ames had always said so."

"Oh, you knew that, did you?" his eyes studying her face deliberately.

His tone brought Aunt Addie up erect now. She gave him glance for glance, her blue-gray eyes like steel. "What do you mean?"

"You were alone with your husband when he took the sleeping powder?"

"Naturally. He always took them at bedtime," Aunt Addie answered with dignity.

"And if you had prepared them for him," suggested Thornberry softly, "he would not have known how many he was taking? He took them in water, didn't he?"

In my amazement, I could find nothing to say. I had seen it coming, but the horror of the actual words caught at my breath like the shock of a sudden explosion. I felt as if there had descended upon all of us a smothering cloud of evil from which no one could escape. We seemed to be fighting only fog and darkness. There was no tangible enemy.

That Aunt Addie, of all people, should be suspected—the thought left me dizzy—Aunt Addie, who had been almost like a mother to us.

It was Aunt Addie's voice, calm and collected, that brought me back to my senses.

"No," said Aunt Addie evenly. "Matthew would not have known how many powders I gave him. He would have taken anything I gave him without question."

Her composure seemed to shame even Thornberry.

"You've nothing to be alarmed about now," he hastened to say. "But it's fortunate for all of you—" his glance included me—"that this didn't happen last week when it was believed that Anthony Sheridan had been murdered. When a man as rich as Matthew North dies under peculiar circumstances and one of his heirs is murdered, it looks bad for the other heirs. However, I can see no connection between Pat Brace's murder and Matthew North's death—except the shock to Mr. North of learning his nephew was probably the murderer instead of the victim. And I feel sure my theory will be proved correct when the body is exhumed. I have an order and am making arrangements to have that done to-morrow. After that, there will be no doubt."

His words left me floundering again. What if, after all, Rush had been mistaken? The scar on Tony's leg was small; the body had been exposed to smoke and flame for five weeks; it would not be strange, after that, if the scar were invisible—or at least not easily discovered. We had no actual proof yet—except Ruth's word there was no scar on the body. We see largely what we expect to see, Thornberry had said. Rush had not expected to see Pat's body but he was so convinced Pat was dead, the idea might easily have influenced his judgment. The others had not questioned that it was Tony. It might be Tony. Hope and dread gripped me. I wanted to believe Tony alive, but hope mocked me with the fear of justice. To know the truth either way would be a relief.

I tried again to reason it out, but I could reach no conclusion. All the evidence pointed to Tony as alive and guilty. Yet I could more readily believe Pat the murderer. What, after all, are mere facts against one's knowledge of a person's character? But if Pat were guilty, Tony was dead. And I did not want to believe Tony dead. So whirled the grim merry-go-round of my thoughts, leaving me dizzy and unnerved.

XXIX
"A SHOT IN THE DARK"

Sheriff MacFarland brought Regina back that afternoon. There was a crowd around the courthouse. Some people had been waiting for hours.

I was in the sheriff's office with Regina's father, the lawyer he had brought, the district attorney, and Captain Thornberry and his assistant. Regina's father sat with his hand over his eyes like a man suffering physical pain. His face seemed almost as gray as his hair and his clothes. There were dark circles under his eyes.

The office was a big high-ceilinged room with tall narrow windows unwashed for years. The walls, above the dark wainscoting, were covered with dingy red paper, once disturbingly garish, now mercifully smoked and faded and half-hidden by ancient calendars and pictures of men wanted: "Reward—". I studied those hard faces when I was not watching at the window for the sheriff's car.

When at last the big touring car came down the street in a cloud of dust, everyone on the sidewalks stopped and turned. And people came out of the stores to look. I stood at the window watching. The car stopped in front of the courthouse instead of the jail. I was thankful for that. Sheriff MacFarland helped Regina out with as much courtesy as if he were escorting her to a ball, but his lower jaw was thrust out resolutely, and there was a forbidding look about his austere, weathered old face.

Regina came up the tree-lined stone walk between the rows of curious staring eyes. Her little tan hat was pulled low over her face, and, in spite of the warmth, she held the collar of her tan coat close about her chin. A man with a camera sprang out suddenly before her.

Regina ducked her head lower and shrank nearer to the sheriff. She stumbled a little on the stone steps, but MacFarland's grip on her arm saved her from falling.

I opened the door of the office. Regina came in wearily, no trace of emotion on her white face.

Her father took her in his arms. "Gina, Gina! Baby . . ." His voice was husky.

Regina said nothing. She kissed her father's cheek, held out a limp hand to me, and sank down in a chair. I had never suspected Regina of so much stubbornness, but there was obstinacy, quiet and immovable, written in every line of her face. Her brows were drawn together in a little frown; her small round mouth was pressed tight.

The attorney Regina's father had engaged drew his chair up beside her. He was a big homely man with thin sandy hair parted in the middle, a short nose, and an extraordinarily long upper lip which gave him a gloomy appearance, though, actually, he was a humorous sort of fellow. He was never excited; his voice was low and drawling. His name was Bob Darnley, and I had admired him since I was eight and he was fullback on the high school eleven, He was a good lawyer.

"Now, Regina," he began in his slow way, "maybe it'll be better if you refuse to answer any questions this afternoon. You're tired now, and it's easy to get mixed up on little things, and you might say something that could be twisted to mean something entirely different."

Regina nodded gravely.

Yeager, the prosecuting attorney, cleared his throat nervously. He was a kindly-faced man with soft, plump, wrinkled cheeks like an old woman's. He had known Regina all her life and seemed rather terrified at the idea of having her for a defendant, but determined to do his duty.

"It's always best to tell the truth, Regina," he advised sententiously. "As a matter of form, I got to warn you, anything you say may be used against you. But you've always been a good girl, Regina, and I hate to see you get into trouble trying to protect a man that ain't man enough to give himself up."

I felt myself growing warm at this insinuation that Tony was a coward as well as a murderer. Yet, I did not want Tony to give himself up. I wanted him to escape.

Regina's face went a shade paler. She twisted her gloves in her hands. Without looking up, she answered: "I've nothing to say."

"If you'll let me talk to Regina alone—" Bob Darnley began.

"Wait a minute," Yeager interrupted. "I'd like to see Regina cleared as much as you would. Why, man, I held her on my lap and let her listen to my watch before she could talk. And I ain't going to twist things she says to prove her guilty. You know that, don't you, Regina?"

Regina said: "Yes," faintly.

"But it's my duty to get at the truth," Yeager went on uncomfortably. "And it'd look better for Regina, too, if you'd let her talk now. When a person won't talk till after they see their lawyer, it always looks guilty."

"Guilty," Darnley drawled. "You know Regina's not guilty of anything."

"Then why won't you let her talk?" demanded Yeager.

"Well, I've got to do something to earn my fee," Darnley said dryly.

But I knew he was afraid Regina might involve herself too much. So did the others. No one smiled.

It was Thornberry who took charge of the situation. "Surely, Mrs. Brace will be willing to answer a few simple questions?"

At the sound of the unfamiliar, clear cut voice, Regina glanced up. Her gaze met Thornberry's, and I saw her greeny-gray eyes widen slightly as she sensed his challenging suspicion. Before she could say anything, Thornberry went on:

"There really isn't much you can tell us. We know you and Anthony Sheridan had been meeting at this unfinished house in the country and that your husband surprised you there. That's true, isn't it?"

Regina's gaze dropped. Her fingers writhed in her lap. Her voice was barely audible. "I don't want to say anything to-day."

Thornberry ignored her protest. "Where is Anthony Sheridan now?" he inquired, his narrowed gaze fixed upon her.

Regina's Lashes quivered. Under the narrow brim of the tan hat, her eyes darted to one side, but she did not look at the detective.

"Tony is dead," she said.

"I know that's what you wanted us to believe," Thornberry told her crisply. "And until yesterday, it's what we did believe. But we know now it was your husband who was murdered, and Anthony Sheridan who was the murderer."

By Regina's startled look, I knew Tony was alive.

Thornberry, too, realized he was on the right track, and pressed his advantage. "To-morrow the body will be exhumed and we'll have definite proof. So, you see, Mrs. Brace, your silence has been to no purpose. A murder charge has already been filed against your lover." Thornberry leaned forward, eyeing Regina narrowly. "Rush Sheridan has confessed that he knew the dead man was Pat Brace, but identified him as Anthony Sheridan to help his brother escape."

Regina's eyes met mine pleadingly. "Is that true?" she whispered. "Did Rush—?"

I nodded dumbly.

"Where is Anthony Sheridan now?" Thornberry repeated sternly.

"Don't let him frighten you," Bob Darnley murmured, drawing his long lip down. "If he's such a good detective, he can find that out, too."

Thornberry's cold blue eyes never left Regina's face. "Did you see Anthony Sheridan kill your husband? We have your lover's revolver and proof that the fatal bullet was fired from it."

"No, no; that isn't true! There must be some mistake!" Regina cried, startled out of her silence and sitting forward in her chair. "It couldn't be Tony's revolver. Tony didn't kill him."

"Then who did?"

Regina drooped in her chair again. Her voice was lifeless. "I don't know."

"Then how do you know Tony Sheridan didn't?"

"Because—he was with me."

"Did you see the shooting?"

"No."

"Then how do you know Tony Sheridan didn't do it?"

Bob Darnley leaned forward in his chair. "We aren't arguing the case to-day, Captain Thornberry," he drawled. "But since you don't seem able to figure it out, yourself, I might point out that if the murder was committed while Tony and Regina were together, she'd certainly know Tony didn't do it without knowing who did. That's simple enough."

"It's apparent you don't want your client to talk," Thornberry returned. "Perhaps you can explain away the fact that Anthony Sheridan's revolver was used."

"Well, of course, it's news to me about the revolver," said Bob Darnley thoughtfully. "But if it's true, I'd say that anybody wanting to kill Pat Brace could save his own skin easy enough by just using Tony's revolver and leaving it around handy like to be found because everybody in town knows that Tony and Regina have been sweethearts since they were kids."

"All very ingenious," was Thornberry's unsmiling comment. "Perhaps you'll be good enough to tell me who this mythical murderer is."

Darnley appeared to consider the question. "You've got me there," he admitted slowly. "I guess that part of it is up to you and the district attorney."

Regina straightened up, deliberately facing us all. She pushed back the little tan hat with an impatient gesture. One hand gripped her gloves tightly.

"It's true—what Bob Darnley said. That's just what happened. I don't know about the gun, but the rest of it—that's true."

Darnley made another effort to stop her, but she brushed aside his admonition.

"I can't say anything to hurt Tony now. He didn't do it, but everything was against us. We didn't know who did it. We knew Tony would be accused. So we ran away. I wanted to leave the country—there was time. But Tony wouldn't. He said he was going to get evidence to clear himself if it took the rest of his life. And I wouldn't go without him, because—because it was my fault—for meeting him. I knew it was dangerous—but I—I didn't think of—this—"

For a moment Regina faltered. She pressed her handkerchief tight against her quivering lips. Then went on, her gaze meeting Thornberry's unflinchingly.

"I had to talk to Tony. Pat had been acting so strangely, I was afraid. Sometimes he laughed suddenly to himself. Once I asked him what was funny, and he said: 'I was just wondering how old Matthew North would like something I have to show him.' Pat was working up a case against Mr. North, so I didn't think much about it till he began talking about running Haunted Mine and living in the North house.

I knew that his suit couldn't ruin Mr. North. Pat said when he took charge of Haunted Mine he'd put in a new fan. And once when I said I was going to leave him, he said: 'Wait; you won't want to marry Tony Sheridan when I get through with him.' Then one day I saw Pat loading a revolver. I warned Tony, but he said he wasn't afraid of Pat, and he wouldn't carry a gun.

"Then Friday, the day of the rehearsal, I found an alarm clock in the basement, back under the stairs. It was a brand new clock. I brought it up and asked Pat about it, and he said he didn't know how it came there, that it must've been there for years. But it hadn't. It wasn't even dusty. I was afraid Pat might be planning to blow up the mine—because he acted so queerly about the clock. After he left the house that evening, I looked in his chest of drawers—and the revolver was gone. I had to tell Tony. I had to make him realize his life was in danger. I tried to talk to him at the rehearsal, but we were interrupted. There was no place we could talk by ourselves except in the car or at Happy House."

"Do you know where your husband went that evening while you were at the rehearsal?" Thornberry interrupted.

"No," said Regina faintly.

"What time did he leave?"

"About eight o'clock."

"And what time did you and Anthony Sheridan leave the rehearsal?"

"About ten. We stopped by my house and got some coffee and bacon and cheese and crackers and some candles. Then we drove straight to our house—we still called it our house because Tony built it for me," Regina confessed a little tremulously. "We made a fire in the fireplace. And Tony drew some water—there's a pump in the yard—and put the coffee pot on. And I broiled the bacon on a stick."

"Was all this supper necessary to telling your troubles?" Thornberry inquired ironically. "It doesn't look as if you were very worried."

Regina caught her lip in her teeth. "Tony enjoyed it," she said apologetically. "It wasn't much supper. We ate with our fingers, and we just had one cup."

"Weren't you afraid your husband would return home and miss you?"

"Pat knew I intended going to the rehearsal, though he told me not to. I expected to be home by eleven-thirty. Our little fire had gone out. We were just ready to leave when—it happened. We heard a shot outside in the dark somewhere—not very loud. And I thought I heard a cry or a groan that seemed to end in a cough, but I wasn't sure. We were talking, I suppose. The sound just made me catch my breath—then it was all over."

XXX
"PAT HAD A GUN IN ONE HAND"

"We stood there a minute, just listening and looking at each other in the dim light," Regina went on. "There was only one candle burning on the mantel. Somehow the sound frightened me, coming out of the darkness and stillness like that. 'Was that a gun?' I asked Tony. He looked anxious, too. But he said: 'Maybe it was just a car backfiring.' I thought it sounded too near for that. And that cry seemed to be echoing in my ears, too. But I didn't say anything. Tony was frowning a little. He picked up my shawl from the window ledge and put it around me. Then he went to the door and looked out.

"I followed him, but he said: 'Don't come out yet. I'll just have a look out here.' He walked around the house. Everything was quiet now and still in the moonlight. 'The coast is clear,' Tony said when he came back. He stood at the bottom of the steps and smiled up at me. Then I heard something. I grabbed Tony's arm. 'Listen,' I whispered.

"What I heard sounded like the cracking of a dead branch—then another, as if someone were running through the wood. But it seemed to be on the other side of the ridge—it was very faint. Tony put his hands to his mouth and shouted: 'Hallo, who's there?' Nothing but the echo came back to us. Then we heard something else. A car started. The motor was raced a moment. Then the sound died away. 'I believe it was in our lane,' Tony said. He was thinking of Pat, I knew. 'Do you suppose he could have followed us?' I whispered. Tony shook his head. 'He wouldn't turn back,' he answered.

"I was really afraid now. 'I believe it was a shot,' I insisted. 'I think it came from the wood.' Tony started towards the path. I begged him not to go. 'It might be bandits,' I said. But he laughed. 'Maybe we'll find some buried treasure,' he said. 'At any rate, they've gone.' But I couldn't forget the cry I'd heard. I don't believe Tony had heard it, or he wouldn't have taken the matter so lightly. I ran back into the house and snatched up the little candle and followed Tony up the path.

"He stopped and waited for me. 'That's no sort of light to go treasure hunting with,' he said. 'You ought to have a lantern. And where's your pick and your chart?'

"Tony went ahead, thrusting some of the branches aside for me. I held my hand around the candle to keep the wind from blowing it out. Tony stopped suddenly. He was staring at something in the path before him. He motioned me back with one arm. 'Wait,' he said. 'Wait. Let me have that candle.' He half turned and took the candle out of my hand. 'You'd better go back,' he told me.

"But I'd already seen the form of a man lying there in the path, his feet towards us. 'I'm not afraid,' I said. Tony leaned over and held the candle close to the man's face. I saw it was Pat. His eyes were open, and a little stream of blood had run out the corner of his mouth. There was no need to see if he was dead. I started to scream. Tony dropped the candle and caught me."

Regina pressed her handkerchief tight against her lips again. Her eyes were wide with the horror of the scene she was reliving. In the silence of the sheriff's office, a blue bottle fly buzzed noisily at the top of one of the high windows. Presently Regina went on in a barely audible voice:

"But I didn't faint. I just kept whispering, 'What are we going to do? What are we going to do?' Even then I knew that Tony would be blamed for it. 'Do you think you can stand it while I look around a bit?' Tony asked. 'Or shall I take you home, first?' I told him I'd stay with him.

"Tony struck a match. The candle was too near gone to light again. We saw then that Pat had a gun in one hand. His fingers were gripped tight around it. We thought at first he'd killed himself. But Tony said: 'He's been shot in the back. He couldn't have done it, himself.' Tony picked up the gun and broke it. One shot had been fired. Tony said it had been fired recently because the barrel smelled of gun powder. We couldn't understand it; we hadn't heard but one shot. 'Why did he come here with a gun?' I asked. But I knew. 'Looks as if he meant to get me,' Tony muttered. 'But who stopped him?' I whispered.

"The wood about us was dreadfully quiet. The darkness began to frighten me. I felt as if some enemy were moving about in the shadows watching us, ready to kill us, too. Tony seemed to know what I was thinking, for he said: 'Never mind, there's no danger now. Whoever did it drove away. That was his car we heard. It might have been a stick-up. Some bandit followed him. You hold the gun.' Tony put the revolver in my hand. Then he struck another match and cupped it in his hand. Pat's pockets had been searched, we saw now. Some papers and letters and his pocketbook were lying beside him. But his watch was still in his pocket. Tony picked up the billfold. There was fifteen dollars in it.

"'It wasn't a bandit,' said Tony, 'but somebody was hunting for something. Look—' He picked up a little match half burnt. Tony had used nothing but big matches, and there were several of these little ones about. I couldn't understand it. Pat didn't have anything very valuable. I couldn't think of anything anyone would want except his money and his watch. 'It wasn't an ordinary thief, anyway,' Tony said: 'Let's see if there's any sign of him farther along. He must've followed Pat up the path.' Tony took the gun, and we went down the path on the other side of the ridge. But it was too dark to see anything. Only a little moonlight came through the trees.

"When we reached the road, there was Pat's car. He had driven it off the pavement and stopped near the path. I was glad to get out of the wood into the open. We walked back along the lane to the curve where we could see the house. But there was no sign of anybody. We stopped there bewildered, and not quite knowing what to do.

"Tony was worried. 'It looks bad—our being here,' he said. 'People will think I did it.' I knew it was true. But I tried to tell him no one would know we'd been there. 'Someone must know it,' Tony said, 'since Pat came here. Besides, we can't prove we weren't here when this happened. Pat came here with a gun. He must've meant to get me. If it weren't that his pockets have been searched, I'd think somebody followed and shot him to save me. But whether that's what happened or not, we're going to get the blame for it, Gina. Do you realize what that means? We'll be tried for murder.'

"I clung to Tony. I begged him to run away. I told him I'd go with him anywhere. 'It's about all that's left for us to do,' he said. And his voice sounded bitter and harsh. 'I don't know whether it was a friend of mine or an enemy who stopped Pat,' he said. 'But I know if it's proved we've been meeting here, our lives won't be worth thirty cents. But we'll need a few days start. You'd better go home in Pat's car and I'll come later.' He wanted me to take Pat's revolver, but I made him keep it. I wasn't afraid. I knew nobody would harm me now that—Pat was gone.

"Tony didn't tell me what he meant to do, but I guessed. He walked back to Pat's car with me. He told me to go home and throw a few things in a suitcase and he'd come a little later. 'And if you see anyone, you'd better say Pat left on the midnight train,' Tony told me. He looked at his watch. It was ten minutes of twelve. 'Drive slow,' he said, 'and go down through town and past the station, so it will be after midnight when you get home. Some of the neighbors might see you.'

"I did as Tony told me. When I reached home, Cappy was sitting on the steps waiting for me. He knew Pat was looking for Tony and me and was worried. I told him Pat wanted me to take him to the train, and, as soon as I could, I sent Cappy home. I packed a suitcase. It was nearly one when Tony came. He told me he'd buried Pat's body in the sand pile. 'It'll be safe there for a few days—maybe forever,' Tony said."

Regina closed her eyes and pressed her hand wearily to her forehead. She pulled off the close-fitting hat with a tired little gesture, and pushed back the hair from her face. Bob Darnley brought her a glass of water, and after a minute, she went on:

"Tony thought we'd better not leave that night after all. We'd need some money to go far, and it'd be better if we'd go separately, he said, instead of together. We'd meet somewhere. And before anyone was suspicious, we'd be safe in another country. Besides, if we should wait something might turn up, Tony said, and maybe we could find out who the murderer was and wouldn't have to sneak away. I thought he was right, though I wanted awfully to go at once. But we didn't have any money.

"We planned then for Tony to take the pay roll. Tony said Cappy always put it in the safe while he made out the envelopes. I went to the office the next morning. Tony gave me the money. I put it in my shopping bag and carried it home. I told people Pat had gone to the city. But I was nearly crazy with fear.

"Then the explosion came. In a way, it was a relief. People wouldn't pay any attention to me or wonder about Pat's absence. It would give Tony and me more time to find out who had killed Pat. I went to the mine for Tony that evening. He came home with me for supper, and told me he had a better plan. You know how he went down into the mine and disappeared. He had thrown a pair of overalls and a coat down the air shaft. And he had a beard Cappy was going to use in the play. We had stopped by Tony's house and he went in and got it and cut it off short. And he had some grease paint in his handkerchief and a little mirror he'd taken from Cappy's make-up box.

"Tony showed me the things while we ate supper, and he tried the beard on. He pulled the ends he had cut off out of his pocket and threw them in the trash box. Then I trimmed the beard a little more for him, so it looked better. He said it was becoming, and tried to joke about it. But I knew he was desperate.

"I was awfully afraid. But Tony told me there was no more danger than he'd already been in—not as much—because he could reach the air shaft in a minute or two, and once there he'd be safe because there's an air tight door to the emergency exit, and it's walled off separately from the rest of the shaft. While Tony waited at the bottom of the shaft, he made himself up and put on the overalls and the coat and pulled his cap down over his eyes. After the fan was shut off, Tony came up. He waited till Big Bill left, and walked out through the crowd.

"He came to my house and stayed there till Tuesday night. Sunday and Monday we went through all of Pat's things hunting for something that would give us a reason for the shooting. I went to Pat's office and searched his desk and files, but there was nothing. We had no idea who had killed Pat.

"We had to go through with our plan. And there was no time to lose because I knew the mine would soon be closed. Our principal difficulty was getting Big Bill away. We thought of giving him a sleeping potion, but I didn't know how to obtain the drug without a prescription, nor how much to give him. It might arouse suspicion, too, if Big Bill should guess what had happened. It was Tony who thought of the harmonica. Monday night I climbed Moon Mountain and played *Auld Lang Syne* very softly. Big Bill listened a few minutes, then started towards the sound. There were still a few people around the mine shaft that night waiting and hoping the fire would burn itself out. But nobody except Big Bill seemed to hear the harmonica, and I felt sure he wouldn't say anything.

"Tuesday night there was no one about the shaft. And it was the night of the memorial service, so it seemed the safest night we could choose. About nine o'clock I went to the North house and got Tony's car out of the garage. We had decided it would be better for me to do that because if Tony were seen, it would ruin everything, and if I were caught, I could say I was just borrowing it because my own car wouldn't run, and though Tony's family might be surprised, I knew nothing would be said.

"Tony was waiting for me on the Hill Road. He took the car and went on to Happy House. And I drove Pat's car down to the mine—that's why we needed both cars. I drove a mile or two up the valley past the mine and parked the car in a side road. Then I walked back and lured Big Bill away with the harmonica. I led him slowly along the stream and the foot of the hill back towards my car, taking as long as I could. When I reached the car, I drove back to town and out the Hill Road to Happy House, where I was to meet Tony.

"He was not there, and I was dreadfully afraid I had not kept Big Bill away long enough and that he, or somebody, had seen Tony. It seemed as if I waited hours, but I suppose it wasn't more than ten minutes before Tony came. He was rather shaky. I never saw him so all in before."

Regina paused, leaning her head over on her hand. She was silent so long that Thornberry asked: "How did he lower the body into the mine?"

Regina looked up, brushing the hair back from her forehead. "Big Bill had a bucket there he had used to let a mouse down. It was a big bucket on a windlass. Tony tied a little rope to the bottom of the bucket, so he could tip it when it reached the bottom. Tony was so unstrung when he got back to Happy House, he was actually trembling. He ran his car behind the house, and I heard him pumping water.

"Then he came over to me. I was sitting at the wheel of my car. Tony got in beside me and leaned his head over in his hands. That was when I saw he was trembling. I put my arms around him, and he said: 'God! why don't we wake up? Is this nightmare going to last forever?'

"He hardly spoke all the way to the city. I did the driving. Once when we stopped at a garage, Tony put on the beard so anyone who tried to trace us would be thrown off the trail. We went to a hotel in the city. I wanted to go on to New York the next day, but Tony wouldn't give up so readily. After a day or two he recovered some of his old spirit and began to talk about discovering the murderer and clearing himself.

"'If we go away now, it means living under a cloud the rest of our lives,' he said. 'There ought to be some way of finding out who killed Pat.' I begged him not to take the risk, but he said he wouldn't be beaten so easily. 'There won't be much risk,' he said, 'as long as everybody thinks I'm at the bottom of Haunted Mine.' He was so determined I didn't have the heart to oppose him. But I wish now I had."

Regina sighed and gazed down at her hands.

Thornberry said: "You haven't answered my first question yet." His voice was still cold. "Where is Anthony Sheridan now?"

"I told you I don't know," Regina repeated listlessly. "He went away. I haven't seen him since."

"Did he take the car?"

"Yes."

Sheriff MacFarland spoke up: "That funny looking car ought to be easy to trace."

"What about Mrs. North's diamonds?" Thornberry asked Regina. "You haven't explained how you happened to have them."

"They were sent to me in a parcel post package."

"Oh—and when did you receive them?" Thornberry inquired in a tone of disbelief.

"Yesterday morning."

"Just before you were arrested?"

"Yes."

"Did Anthony Sheridan send them to you?"

"I suppose so. The address was printed, and there was no return address. But no one except Tony knew where I was."

"Where was it mailed from?"

Regina hesitated. "From the city."

"A very remarkable story you've told, Mrs. Brace," Thornberry commented unsmilingly. He leaned back, stroking his little dimpled chin thoughtfully. "But it has one disadvantage. It isn't true."

Regina started. She flashed him a look of indignation, then seemed suddenly to wilt. "Tony said nobody would believe it. Oh, I wish I'd made him go!" Her fingers gripped the chair arms. "But you must believe it. It's true! There must be some way of proving it."

"It's just the sort of story a guilty person would tell— and does tell frequently," Thornberry went on, ignoring Regina's plea. "A story of a mysterious murderer whom nobody saw, and who, apparently, had no motive. In fact, the kind of story which is difficult to prove or disprove."

But I knew Regina's story was true. Tony was not a murderer.

XXXI
"A STEP ON THE STAIR"

It was dark when I left the courthouse, after having seen Regina led away by Sheriff MacFarland to the jail. I tried to put that scene out of my mind and keep my thoughts on the strange story Regina had told. Tony was not guilty. And yet without some tangible proof, he might be tried for murder—convicted even—sentenced—to what fate I dared not think.

I wandered out into the twilit streets trying to find some explanation for the murder. Pat had been killed for something he might have had with him—something that had more than a monetary value for the murderer. Vague ideas of secret organizations and stories of Bolshevism floated through my mind. Pat was radical in many of his ideas. Was it possible he had belonged to some revolutionary or communistic society that was planning to take control of the mines? Was that what he had meant when he talked of running Haunted Mine? It was not difficult to believe that Pat would join some such organization, especially in view of his hatred for us.

If Pat had had a part in any plot against us, he had not given it up or withdrawn, because he had talked of ruining us till the last. Why, then, had he been killed?

The idea of revolution brought my mind back to the alarm clock Regina had found. Was it possible that Pat had meant to plant a time bomb in the mine? But the alarm clock had not been used. But for that, I could almost believe that Pat was responsible for the explosion that occurred after his death. But he would not have been killed by members of his society unless he had been about to warn Tony or Uncle Matthew. And Pat had not relented to that extent. It was evident he had gone to Happy House with murder in his heart. His shooting of Dr. Ames proved that.

Though Tony was accused of murder, it was only that murder which had saved him from Pat's gun. And Pat, dying, had spared the life he had meant to take. I found some satisfaction, at least, in those thoughts.

But for what mysterious reason had Pat been killed? Perhaps he had overstepped the bounds of his organization, had been too zealous in his plans for revolution. But if he had, his attitude would not be so entirely secret. Someone would know he was a revolutionist. I put that possibility aside.

Had I not known Dr. Ames so well, I might have believed he had followed Pat that night after being wounded, and fired in revenge. It would have taken but a few minutes to reach Happy House; he could have driven there before he came to the drug store. But that was not in Dr. Ames' character. And Miss Dunlap had been with him, too. I checked off that theory also.

I remembered now that Pat's house had been searched. The murderer must not have found what he wanted in Pat's pockets. Perhaps he had not found it at the house, either. If I could find it—! The thought filled me with new hope. I should have searched before.

I hurried now towards the stone cottage. I had no key, but the catch on the dining room window was still loose, and I had no difficulty in lifting the sash. I threw one leg over the sill, pulled myself up and stepped into the darkened house.

I struck a match. Someone had been there since my last visit. The dining table and the chairs were shoved back against the wall, and the rug was rolled up. I was confident now the murderer had been here. If only I had thought to watch the place!

I had no idea what to search for, nor where to search. But if it was something which Pat might have carried in his pocket, it was something small. And since the mysterious visitor had looked even under the rugs, it must be something flat. It must be a paper of some kind,— perhaps a letter or a picture, I decided. And the places where such a thing could be concealed were innumerable. But the other searcher had saved me much trouble. The most obvious places had already been searched. I remembered that even the books in the living room had been disarranged. And Pat's room had been thoroughly explored even before my previous visit.

My match flickered out, and I found only one other in my pocket. The electricity had been cut off in the house since Regina's absence. I pushed open the kitchen door and struck the match on the range which I knew to be just to the right. I found a box of matches half full there on top of the stove, and beside it, a saucer with a candle stuck in it—one of those red Christmas candles. I lit it and looked about the room.

Even the kitchen had been searched. The things on the shelves had been piled up any old way. There was none of the prim orderliness Regina loved. Dirty dishes were stacked in the sink; empty tin cans were piled in a box in the corner. The intruder had been making himself at home.

I went into the hall, holding the candle high. The shadows danced around me, and fled back with every step. A draft whipped at the little flame. I cupped my hand around it, but too late. It flickered out.

Somewhere above a door was opened. I stood there a second paralyzed. Instinctively, I felt in my pockets for matches, then remembered I had used my last one as I entered the kitchen, and had neglected to take any more. I heard a step in the hall above me. Someone was feeling his way towards the stair. My first impulse was to run. But I could not hope to get out through the window without being heard. And if the man coming down the stairs were murderously inclined, he could put a bullet through me before I could cross the lawn. I seemed to feel I would have less chance in the open than here in the dark. Perhaps it is the instinct of the hunted animal to efface itself as nearly as possible, but fear numbs the legs and checks the breath, while the mind sometimes works with abnormal rapidity so that seconds seem like minutes, and a minute like ten.

I pressed myself back against the wall. My eyes strained through the darkness for a glimpse of the descending figure, but the impenetrable blackness was like a velvet curtain around me. The steps came slowly down the stairs.

Wild plans raced through my brain—plans for attacking this man and tripping him as he reached the bottom of the steps, for throwing myself upon him from behind, for hurling a chair at him and overpowering him in the dark—plans I discarded before he reached the bottom step. It would be better, I decided, to obtain a glimpse of the man's face, if possible, and escape with my life, than to risk everything in a fight with a man who was probably armed and desperate. I was sure it was Pat's murderer come here to continue his search for what he had failed to find on Pat. The fellow must've heard me. He was coming down to look for me. I could not hope to hide. If I was to escape, I would have to pretend ignorance of his errand. I might pretend to believe him an ordinary burglar, and might possibly speak to him of reform. I had excuse enough for being there, myself. I could say I had come for some things for Regina.

My life might depend on my wits now, I thought. I upbraided myself for not bringing a weapon, but was determined to see the fellow at any cost.

I cleared my throat. I tried to say: "Who's there?" but the words sounded dry and queer as if I had cotton in my mouth.

I heard a match scratched. I saw the yellow flame sheltered in the palm of a hand. The light flared up. And I saw Tony's face painted against the darkness.

"Tony!" I cried.

The match was dropped. The curtain of darkness fell between us. I heard Tony's startled: "Who's that?" He evidently had not heard me before.

I threw myself upon him.

"Tony, Tony!"

I felt his hands on my shoulders shaking me. His voice was muffled, but joyful.

"Cappy, Cappy, you old son-of-a-gun! What do you mean—scaring me like that?"

"Didn't you hear me come in?"

"No—must've dropped asleep."

"What are you doing here?"

"Hunting for evidence. Let's get a light. I went upstairs this afternoon and forgot to take a candle."

I put mine in his hand, and he lit it. In its dim glow we stared into each other's eyes. Tony's mouth twitched into that happy, one-sided smile he could not repress. He set the candle on the newel post and shook me again.

"Tony, they're hunting for you," I said.

He was instantly grave. "I know."

"You mustn't stay here."

"How much do you know about it, Cappy?"

"Everything you do. Regina told everything."

"Regina?"

"Yes; they brought her back to-day."

Tony gripped my arm. "You mean—she's been arrested?"

"Yes."

"I haven't seen a newspaper for a week," Tony said bewilderedly. "Where is Regina now?"

"In—jail." I couldn't meet his eyes.

"Then I've got to go," said Tony determinedly. "I'll give myself up."

"That wouldn't help Regina—it would only make it harder for her," I pleaded. "They don't believe her story. They think you killed Pat. You can't give yourself up without some proof of your innocence. Don't you know who did it?"

Tony shook his head, then answered slowly: "I know more than I did when I came back here. I know—" he broke off. "Have you noticed Uncle Matthew lately—has he been acting strangely, I mean."

"Uncle Matthew died last night," I told him. The memory came back to me with a fresh shock now, as I thought of his death for the first time since I had entered the house.

"Died? How?"

"He took an overdose of sleeping powders."

"On purpose?"

I hesitated a moment, dreading to add to Tony's worries, before I answered truthfully. "I think so. But Aunt Addie doesn't know it. You mustn't feel responsible, though," I hurriedly assured him. "I don't think Uncle Matthew believed you did it—not even with all the proof the detectives seemed to have. It was just the worry and uncertainty that made him do it. And you couldn't help that."

Tony didn't seem to hear. He was silent a minute. Presently he asked: "Did Uncle Matthew tell you he was searching Pat's things?"

It was my turn to be surprised. "Here?"

Tony nodded. "I've been staying here off and on most of the time. I left the car—Pat's Tiger—in the barn of an old abandoned farm on the other side of the hill. I walk over the hill at night and come here. One night I found Uncle Matthew upstairs going through Pat's clothes."

"But why? What did he want?"

"He said he was looking for evidence against Pat's murderer."

"But how did he know it was Pat who was killed? Why did he come here at night? Why didn't he tell Rush and me?"

"He said he recognised the body as Pat's and knew I must be alive, but he didn't think I'd killed Pat, so he was hunting for something to show who Pat's enemies were." There was disbelief in Tony's voice.

"Do you think he was looking for something else?" I asked, dazed by the new vista that opened up before me and not daring to put my fears into words. "Do you think Pat had something Uncle Matthew wanted?"

Tony shrugged. He lighted a cigarette from the candle flame and sat down on the steps.

"Where was Uncle Matthew that night—the night it happened?" he asked.

"He followed Pat because Pat had come to the house looking for Regina and you," I answered. "The sedan was just turning out of the drive when Aunt Addie and I came home from the rehearsal."

"How long was Uncle Matthew gone?"

"I'm not sure. He got home before I did, but—" I remembered how Aunt Addie had scolded and questioned him—"he must've been away about an hour. Aunt Addie didn't like his being out so late. He'd been drinking, too."

Tony looked up with a puzzled frown. "Had he been drinking much?"

"He was just a little drunk."

"Did you ever see him like that before?"

"No. But—" I forced myself to say it—"you don't think Uncle Matthew had anything to do with—Pat's death?" I felt myself guilty of ingratitude and disloyalty in saying it even to Tony.

"Where was he all that time?" Tony countered. "He wasn't used to driving around in the middle of the night. He started out to follow Pat—"

"Uncle Matthew said he turned back when he saw Pat was going towards the Townsends'. And Pat went that way, I know. I met him coming down the hill. I suppose he just drove by the Townsends', then he went by the mine and shot Dr. Ames."

"But if Uncle Matthew started to follow Pat," Tony persisted, "why would he turn back? He wouldn't drive about aimlessly for nearly an hour."

"He passed here once—while I was hunting for you and Regina."

"Maybe he thought of coming in then," Tony pondered, "but couldn't because you were here. Was that long after you saw Uncle Matthew leave the house?"

"Just a few minutes."

"Then it must've been before the murder. Which way was he going?"

"Away from town."

"If Pat drove out to the Townsends' and by the mine, too, Uncle Matthew would have time to reach Happy House first. There are places along the lane where he could run his car into the brush so it would not be seen. And if he hid in the thicket, he could watch both the lane and the path, so he could get Pat either way, whether he drove up to the house or walked over the ridge. Uncle Matthew must've seen our light in the house and realized he'd have to get it over with before Pat could reach the clearing."

"But you can't be serious," I protested, shocked. "Uncle Matthew's been almost like a father to us. He's no kin to us—except through marriage—but we ought to be that much more grateful for all he's done for us. And now he's dead—"

"We mustn't let gratitude and sentiment blind our eyes to facts," Tony answered, his voice hard. "Pat was killed on the path over the ridge. He must've been trying to slip up on Regina and me. But the murderer was there ahead of him—waiting for him, not following him as I supposed at first."

"Why are you so certain?"

"Nobody but an Indian—and a good, old-fashioned, storybook Indian at that—could follow over a rough path like that without being heard—you know how dead leaves rustle underfoot. He'd have to follow pretty close, too. The path is crooked, and the undergrowth thick, and it was night. The murderer couldn't have been more than a few feet away when he fired. And yet the bullet caught Pat squarely in the back, showing Pat had no idea of the fellow's presence behind him. So I think it's safe to assume the murderer was there first, waiting."

I nodded. That part seemed clear.

"But there were very few people who knew of that path," Tony went on. "It was almost overgrown and not visible at all from the road because it slants down through the thicket on that side. A stranger would never find it at night."

"Bandits might've used the place for a rendezvous," I offered weakly.

"Suppose a stranger did know about the path then," Tony conceded. "Who could've known Pat would come to Happy House that night? Nobody except Uncle Matthew who told him about it, and Rush, who overheard his threat. And I can't quite imagine Rush as a murderer."

"But I can't believe Uncle Matthew—"

"Oh, I know it's a shock," Tony interrupted. "I tried not to believe it, myself, at first. But you can't get away from it. Why do you think Uncle Matthew gave me Aunt Addie's diamonds and urged me to leave the country?"

"Did he do that?"

"The night I found him here, he said he was interested only in saving me. He advised me to run away, take Regina and go to South America or somewhere. He said I'd need more money, and he wanted me to take my inheritance now. He urged me to take the diamonds— he said that would be the most convenient form to carry it in if I wanted to disappear. And why do you think he kept quiet about the pay roll? He pretended it was through kindness, but Uncle Matthew isn't so generous and forgiving as all that—he'd be a fool if he was. He *wanted* me to get away—don't you see? I should've seen through him at the time, but I was so relieved, I didn't think about his motive. But when he urged me to run away—"

"When did he give you the diamonds?" I asked.

"Tuesday night I went to the house, and he gave them to me."

"I saw you crossing the lawn as you left," I put in.

Tony nodded. "I didn't want the diamonds for myself. But I intended to hire a good detective to investigate if I didn't uncover something pretty soon, and I'd need money for that. So I took the diamonds and put them in a box and mailed them to Regina for safe keeping."

"From here?"

"Yes; I dropped them in a mail box that night. Did Regina get them all right?"

"Yes; she said they were mailed from the city."

Tony smiled wistfully. "Good girl. She didn't want anyone to guess I was here, of course. I intended writing her a letter to-night and asking her to get some good detective we could trust to take the case. But I suppose it's too late now."

"No; it isn't. We won't stop till we find—"

Tony interrupted me with: "Uncle Matthew is dead now. And I think he's the only one who could tell us about it—"

"We mustn't be too certain yet," I protested, fighting against the growing conviction that Tony was right.

XXXII
"PAT KNEW HOW TO MAKE NITRO GLYCERIN"

"Pat had been boasting recently to Regina that he would own Haunted Mine and make beggars of us all," Tony went on.

"I know—"

"You remember Pat always said Haunted Mine should be his, that Uncle Matthew had cheated his father out of it, and that his father was always hunting for some evidence—some papers or something that would prove it."

"Yes," I admitted reluctantly, "but that was so long ago. Later Pat looked it up and satisfied himself that all was legal. He saw the papers himself at the courthouse. He told Uncle Matthew so. What could it be?" I was almost as loath to believe Uncle Matthew guilty as I had been Tony. "Uncle Matthew simply foreclosed the mortgage," I argued.

"I don't know what it could be," Tony said. "But since I've been in the office, I've seen things that have worried me. That deal that ruined Regina's father, for instance. I think Uncle Matthew could've supplied the coal at that price, and I believe he intended to—until—" Tony hesitated, frowning.

"You don't mean that Uncle Matthew gave his word and then—changed his mind? You don't think Uncle Matthew did that—went back on his word—because coal went up and he saw a chance to make a bigger profit?" I demanded indignantly.

"I don't know. Uncle Matthew said he'd lose money if he delivered the coal—but it wouldn't have broken us. I tried to believe him then—he said he couldn't do otherwise. But Pat said Baker gave Uncle Matthew a cash deposit on the deal—to bind the contract.

Uncle Matthew denied it, and I believed him, of course. But now—I don't know what to think. That case hasn't anything to do with this, of course—except it started me to wondering.

"Regina said Pat brought up a box of old books from the basement about a month before he was killed—books that had belonged to his father. And it was since then that Pat had become so confident of ruining us. What if he found something—the paper his father was always looking for—in one of those books? What if he had found proof of some crooked deal, whether it had anything to do with the mine or not, that would send Uncle Matthew to the penitentiary? What if he saw an opportunity to blackmail Uncle Matthew?"

"Have you looked in the books?" I asked.

"I've looked between all the leaves of every book in the house," Tony answered.

"Had Uncle Matthew looked through them before?"

"I don't know. If he did, he didn't find what he wanted because it was only a few nights ago I found him upstairs."

"Let me see the books now."

I carried the candle into the living room, and Tony followed. The books were ranged in straight, even ranks now; none was upside down.

"You always liked everything neat and orderly, didn't you?" I questioned. "These books weren't like that when you came, were they?"

Tony frowned thoughtfully. "Now that you mention it, I believe they were rather scattered about and piled up."

"Someone had searched them before." I told Tony of my previous visit to the house.

Tony nodded. "It sounds like Uncle Matthew all right. You know how sloppy he always was. Aunt Addie always had to hang up his clothes, and his desk looked like a cyclone had struck it. He couldn't put anything back straight."

"Still, that isn't much proof," I objected.

"It shows we're on the right track, though," argued Tony. "Uncle Matthew wasn't hunting merely for evidence against Pat's enemies. He knew what he was looking for—he was hunting for something definite."

"But both of us came here hunting, too," I pointed out.

"Why did you come to-night?"

I told him how I arrived at the conclusion that the murderer had searched the house after failing to find what he wanted on Pat.

Tony said: "That's what I hoped had happened. But you didn't think of that until after you heard Regina's story. And Uncle Matthew never heard it. How did he know that Pat might have something of importance?"

I could not answer him.

Tony dropped into a chair. "You say Pat had been to our house looking for Regina and me. Queer he'd look for us there." Tony pondered the problem. "Who saw him?"

"Only Uncle Matthew. But Rush heard him." I repeated all that Rush had told me.

"How long did Pat stay in the library with Uncle Matthew?"

"I don't know exactly. I believe Rush said 'a long time'. I imagine it was about half an hour."

"And Pat was there before Rush came home, so he might've been much longer with Uncle Matthew. They surely weren't talking about Regina and me all that time."

"Uncle Matthew said he was trying to persuade Pat not to do anything rash."

"But if Pat started out to murder me that evening, why did he go to our house first? It isn't customary to notify a victim's relatives before the shooting," Tony countered wryly. "I don't believe Pat had that gun for me at all. He might've told Regina he was going to get me to frighten her. But I don't believe Pat even thought of looking for Regina and me till Uncle Matthew told him we were at Happy House. Of course he blew up then. But how did Uncle Matthew know?"

"He said he saw your car turn into the lane there one night."

"He may have," Tony admitted. "But he couldn't have known we were there that night because we didn't think of it ourselves till after we left the rehearsal. It's possible Uncle Matthew told Pat that without knowing anything just to get him out in the country—"

"But Rush said Uncle Matthew was begging Pat not to go," I interrupted hurriedly. "Uncle Matthew begged him to wait."

"Don't you see?" said Tony in a tortured voice. "Don't you see it would only make Pat more anxious and worried, more determined to go?"

"You don't think Uncle Matthew did it for that purpose?"

Inwardly I rebelled against the thought. It seemed treacherous to accuse Uncle Matthew of such cunning and duplicity after all he had done for us. And yet, the idea, once started, went on gathering momentum and substance, like a snowball rolling downhill, till it seemed impossible to escape it. Every detail seemed to cling to it and add to its hideous weight. I searched for some circumstance that would refute it. But I could remember only that Uncle Matthew had given Tony the diamonds and urged him to leave the country. It looked as if Uncle Matthew had not wanted Tony to tell his story. Then another memory crept unbidden into my mind, like the shadow of a dark cloud. The memory of Rush's words: "Uncle Matthew came upstairs. He looked into Tony's room . . . and went down again hurriedly. . . ." I heard Rush saying that again. Rush had supposed that Uncle Matthew was looking for Tony, wanting to make sure Tony was not at home before following Pat. But in the light of this new theory, the action took on a sinister significance. Uncle Matthew, for the past few years, had disliked climbing stairs and never did it when it could be avoided. He would not have gone upstairs to see if Tony were there—he would have called. He had not gone on to his own room. He had looked into Tony's room and hurried downstairs again.

I told Tony about it. But he only looked at me blankly.

"What do you make of that?" he asked.

I had forgotten that Tony had not read the newspapers recently, and it had been only two days since Thornberry had made the discovery.

"Pat was killed with your revolver," I said, "the nickel-plated thirty-eight."

Tony sprang to his feet. "That settles it. I wish we'd never found out. It clears me—but at what a price! Poor Aunt Addie—if only we could keep it from her. But we may as well face it ourselves, Cappy. Uncle Matthew killed Pat."

I couldn't answer.

Tony was walking up and down the room excitedly. "The thing we must find out is why Pat went to see Uncle Matthew. Pat went there with a gun. He must've threatened Uncle Matthew." Tony turned suddenly. "Did Regina tell you about the alarm clock? Do you think Pat could've caused the explosion with a time bomb?"

"But he didn't use the alarm clock," I pointed out.

"He might've used something else. He might've bribed someone to cause it. It's queer—its happening the day after Pat was killed. Do you think he used that as a threat to get something out of Uncle Matthew? 'Pay me or I'll blow up the mine'—that sort of thing. Maybe he forced Uncle Matthew to sign a deed giving Haunted Mine to him, and Uncle Matthew followed him to get it back. I believe that's it, Cappy! I believe that's it! But Uncle Matthew didn't find it—deed or money or whatever it was—because he was still searching for it the other night. That means we've got a chance to find it. But first—let's see if there's anything else under the steps where Regina found the alarm clock."

Tony led the way to the basement, shielding the candle from the draft with one hand. Leaning over he held the candle low in the dark angle under the steps. Nothing was visible at first. Then as Tony moved the candle, the light was reflected from something shiny. I found a broom and swept it out. It was a little vial, quite fresh and new in appearance. Tony picked it up and held the label close to the candle flame.

"Nitric acid!" he exclaimed. "See what else you can fish out."

I ran the broom under the lowest step. Another small vial and a bottle, slightly larger, slid out.

"Sulphuric acid and glycerin," Tony predicted before he picked them up. Then as he glanced at the labels: "Right. Pat knew how to make nitro glycerin."

"He couldn't have made much." The little vials were still half full.

"It wouldn't take much," said Tony grimly. "A match would cause an explosion in some parts of the mine. Pat probably intended just to start the fire. He knew there'd be some real explosions before long with so much fire-damp. He must've put his time bomb in the mine the day before."

"He couldn't have done that," I objected. "Pat was killed more than twelve hours before the explosion."

"Right," agreed Tony. He stood up, looking at the little bottles in his hand. He nodded thoughtfully. "Pat wouldn't need the alarm clock. He decided not to use it, I guess—afraid it would be found. He just put a little more nitro around in the workings somewhere, knowing it would be exploded sooner or later. He wouldn't have any trouble going into the mine. He probably said he wanted to see some-body—"

"Pat was down in the workings the day before the explosion," I remembered suddenly. "Big Bill said he was snooping around asking questions."

Tony nodded. He thrust the bottles in his pocket. "But what hap-pened between Pat and Uncle Matthew that night? What is it Uncle Matthew was hunting for? If we can only find that now, we'll have proof enough—"

"But if it's money, we can't prove where Pat got it," I reminded Tony.

"I don't think it was money," Tony said. "Uncle Matthew wouldn't have much cash with him, and he didn't give Pat the diamonds. A check wouldn't do because Uncle Matthew could stop payment on that."

"A deed could be set aside, too, if Uncle Matthew was forced to sign it at the point of a gun," I added. "It wouldn't be any good any-way unless it were acknowledged before a notary—Pat would know that."

"But maybe he thought he could make Uncle Matthew acknowl-edge it the next day," Tony argued. "What if Uncle Matthew were afraid to complain—to tell? Whatever Pat obtained, whatever he did, he knew he was safe. Pat wouldn't be fool enough to threaten Uncle Matthew and obtain a signature or anything else, unless he knew he could get away with it. He'd been planning this thing for weeks. He waited for a night when Uncle Matthew would be alone in the house. He must've waited till Hilda left, too. He knew she and Ezra couldn't hear anything from their rooms over the garage. If Rush hadn't hap-pened to go home early, we wouldn't have known how long Pat was shut up in the library with Uncle Matthew, nor that Uncle Matthew went to my room before he left," Tony finished grimly.

We were in Regina's living room again now. I glanced around for a possible hiding place of the thing which Uncle Matthew—or the murderer—had sought. I couldn't yet concede the two were the same. I tried to put the growing dread out of my mind and think only of saving Tony. My joy in seeing him again was dulled by the ever present fear that the sheriff or one of his men would find us here.

It was fortunate after all that Thornberry had not believed Regina's story; for if he had, he might have reasoned that if Tony was searching for evidence to clear himself, he had returned to Genesee and was probably hiding in Regina's house. At any rate, no one came while we were there, though we were listening constantly for the ring of the bell or a peremptory pounding at the outer door.

"You'd better go back to your abandoned farm," I told Tony. "I'll stay here and hunt."

"But where are you going to look?" Tony asked. "I've turned the house upside down, and so did Uncle Matthew, I expect."

I remembered the pictures all awry and the rumpled rugs I had seen on my first visit. Uncle Matthew must have made a thorough search.

"I'll tear the house down if necessary," I declared.

Tony smiled crookedly. "Pat didn't have time to tear up the floors or rip open the upholstery. He couldn't have been in the house but a minute or two after he left Uncle Matthew if you met him at the foot of the hill. He just came in to see if Regina was here, I suppose. If he didn't have the papers on him when he was killed, he must've dropped them in some convenient place near the door. That's the conclusion I reached after I suspected he'd got something from Uncle Matthew. Before that I just hunted blindly—but I've looked everywhere except behind the wall paper, and I can't find anything. I'm beginning to think Regina must've thrown it out—whatever it was."

"But if Pat came by the house to see if Regina were here, I don't believe he'd stop or come in at all," I reasoned. "He'd just see there were no lights and drive on. Regina wasn't fond of going to bed early, and Pat knew she intended going to the rehearsal, so, most likely, he'd think she hadn't come home yet. Besides, Aunt Addie had just told him Regina might've gone to her mother's."

"And if Pat didn't come into the house at all, where would the papers be?" Tony pondered.

"Have you looked in the car? Maybe he stuck them under the seat," I suggested.

Tony stared at me a moment. "Good boy!" he exclaimed softly. "Let's go!"

XXXIII
"THE OLD PROPHECY HAD BEEN FULFILLED"

Tony and I trudged over the hill together. Though I had had no sleep the night before, I was too excited to notice any weariness. After half an hour of rough going we reached the deserted farm tucked away in a little upland valley. The tired old house leaned quietly to one side as if it were about to lie down. The roof of the barn had already collapsed, but the walls, relieved of that burden, rose gauntly erect.

Tony removed the prop that held the door in place, and we passed into the grass-grown, walled enclosure that had once been a large barn. There was Pat's old racing car fender high in wheat and grass and looking curiously out of place. In one corner Tony had improvised a shelter with loose boards placed across the joists above.

The high grass swished about our legs as we strode towards the car. Tony lifted the seat while I held the candle we had brought. And there, under the cushion, was a long white envelope, unsealed.

Some folded sheets of paper and a smaller envelope slipped out into Tony's palm. He spread out the papers in the yellow haze of the candle. The first two proved to be deeds, which, stripped of their legal terms, assigned Haunted Mine and our house to Patrick Dallas Brace. They had been signed by Uncle Matthew but not acknowledged. The third was headed "Confession". It was dated July 14th, the day Pat was killed. The white surface of two sheets was covered with Uncle Matthew's thin spidery writing.

Our eyes raced down the lines, then, still uncomprehending, moved more slowly through the words fraught with strange meanings.

To WHOM IT MAY CONCERN: (Uncle Matthew had written)
Being advanced in years and nearing the end of my
allotted span, I desire to make restitution, insofar as I
am able, for my crimes.

In 1903 I wilfully and knowingly defrauded Dallas
Brace out of the property known as Haunted Mine. I
agreed to make Dallas Brace a loan of $10,000.00 at
10% interest for a term of three years, taking as security a mortgage on the property. But, unknown to
Dallas Brace, I made the mortgage and the note out
for three months instead of three years. Dallas Brace
believed me his friend and trusted me; and, being an
unsuspecting person, he signed the papers, as I expected, without reading them carefully. It was during
the panic, and I knew that Brace could not borrow the
money elsewhere on short notice to repay me. And I
knew he could not receive any income from the mine
until the following winter.

Dallas Brace was not aware of the trick I had
played on him until he received notice of the foreclosure. He filed suit against me, but when the case
came to trial Brace admitted he could produce no
evidence.

I had known Dallas Brace at school, and, in order that any accusations he might make against me
should be discounted, I circulated the report that, as
a boy, he had been called Mad Dal Brace and was not
altogether responsible for what he did or said, with
the result, as I hoped, that his complaints met with
laughter and he soon became silent. I even went so far
as to tell his wife that Dallas Brace had often showed a
strain of insanity. His suicide, a year later, seemed to
bear out my statement. And whatever Mrs. Brace had
heard about the deal, she was apparently too much in
doubt to attempt any action.

For many years I have lived in security, but now,
being in mortal fear of damnation, I hereby confess

the greatest of my crimes and make what amends I can by restoring the property to its rightful owner, Patrick Brace, son and heir of Dallas Brace. May God have mercy on my soul for the suffering I have caused, the lies I have told and for the death of Dallas Brace.

Matthew North.

Tony's gaze met mine as we finished the strange document. The hot dripping from the candle ran down on my hand. I hardly noticed it, but mechanically I stuck the candle on the fender of the car and sat down on the running board. For a minute we were silent. My first thought was for Tony.

"You're safe now—you've nothing to fear."

Tony said: "We must go tell Regina."

"It doesn't seem possible yet," I muttered, slashing at the grass.

"Why did Uncle Matthew write it then?"

"Pat threatened to kill him. He had to write it to save his life," I defended.

"Uncle Matthew didn't make any outcry or resistance," Tony pointed out. "Rush was in the house, remember. He would've known. Uncle Matthew was afraid even to raise his voice—afraid of the penitentiary."

Tony was fumbling with the little envelope. He held it close to the candle, bending over to examine the faded address. "This is postmarked April 7, 1903!" he announced excitedly. "It's addressed to Dallas Brace—and from Uncle Matthew!"

I was beside him, bending over the yellowed slip of paper. It, too, was in Uncle Matthew's thin, angular writing. We read:

Dear Dal:

Replying to your request for a three-year loan of $10,000.00 on Haunted Mine, will state that I am able to make it and glad to accommodate you. I regret that I must ask for 10% interest; but that is the rate everyone is getting here, as you are no doubt aware. Money is tight now, and it is probable interest rates will go even higher.

But I suppose in three years you will be mining thousands of tons and well on your way to becoming a millionaire and able to pay me off with any amount of interest. I have heard you are making some great improvements in the mine and are going to open up a new vein. And here am I struggling along trying to sell real estate and saving my pennies. But you always did have big ideas, Dal, and I wish you all the success in the world.

Well, if you want the loan, come down to the city any day next week, and I'll have the papers ready for you to sign.

How is the young future president? A boy named Pat ought to make as good a fighter and rough rider as Teddy. Give my regards to Mrs. Brace.

Yours sincerely,

Matthew North.

Tony and I were silent as he folded the letter and put it back in the envelope. We were thinking of that treacherous bit of artifice of so long ago that had led to three deaths, Dallas Brace's, Pat's and Uncle Matthew's.

"That was the evidence Pat's father couldn't find," I mused. "He didn't think of keeping the letter when he received it, of course. And three months later he couldn't find it. But he remembered Uncle Matthew had written promising a loan for three years. Where do you suppose it's been all these years?"

"Probably between the pages of one of those books Pat brought up from the basement a few weeks ago."

"I can understand Pat's hatred and bitterness now," I said. "He knew there was some irregularity, though he didn't know just what. If his mother knew, she probably thought it useless to tell; she might've been afraid Pat would brood over it as his father had done." I was sorry for Pat now, hot-tempered, rebellious, embittered Pat, succeeding at last in righting a wrong, only to pay for triumph with his life. "And we thought it was all jealousy and envy," I said.

"Because Uncle Matthew impressed that on us when we were little."

"Do you think Uncle Matthew realized what a terrible thing he had done and that all these recent troubles sprang from that old crime?" I asked, still rather shaken.

Tony shook his head. "He thought it was just hard luck, I believe, and that fate was against him."

I remembered how Uncle Matthew had told me that he had been in some hard places and forced to do things he didn't want to.

"I imagine he had pretty well succeeded in forgetting just how he had obtained Haunted Mine," Tony continued. "Some people have that trick of fooling themselves—seeing only what they want to see and remembering only what they want to remember."

"He must've put in a few bad minutes, though, when Pat showed up with that letter and threatened to ruin him and send him to the pen probably," I reflected. "That's what broke him and aged him so— writing that confession—that and the things Pat must've said to him."

"But Uncle Matthew had a lot of fight left in him yet. He knew that if he let Pat get away with those papers, he was done for. Pat could force him to acknowledge those deeds—or send him to the pen. Pat would probably do both. His hatred wouldn't be appeased with just the property. Uncle Matthew saw ruin and prison staring him in the face. His only chance was to destroy that old letter. He was quick-witted, too, to think of telling Pat to look for Regina and me at Happy House. All the time Uncle Matthew was writing, he must've been planning how he could trap Pat, kill him if necessary, and get the confession and the letter. It's lucky for me Pat thought to hide the envelope in the car. And yet, I'd almost rather take my chance with a jury than—know this."

"But why would Pat try to blow up the mine when he had this letter?" I asked. "That seems to be threat enough."

"I suppose he wanted to make doubly sure," Tony said.

"I don't believe Uncle Matthew knew anything about that," I said. "If Pat had threatened to blow up the mine, Uncle Matthew surely wouldn't let the men go down—he wasn't that inhuman."

Tony picked up the cushion and was about to replace it in the car, when he suddenly exclaimed: "What's this?"

He picked up a small sheet of paper torn from a notebook. It had been folded in a neat little packet and tucked down behind the seat. On it Pat had scrawled in pencil:

> Waiting outside Matthew North's house for the servant to go to bed. There's a chance old North might get the better of me yet, old as he is. He may keep a gun handy for some of the men he's cheated who might want revenge. So I'm leaving this note. If anything happens to me, ask Matthew North about it. If he puts up a fight or tries to take the letter away from me, I can manage him. This afternoon I smeared a little nitro over the face of the coal in the lower level. The cutting machines will get to it in a day or two. And nobody can find it except me. I guess that will bring old North around if he tries to get rough. If everything turns out as I've planned, I'll go down and remove it to-morrow morning first thing. If not—it's my last word to Matthew North.
>
> Pat Brace.

"Pat's last gesture of defiance," Tony commented. "He did things thoroughly. I don't suppose he told Uncle Matthew about the nitro— he was holding that in reserve in case Uncle Matthew tried to destroy the letter or call for help. Then Pat would say: 'If you do that or if any harm comes to me, Haunted Mine will be blown up to-morrow. Nobody can save it except me.' Only a thin film of nitro glycerin over the coal would cause an explosion when the cutting machine struck it. And any kind of explosion would start a fire. The men who could tell how it started were trapped down there, and, but for this, we'd never be sure it wasn't an accident."

But the old prophecy had been fulfilled, and Pat, rightful owner of Haunted Mine, had lain cold and dead in its black depths.

EPILOGUE

"It all seems like a nightmare, and we're going to forget about it, aren't we?" The words were meant to include Rush and me, but Tony looked only at Regina.

He drew her closer to him on the couch and tousled the silky ash blond hair.

"Tony!" she reproved. "I'd better go see how Aunt Addie is."

"No, you don't. Wait a minute."

Aunt Addie, for all her self-control and calm, had collapsed under the shock of the news which could not be kept from her. In a few weeks her hair had turned white and her eyes had taken on a haunted, staring look. Dr. Ames had said we must keep her interested in something if her reason was to be saved. And Regina it was who had done the most for her.

Regina had whispered to her: "Tony and I want to be married in November and go south for our honeymoon. We haven't told anybody yet but you because we can't go unless you are better."

And now Aunt Addie was beginning to improve.

Regina tried again to rise, but Tony pulled her down beside him and shamelessly took a kiss from her little round mouth.

Rush, lolled back in his chair, legs stretched out in front, remarked lazily to the ceiling: "I thought this was to be a business meeting."

"Get on with your business then," Tony returned, "but don't expect us to listen to you."

Rush drew in his legs and sat up. "Since Regina is Pat's sole heir, and Haunted Mine was rightfully his, I thought we'd better deed it to her." He took a paper from his pocket.

"Then you can just tear up your deed," Regina returned. "There's enough for all of us, isn't there, Tony?"

"Yes, dear. What did you say?" Tony answered.

Rush shrugged. "You can fight it out between you. But—there's another thing—" he hesitated, frowning down at his shoes. "I wonder if you could get along without me at the office? I wonder if there'll be enough—income—for me to study music? You see—Norma thinks I'd do better with music than the law. And I've always wanted to have a try at it—for a while anyway—composing, you know."

"Norma's right," Regina agreed.

Rush's dark eyes flashed her a grateful look.

"The Professor shall have his music lessons," Tony declared. "Cappy can go back to school. I'll run the mine. I'm the head of the family now. And I'll be obeyed." He took Regina's chin in his hand. "Do you understand that, Mrs. Anthony Sheridan?"

COACHWHIP PUBLICATIONS
COACHWHIPBOOKS.COM

THE
RUMBLE
MURDERS

Henry Ware Eliot, Jr.

COACHWHIP PUBLICATIONS
COACHWHIPBOOKS.COM

ANONYMOUS FOOTSTEPS | JOHN. M. O'CONNOR

COACHWHIP PUBLICATIONS
COACHWHIPBOOKS.COM

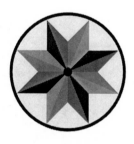

THE HEX MURDER

Alexander Williams

COACHWHIP PUBLICATIONS
COACHWHIPBOOKS.COM

COACHWHIP PUBLICATIONS
COACHWHIPBOOKS.COM

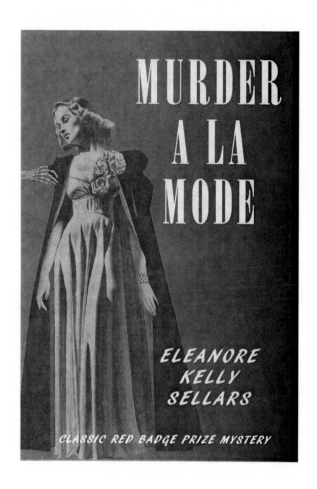

MURDER
A LA
MODE

ELEANORE
KELLY
SELLARS

CLASSIC RED BADGE PRIZE MYSTERY

COACHWHIP PUBLICATIONS
COACHWHIPBOOKS.COM

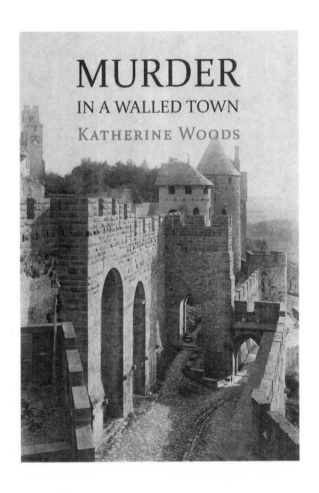

MURDER

IN A WALLED TOWN

KATHERINE WOODS

COACHWHIP PUBLICATIONS
COACHWHIPBOOKS.COM

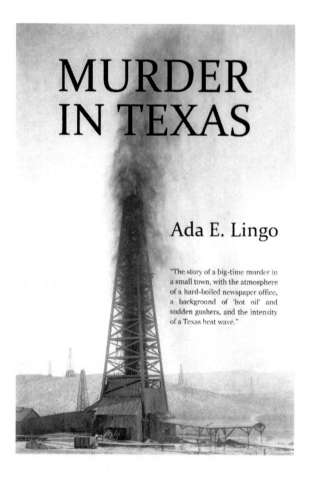

MURDER
IN TEXAS

Ada E. Lingo

"The story of a big-time murder in a small town, with the atmosphere of a hard-boiled newspaper office, a background of 'hot oil' and sudden gushers, and the intensity of a Texas heat wave."

COACHWHIP PUBLICATIONS
COACHWHIPBOOKS.COM

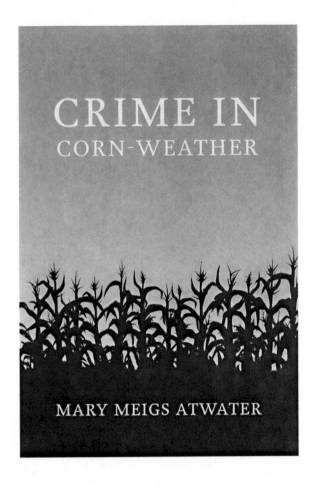

CRIME IN
CORN-WEATHER

MARY MEIGS ATWATER

COACHWHIP PUBLICATIONS
COACHWHIPBOOKS.COM

THE GOLF CLUB MURDER | OWEN FOX JEROME

CPSIA information can be obtained
at www.ICGtesting.com
Printed in the USA
LVOW11s2146260617
539413LV00003BA/763/P